PROPHETS OF DEATH AND MADNESS

THE BOOK OF ANCIENT EVIL
BOOK 3

JOHN HAAS

WFP
WORDFIRE PRESS

EBook ISBN: 978-1-68057-606-1
Trade Paperback ISBN: 978-1-68057-607-8
Dust Jacket Hardcover ISBN: 978-1-68057-608-5
Case Bind Hardcover ISBN: 978-1-68057-609-2
Library of Congress Control Number: 2023946617
Cover design by Janet McDonald
Kevin J. Anderson, Art Director
Vellum layout by CJ Anaya
Published by
WordFire Press, LLC
PO Box 1840
Monument CO 80132
Kevin J. Anderson & Rebecca Moesta, Publishers
WordFire Press eBook Edition 2024
WordFire Press Trade Paperback Edition 2024
WordFire Press Dust Jacket Hardcover Edition 2024
WordFire Press Case Bind Hardcover Edition 2024

Printed in the USA
Join our WordFire Press Readers Group for
sneak previews, updates, new projects, and giveaways.
Sign up at wordfirepress.com

THERE ARE WORSE THINGS THAN CTHULHU

The *Necronomicon* lies on the ocean floor, but there are other dangers, other hidden copies. In that loathsome tome lie ways to contact creatures as far above Cthulhu as Cthulhu is above humankind. Elder gods who could destroy all reality in the blink of an eye.

Death lies in wait for Doctor Archibald Shaw, recent survivor of the *Titanic* sinking. Dangers, both new and familiar, unseen and overt, conspire to drag him deeper into the dark secret world. Shaw finds himself struggling to resist an undeniable pull toward Arkham, Massachusetts and whatever new nightmare awaits there.

Meanwhile, Singh crosses the Atlantic in pursuit of his only friend, convinced he is already too late. What other option than to continue forward? He faces his own dangers in the ocean's depths, dangers which may prevent him from ever reaching Shaw.

Separated for the first time in decades, the two struggle against impossible odds, alone. Monsters. Nightmares. Strange portals. Elder gods. A strange new cult.

Will Shaw and Singh reunite before death claims them all?

For my wonderful lady Michelle.
Thank you for your unceasing support for my dream.
Love you.

*"Wise men interpreted dreams,
And the gods have laughed."*

—H.P. Lovecraft

WHAT CAME BEFORE

Between the previous novel, *Book of Death and Madness,* and this one the novella *Damned Voyage* takes place. That story was the first written but is now third in sequence. For those of you who may have missed it, or read it a while back, here is a quick recap.

A much older Shaw and Singh arrive at the docks of Southampton in pursuit of the thieves which have stolen the Necronomicon. They've been living a quiet life, protecting this evil book and keeping it from the hands of those who would use it. Shaw boards the ship while Singh goes off to alert those in power of what has happened. Shaw reluctantly kills a man to gain the necessary passage aboard the ship, to find the thieves. Through the course of that story the book affects people aboard ship and many disappear, others go mad. One who goes missing is the ship's doctor whom Shaw fills in for, using his new position for better access to the passengers. In the end the mastermind of the theft, James Wilson, and his henchmen attempt to wake the elder god, Cthulhu. Shaw prevents this and sends Cthulhu back to its slumber, but not before the god's thrashing destroys and sinks his ship, the Titanic. Shaw is pulled from the ocean into a lifeboat where he finds an elderly woman he had encountered earlier, Mrs. Hooper. Those passengers who saw what had actually sunk their ship don't want to believe it, their minds refuse, and they're only too happy to allow Shaw's concocted story of an iceberg to replace those memories.

Dread Cthulhu loomed over the ship as it cracked in two. It gazed off to the west, paying no particular attention to its handiwork, or to the insignificant speck named Doctor Archibald Shaw, floating nearby.

No! This was not how it had happened.

"I sent you back!"

Slowly, ponderously, the elder god turned from the sinking ship, heading west, toward the nearest city.

"No!" Shaw screamed around mouthfuls of freezing ocean water.

He had failed. Failed!

CHAPTER 1

Shaw awoke with a start and a sharp slash of pain which filled his body. He tried to shout, to call out, to curse the nightmare and that damned god. Only a stuttering, incoherent blabber escaped his lips.

Where ...?

With effort he turned, taking in the bed after bed which lined the room. Still more existed beyond his feet in neat, uniform lines leading to two massive doors. A hospital ... A makeshift one at least, temporary. Judging by the chandelier and stacks of chairs and table off to one side, this was a dining room until recently.

A slight rock to the world around him confirmed he was aboard a ship ... but not the same one. No, that one had sunk, the damage too severe. He did not remember being rescued. Last he recalled was being pulled from the ocean into a lifeboat, blankets being pressed to cover him. The ship had sunk, destroyed by ancient Cthulhu before it returned to sleep.

A shiver passed through his body at the memory, and Shaw was unable to bring it to a stop. He fumbled one hand from under the covers, struggling to bring it into view. It shook violently before falling back to his side.

"Hypothermia," he whispered, but it was all unintelligible babble. "Unnn—"

A blurry face passed into his view, looking down with clinical interest. Black thin moustache. Receding hairline. Somewhat pudgy but hardly overweight.

"You're awake," the man said needlessly with a slight accent. "Good."

Good came out as *goodt*.

"I am Doctor Lengyel. Ship's doctor aboard the RMS *Carpathia*."

"*Carpathia*?" Shaw slurred. It sounded nothing like the word he wanted.

Lengyel nodded. "You are suffering the effects of hypothermia. It should wear off in a day or so."

Annoyance rose in Shaw. He knew damn well the symptoms of hypothermia.

"The *Carpathia*," Lengyel said while checking Shaw over, "sped to the *Titanic* after it struck an iceberg."

An iceberg. Good. His words had affected those few who had seen the great monstrous god. Word of mouth spread it afterward. Better everyone believe that fiction rather than know what had actually sunk their ship.

"We pulled you from the ocean this morning." The doctor forced a thermometer into Shaw's mouth and continued on. "You and a little over seven hundred of your fellow passengers."

Seven hundred? Shaw closed his eyes against the fact. Not even a third. When he reopened his eyes, Lengyel was making a note on his chart. The doctor glanced toward the next patient, then pulled out his pocket watch.

"As you can imagine, seven hundred patients keep a ship's staff busy."

Shaw shifted and was rewarded with a fresh spike of pain through his right side. He exhaled sharply and coughed, bringing pain he hadn't felt since breaking his leg decades earlier.

"You will want to remain still as much as possible," Lengyel said.

"Your right side is one massive bruise, and I suspect a broken rib. You have been wrapped in compression bandages, but they can't be too tight because of the hypothermia and your need to breathe. It is a balance."

"Hnnn," Shaw managed, the closest he could come to an agreement.

"On your other side you have slashes to your abdomen and side. They look more like knife wounds than anything else."

Knife wounds? He remembered the furrow along his left arm, received from one of Wilson's associates, a bandage confirmed that. A long thin knife which he'd barely managed to deflect. Had the man stabbed him a second time? He couldn't remember. Shaw repositioned and let loose a hiss of pain, but managed to avoid coughing this time.

Lengyel gave him a look of *I told you not to move, didn't I?*

"There is also trauma around your eyes. Scratches, but nothing on the eyes themselves."

Now that Shaw remembered. Wilson's lacky grinding two thumbs into his eye sockets, trying to blind him. All in an effort to keep Shaw away from his master. Wilson. Damn the man. He'd gotten his hands on the *Necronomicon* and read from it, almost raising the worst of the elder gods.

Cthulhu.

A shiver ran through Shaw's body which refused to stop. The doctor tucked the coverings around Shaw more securely.

"Mrr-rr?"

"A mirror?" The doctor reached over to the next bed and brought one where Shaw could see himself.

Briefly he tried to raise one arm to take it but that was out of the question. The scratches around his eyes were not too bad and would fade away in a few days. Other than that, he looked much the same. Receding gray hair. A bit of pudginess to his face which came with age. Often he wore glasses for reading or to provide a disarming effect. He hoped they were with his belongings … If he had any.

"You must stay in bed and under the warm blankets until we

reach New York. We have patched you up as much as we have time to, but they will be better staffed for treatment in a hospital. Stabilization and ensuring no one should die, that is our focus."

The man's eyes took on a sad expression and looked away. Shaw would bet that more than one of those rescued had not made it.

"You are a doctor," Lengyel continued, "so I am sure you understand all of this."

Shaw's eyes focused on the man. "Hrnnww?"

The closest he could come to "How?"

"Another passenger named you."

Another passenger? Ah, Mrs. Penelope Hooper who he had boarded with. She'd been in the lifeboat with him as well.

Shaw looked aside.

That might cause problems. No Archibald Shaw was listed on the passenger manifest, and any list made would be compared to that original one, his identity scrutinized. Could he claim he took the place of someone unable to sail? The man he'd murdered for his room perhaps. Stephen … Stephen … No, the family name wouldn't come, though it was sure he'd seen it on his luggage.

Shaw's eyelids dipped, opened, closed again. Exhaustion covered him like the blankets on his bed, dragging him back under.

"Sleep," Lengyel said, patting his shoulder. "You need it."

CHAPTER 2

April 17, 1912
RMS Carpathia

The next time Shaw awoke a nurse attended to him, helping him upright enough to eat soup. It was not worth the pain. He found himself able to say simple, one-syllable words in a low whisper.

Minutes later he returned to a nightmare-filled sleep. Each dream played out with him not succeeding to stop Wilson from reading that damned book.

The book.

The *Necronomicon*.

He woke with that one thought in his mind ... and something else. A fragment. Something about a door ... the number six?

No. That part wouldn't come.

His very reason for continuing to exist these past decades lay on the bottom of the ocean. No longer was he the keeper of the book, the protector of humanity. Perhaps he should have gone down with the book, the way Captain Smith had with his ship.

Shaw's eyes opened.

Had he fallen asleep again?

He'd been dreaming of England. Of his doctor's practice. Of Singh.

Singh! The one thing he was certain of was letting Singh know he was alive.

"Tel," he said in a whisper. "Tel."

The nurse attending him, one he hadn't realized sat beside him, patted his arm. "Tell who, dear?"

He'd wanted to say telegram, but *tel* was as close as he could get. The word was too complex, too many syllables. He could come back to that.

"Sng …"

"Sing?" the nurse cackled. "I'm afraid I don't have the voice for that."

Shaw clenched his eyes shut. Hadn't he made the same mistake himself on first meeting the lad?

"Son," he said, proud for speaking that one word. He opened his eyes to find the nurse had moved on to the next patient.

The telegram would have to wait for now.

Would his name be listed among the survivors? It wasn't on the manifest, but if Mrs. Hooper had given his name … Another problem for later.

To distract himself from not being able to contact Singh, Shaw made small movements, self-examination of his own injuries. The right side hurt most, but he suspected the rib was not broken. Cracked maybe? The stitches on his left were something else. No denying them. He would need to be careful.

Slowly dragging one hand from under the blanket, he found himself able to hold it up for a few seconds. It shook constantly, and when the hand dropped back to his side he was unable to return it under the blanket.

The nurse would remedy that when she passed again.

What had he been thinking about?

Singh.

Home.

Could he return home? Then what? What was he to do with his remaining years? His reason for existing these past decades was gone. Could he return to a medical practice in England? He *was* still a doctor, and there should be many remaining years left. He wasn't so old.

Maybe.

He would need to do something.

Prince Eddy had left a fund, set up for him and Singh to protect that book while living in Cambridge. That fund had survived the prince's passing and looked after them still … Quite some protector he'd turned out to be.

No.

Enough self pity! Was twenty-five years of it not enough?

It was true that he'd lost the book, but he'd still managed to prevent the return of the monster which would have sent humanity to extinction. The cost had been great. More than a thousand innocent passengers but, God help him, he would pay that again.

He'd sent Singh to spread the word, to contact the prince's son, to get a message to the king. Evil was loose in the world once again. Someone needed to be alerted. It was too important for both people aware of the danger to be aboard that ship. As it turned out the point was moot, but he was glad Singh had not been aboard. Hard to convince himself they would have both escaped when two-thirds of the passengers had not.

Would that evil stay at the bottom of the ocean? The *Necronomicon*? Cthulhu? Surely for the rest of his lifetime. When it returned, it would be another's problem.

"Nuh," he croaked out.

No.

That wasn't good enough.

He would prepare someone for its return, someone to pass it on. Would it return in Singh's lifetime?

This time when he dozed off the dreams moved around preparations for his successor. Shaw was surprised to find no memory of nightmares. A pleasant change. He actually felt rested. Another feeling, an outlook on the world, had shifted. It took Shaw several minutes to pin down the exact nature of this change. It wasn't hope exactly. Nothing so dramatic. Optimism maybe? It was the best he'd felt since … since … When? The night at the museum when he'd taken possession of that ugly idol? No. Since leaving India? Earlier than that, too.

Since the night his leg had been crippled more than thirty years earlier.

Yes.

Now, his leg was as maimed as yesterday, but still a wary optimism filled him. Where his life had been determined and bleak, now the future was unwritten with nothing expected of him.

So why did it all feel a bit flat? The loss of his reason in life? Perhaps, but that would not be insurmountable. It was a matter of finding a new reason.

CHAPTER 3

April 17, 1912
RMS Dauntless

Singh leaned on one railing of the RMS *Dauntless*, staring at the passing miles of Atlantic Ocean. Somewhere, far ahead of him, was Doctor Archibald Shaw ... if his friend had somehow survived the sinking of his ship.

Seven days since the *Titanic* had set sail. Two days since she had sunk and Singh had boarded this ship. This was the day Shaw should have arrived in New York, but from the news he'd heard the rescue ship wouldn't dock for another day.

Also days ahead of him was their burden, their obligation. The *Necronomicon*. Stolen from their home while they slept, he and Shaw had pursued the thieves to Southampton.

There, to his eternal regret, Singh had left his oldest friend and went in search of those needing to be alerted that the book was loose in the world. It was a necessity, but the shame still burned deep in his soul, as did that of losing the book in the first place.

Was his friend still alive, and had he retrieved the book? For the sake of the world, Singh hoped this to be true, and for his own sake he hoped Shaw was alive.

They'd been together more than thirty years, ever since the doctor had rescued him from one last vestige of the Kali Cult. Those days before were foggy, whether because he truly didn't remember or simply didn't want to, he couldn't say. Singh remembered pieces, like a nightmare. Awful things he'd been made to do while still a child. Shaw had not judged him for any of it.

Together they'd pursued the cult when the British army refused to acknowledge its existence. It had cost Shaw the use of one leg.

"Doctor Shaw," he muttered, "you must be alive."

When Singh had heard of the *Titanic*'s sinking, he'd already been in the process of boarding this ship in pursuit of Shaw. Others had boarded the *Dauntless* in pursuit of family members aboard the *Titanic*, praying to find they'd survived. Praying as Singh did.

The *Dauntless* sailed directly, not stopping in France or Ireland as the *Titanic* had, but it would still be another three days until they arrived in New York. Three more days until he knew whether his friend survived.

Time crept past.

His fellow passengers had accepted him as some sort of Indian royalty, and Singh did nothing to dissuade them of the notion. He wore a suit of clothes, having lost his usual robe while helping Fred Abberline out in Springbourne. At least his turban had survived that adventure. The other passengers' view of him was beneficial in gathering information. In the two days since boarding the *Dauntless*, Singh had learned more of the *Titanic*'s fate. On the night of April 14, the *Titanic* had hit an iceberg, sinking the next morning.

An iceberg.

The more he considered this, the more it seemed unlikely, unbelievable, given the experience of these ship captains. No. Singh suspected something more sinister, more ancient. When he met with Shaw once again, he would have the full story, and he *would* find his friend again. He had to.

Until then he would wait, the hardest thing. Worry had once again sunk its talons into him. He would return to his room and pass the time until dinner in meditation.

CHAPTER 4

April 18, 1912
New York City, Pier 54: 10:07 pm

Shaw moved from hospital bed to wheelchair in preparation of departing. He had grown tired of lying on his back, staring at the same ceiling and four matching walls. He ached to leave the ship, now docked in New York City.

"I can walk," he said to Doctor Lengyel.

Yesterday he'd regained the ability to speak clearly, though in a low tone. Today was better. Shaw found himself able to speak longer sentences and with greater volume. So much so that he was able to request a telegram be sent to Singh. There'd been a charge, but given he had nothing to his name, members of the crew had gathered the necessary funds to send one word: Safe. When asked for a destination Shaw realized he couldn't know where Singh would be, finally opting for their home in Cambridge.

"That will be for the hospital's doctor to decide," Lengyel responded. "You have regained some energy, but do not push it just yet."

It was the same he would have told a patient. It was logical and realistic, and it irked Shaw no end. The situation was not improved by the presence of another man, this one from immigration. An officious man with a pencil-thin moustache and clipboard.

It was the point he had been dreading.

Shaw held no papers, but neither did many of the survivors. For now they were willing to allow those in need of medical attention to leave, under the administration of Doctor Lengyel, and with a promise to continue at the hospital tomorrow.

That, Shaw was sure, would not be the case if he were not from first class.

Aboard the *Carpathia* they had already known his name, a name which would not be on any manifest. A second danger came to mind now. Thieves had known enough to track him to Cambridge and steal the book. Were there others? Those who would recognize his name on this end and do him harm?

At a few minutes after ten o'clock, Shaw found himself at the ship's ramp, staring out at the tableau before him. Thousands of people lined the streets leading to the docked ship, stretching to the horizon. Somber. Expectant. It had an eerie effect that this many people should gather in such relative silence. No hysteria, no shouting, no wailing. Did they all await word on some loved one, or did many come merely to show support?

"Don't worry," a voice said from beside him. "You won't have to wade through them."

Shaw looked around to see the captain. The man had an amiable look, but haunted as well, as did most of the crew aboard the *Carpathia*. The expectation of a leisurely cruise had become a nightmare.

"There's a section," the captain continued, gesturing to a fenced off area, "where only family will be allowed in."

"No family for me," Shaw said.

"No. I believe you are destined for St. Vincent's Hospital with others who need better care than what we can give aboard ship."

Shaw nodded. Bandages around his chest and stomach area were uncomfortable but doing their job of immobilizing his rib. Doctor Lengyel's crew had triaged him well.

"Thank you, Captain."

The man allowed the crewman looking after Shaw's departure to take over. Gravity sucked at him as they rolled down the ramp, threatening to take his wheelchair from the sailor's hands. The man was up to the task and held the wheelchair's handles tightly. Another death evaded. Shaw's eyes remained on this crowd until reaching ground level. From there he was brought to the segregated area where many were reunited with loved ones, while others like him waited for transport to the hospital. Fences had been set up to provide some amount of privacy, though newspaper reporters shouted questions and snapped photographs. Not all waited with silence and respect.

"The ambulance driver will be here soon," said the crewman who had brought him to shore.

He flipped the brake on one wheel and gave Shaw a last goodbye before hustling back to the ship for his next charge. Shaw watched the man go, not envying the part any of the ship's staff played in this.

Even among all of this excitement, exhaustion threatened to drag him back under. Shaw considered what he knew of hypothermia and decided this was more. This was the exhaustion of more than two decades living under the cloud of that oppressive book. This would take longer to recover from, if that was possible.

"No."

He was the master of his own life, not some book or god. With a moment's effort, using the chair for balance, he forced himself to a standing position. Wobbly and slightly dizzy, he made a deal with himself: five minutes, then he would return to the chair. A quick adjustment of his reading glasses which *had* miraculously survived his plunge into the ocean.

The pain in his side and the tug on his stitches kept him alert. His aching rib howled the loudest, but he was increasingly certain it was not broken.

He scanned the people moving about him. Isolated pockets of those overjoyed to find a survivor, but never complete satisfaction. A mother, but no father. A daughter-in-law, but no son. Shaw felt as intrusive as the reporters.

Through the crowd he saw one woman who stood out. She moved methodically from group to group, not interacting with anyone but stopping near them, listening then moving on. She wore gray pants and a tan pocketed jacket, such as might be worn by men on expedition. A capable woman, not intimidated by those around her. Her complexion was olive, Italian maybe, or Greek, while her hair was loose red curls. An interesting contrast.

Closer. Closer. She looked up and locked eyes with Shaw. In that moment he felt a distinct sense of unease. The way she moved. Her thoroughness. Her calm. She glanced away and Shaw berated himself. Uneasy? From some poor woman looking for a loved one?

Paranoia was not unknown to him, and if he let it go unchecked he would see cultists and assassins in every person. Had he truly been thinking someone might come looking for him by name? Too many years of living in the shadow of that damned book.

He retook his seat, interest in the task lost in the grief of people around him. A minute or so later the woman appeared next to him, her gaze coming to rest on his face before moving on yet again. As she passed from the area, she cast one last glance over her shoulder toward him.

CHAPTER 5

We'll be as quick as possible," the doctor examining Shaw said. The man was half his age, at best. "Then we'll get you to bed and some rest."

Shaw wanted to tell the man he'd had enough rest to last a lifetime, but yawned when he opened his mouth to speak. Perhaps sleep *was* what he needed. Did he have anything better to do? The sharp smells of alcohol and antiseptic in the examination room did their best to make him dizzy.

"What is your name, sir?"

His name?

Shaw saw that no paperwork had been sent from ship to hospital, and that this doctor was starting from scratch, pen poised above the form on a clipboard. Should he give his true name? The encounter with that woman while he waited for the ambulance encouraged him to avoid paranoia. However, a quarter century of habit was not removed over night. Stephen's family name was still a blank in his mind. It would have made most sense to use that, or to at least say he'd taken the man's place ... but, no.

"Wilson."

Why the hell had he used that man's name? The dead man guilty of masterminding the theft of the *Necronomicon*. The immigration man had his true name, and this would lead to complications, but that was tomorrow's problem. At least anyone looking for Doctor Archibald Shaw would not find him, not easily in any case.

More paranoia. Ridiculous twaddle.

Too many years of being victim to every evil which came along. It had taken its toll on his mind. Life had been like a vicious dog, threatening to bite and occasionally doing worse. Yes, there were awful, malicious things in the dark … and yes again, life was certainly not what it appeared … That didn't mean he had to live in abject fear.

Oh, for those days before he'd ever arrived in India, before he'd met Lassiter or saw that ugly idol, before he'd even heard of thuggees or that damned book, or dark gods that only slept.

"First name?"

Ah.

What was Wilson's given name? Shaw had looked through the manifest in search of the mysterious W while aboard ship, while acting as the interim doctor.

"James."

A vivid picture of James Wilson at the *Titanic*'s bow, screaming into the night as he read from tparanoia.ad book. The words came back to Shaw with little effort of his own.

Fhtagn wgah'nagl R'lyeh Cthulhu mglw'nafh Ph'nglui.

"No," he muttered.

"Pardon me, sir?"

He shook his head and gave the man a wan smile. "Sorry. I'm just tired I guess."

Shaw had read from the book, reciting those words backward in an attempt to send Cthulhu back to his slumber. Had that truly worked, or had it simply been the sudden absence of Wilson reciting the spell?

The young doctor started his examination of Shaw. The stitches were given a quick glance and declared sufficient.

"That is quite some bruise."

Shaw agreed. "Doctor Lengyel aboard the *Carpathia* thought I had a broken rib."

More examination. Probing with fingers along the bruised side. Commands to breathe in and out. "No. Just bruised and extremely tender."

As Shaw had thought.

"You fell from the ship, into the ocean?"

"I don't remember much of that."

"Hmm, I would guess you hit something on the way," the doctor explained. "That might have saved your life, slowed the speed at which you hit the water."

The doctor listened to him breathe, getting him to do several more in and out breaths.

"You were treated for hypothermia?"

"I was."

"Good. You may experience some lingering effects, but that will mostly be behind you now. You don't have pneumonia, which is encouraging."

"I …"

Shaw wanted to say he already knew all that, had diagnosed it himself as much as Doctor Lengyel did. He shut his mouth, remembering he was not a doctor right now. He was James Wilson.

"We'll replace your bandages and can do away with the compression around your chest, unless that pressure feels better." The man paused, marking things on his chart. "Best thing is to rest and not move needlessly over the next couple weeks, keep those stitches from reopening."

"Thank you."

"I noticed your leg."

"That is an old wound."

"Yes, of course, but do you walk with a cane?"

"I do. I seem to have lost it in all the excitement."

Another note on the chart.

It was closer to midnight by the time Shaw was wheeled to bed, dressed in a clean white hospital gown which itched his skin. A room full of ten metal-framed beds, all occupied. The one or two still awake were not in a chatty mood, for which Shaw was grateful. He hobbled from chair to bed and lay back, one gasp of pain escaping him. For several minutes Shaw stared at the ceiling above him, pondering.

He had no money. No papers. To return home he was dependent on the shipping company to take care of him. Taking Wilson's name had been stupid. In the morning he would fix that, say he was delirious or some such. Best he could hope for was to bluff his way back home.

Shaw's eyes drooped. He'd had little *but* rest since being rescued and somehow was still exhausted.

CHAPTER 6

April 19, 1912
St. Vincent's Hospital: 2:15 am

erve me! a low voice rumbled inside his mind.

Shaw thrashed in his sleep, and a bright white bolt of pain coursed through his bruised side. He jerked, cursing, sure that by now he would have learned how to sleep without moving, even with nightmares.

Nightmare? What was this one about?

No, it was gone already.

Shaw turned his head and felt cold metal suddenly against his throat. His eyes opened to find the woman he'd seen at the docks. She sat sideways on the bed beside him, dressed in the white skirt and blouse of a nurse, a matching cap on her head.

She pressed a cold blade against his throat while he swallowed involuntarily. Shaw felt the sharpness in that steel.

"No loud noises," she whispered. "You understand?"

Her accent was American. New York? No southern or western inflection.

"Yes," he whispered back.

"Good." Her eyes never left his. They were calm, calculating. "Pleasure to meet you, James Wilson. Now, where's the book?"

"I'm not—"

"Shh-sh-sh." The blade pressed against his skin in warning. "Don't insult my intelligence." She cocked her head toward the clipboard with his details and alias hanging at the foot of his bed. "In any case, I can smell the taint of it on you."

Yes, just as the darkness clung to her.

Annoyance welled inside him. Would he never be free of this?

Enough! Kill me or don't, but get it over with.

"The book," he rasped, a touch too loud, "is at the bottom of the ocean, and good riddance."

She scoffed, eyes narrowing. A lock of red hair dropped in front of one eye. "Strange response considering who I'm talking to."

It occurred to Shaw how little he knew of James Wilson, only caring that he had the book and intended to use it.

"Who am I?"

Teeth clenched, clearly being pushed to her limit. "James Wilson, collector of arcane objects."

"I am *not* Wilson."

She said nothing, made no effort to move. One raised eyebrow spoke to how much she believed the words.

"I needed to take an alias and apparently I chose the wrong one."

"And yet you know of the book."

"I do."

She considered a moment. "Why would you need an alias?"

"Because there are others who may be looking for me by name."

No response. No movement.

"I am Doctor Archibald Shaw, and until a few days ago I was the keeper of that book."

No glimmer of recognition at his name. All those years given and not even the faintest acknowledgment. It annoyed him in some irrational manner. He launched into an abbreviated history. Following the book's trail from India to London. Taking possession of it and keeping it safe for more than two decades. No mention of ugly idols, elder gods, or the horrors which had happened in Whitechapel.

"Hmm."

"I was chasing the book too," he said. "Wilson was a madman."

"Was?"

"Last I saw he'd fallen into the ocean."

"Others survived that."

"Not with three-quarters of a syringe of morphine coursing through his system."

"Hmm."

"Who the hell are you anyway?"

"Who I am is the one with the knife. I'll ask the questions."

The woman scrutinized him a few moments longer before settling back, withdrawing her blade. Now that it was away from his neck, he saw it to be just under a foot in length, the handle brown wood. She stared a moment longer—waiting to see if he would attack?—then pulled open her nurses gown. Underneath were the same slacks he'd seen earlier, held up by black suspenders. She slid the knife into a sheathe at her side, revealing a Colt revolver in a hidden shoulder holster.

"Bottom of the ocean, hmm?"

"For now," Shaw said. "It won't stay there."

"No. Evil can't stay buried."

"It must be destroyed."

She barked a laugh, then looked over one shoulder to confirm none of his roommates had awoken. Though they would see exactly what was presented: a nurse attending a patient in the night. "Evil like this, ancient and eternal, can't be destroyed, Doctor. Best we can hope is to delay its return. Bottom of the ocean will do."

"I knew one man who destroyed a copy, but paid for it with his mind."

She looked dubious, and Shaw considered what he'd always accepted as true. Kosminski was, at best, an unreliable storyteller. *Had* he destroyed a book?

"There's several copies, Doctor." She shrugged. "Some would be more easily destroyed than others. Not all are printed on paper."

"The one I hid was printed on pages of leather."

Leather which he'd become convinced years ago was human skin.

The woman got to her feet, pulling the nurse's cap from her head and tossing it onto his nightstand.

"Who are you?" Shaw struggled to sit up with no small amount of pain.

A pause before responding. "My name's Cassandra. I'm a private investigator."

"You're more than that. You've been touched by this evil just as I have."

"Very perceptive, though we're all touched in our own distinct ways."

"Then—"

"Thank you for your time, Doctor. Best of luck returning to England."

She turned and departed without another word.

CHAPTER 7

April 19, 1912
St. Vincent's Hospital: Morning

After the investigator left, Shaw sat in bed, staring into the dim shadows, wondering once again about his life. His options. She had said "best of luck returning to England" as if it were a foregone conclusion.

Shouldn't it be? This was what he'd considered while aboard the *Carpathia*. *Could* he return to a normal life with all that he knew? Treat patients for sore throats and infections while aware of the hidden dangers all around? The stench of that book would forever be with him, and there would always be those coming into his life for that very reason, like this investigator. Darkness calls to darkness.

What evil had touched her life?

He was unlikely to ever know now.

What time was it? The ward had no clocks, and his watch had gone down with the ship. It was unsettling not knowing the exact time at a moment's notice. Early morning was his best guess. Shaw leaned his head back against the pillows, staring toward the ceiling. Something pulled at his perception, dragging it toward the doorway, like waves at the ocean trying to suck a person away from shore.

Almost a physical pull.

Somewhere, distantly, a low sound of flute playing.

What could—

Doctor Shaw.

A voice, from nowhere. Singh?

Shaw!

No, not Singh. A feminine voice.

Doc!

Wha … Walsh?

Wake up, Doctor.

This voice was more urgent, gravelly and on the edge of panic.

Wake up? He wasn't—

His eyes fluttered open. The room had not changed. The sleepers in every other bed snored on. He *had* been asleep, or at least dozing. In an upright position too. That could explain the screeching complaint in his side.

Had that investigator truly been here, or was she part of the dream?

No, the nurse's cap remained on his nightstand where she'd discarded it. She *had* been here, and now—

"Doctor." A voice from his left. Scratchy. Rough. The voice of age.

Shaw turned.

"Mrs. Hooper?"

The elderly lady whom he'd boarded the ship with, a necessary bit of camouflage at the time. Hadn't she wrapped him in a blanket, in the lifeboat? He owed her a thank you for that at least.

She scowled, glancing toward the door and back. "Flee, Doctor."

"What …?"

"Something approaches."

Shaw forced himself more upright, sucking in a breath at the sudden sharp pain.

"What do you mean?"

"There's no time for questions," she snapped. Another glance toward the door. "My time is done."

"No." With a chill, Shaw realized he could see the chair through Mrs. Hooper.

"Damn you, Shaw!" She leaned forward, bringing her face closer to his. "Move or join me!"

Shaw moved. He forced his legs from under the sheets, ignoring the multitude of pains which assaulted him while scooting forward. This was no dream, no delusion. He'd been visited by the dead before.

"This frightens me, Doctor," the old lady said as her body faded into the shadows of the hospital room. All that remained was her expression, etched with fear. "Run!"

Then she was gone, leaving the lingering scent of her perfume.

No. This was no dream.

Shaw placed his feet against the floor and leaned into a standing position, wobbling. He reached one hand out to the bed, borrowing some balance from it. As he did, his hand brushed against the cane leaning there.

His cane?

No, that was in the ocean with Wilson and the book. This was a simple hospital cane of cheap but sturdy wood. No hidden sword inside. The doctor or one of his staff must have left it while he slept. It would certainly do.

Move!

"Yes, yes," he whispered to the darkness.

Time was short. A prickling up his spine, and a pressure inside his head confirmed that. Something approached. Something malevolent. Shaw grabbed the cane, stumping his way across to the half-open door. His wounds protested, but distantly, drowned out by the danger.

Peering through the open door, he saw what anyone would expect: a clean and non-descript hallway. It was well lit, with wall lamps every few feet, continuing around the corner. Inside his skull a pounding beat echoed, Mrs. Hooper's final words warning him that time was almost done.

Run!

Shaw passed into the hallway, a vague smell of bleach reaching his nostrils. The hall continued in either direction, his room being more or less at the halfway point. Where was the on-duty nurse? There should be one at least. Attending a patient?

Irrelevant. He didn't want to see a nurse.

Flee, yes, but which way?

To the right waited a door with the stairwell beyond, to his left the corner he saw from his room, and a distinct sense of evil and danger. Shaw hobbled to his right. Step by step, glancing over one shoulder as he went. The lights at the far end dimmed, and from that darkness came the click-clack of something sharp against the tile floor.

Familiar.

Sniff!

A deep, breathing, snuffling sound. Like a bloodhound, tracking.

Greater urgency filled him, bordering on panic. It propelled him toward the stairs, threatening to spill him to the floor. A shadow at the opposite end, moving with what light there was. It had paused, sniffing loudly before moving forward again.

"What—"

From around the far corner came a great creature, wings folded against its body to allow passage down the hall. Taloned feet clicking against the floors.

Oh, yes. Familiar indeed.

He'd last seen one at the British Museum almost thirty years ago.

A night-gaunt.

This blind creature came from the nightmare realm and, according to Kosminski, it could exist in the waking world for a short time. Called forth and sent to do some duty. Kill. Retrieve. Destroy.

Sniff! Sniff!

Its head turned in concert to the sound of its breathing. Shaw made no movement, no noise, nothing to attract that vicious monster. The night-gaunt faced him directly, and Shaw felt his knees go weak. It moved forward another click-clack step, following a trail, a scent.

His.

No.

No. No. No. No. No. No. No.

Another step along the hall, following the trail while Shaw held his breath.

The night-gaunt stopped at the first doorway, one away from the room he'd vacated. Its razor claws tapped against the smooth hallway tiles. The ones on its hands flexed, ready to grab at something.

A moment's hesitation …

Sniff!

…and it passed through the open door.

Shaw rushed for the exit, opening it, prepared to step through.

Instead he turned back.

Each of the men in that room would be torn apart. Ten men for the price of his one. He had no excuse. No longer was he the protector of humanity who needed to survive, whose reason was to protect that book in case it fell into the wrong hands. Now he was just some old man who had outlived his function.

Memories of the museum guard, and director Kinkaid, what they'd looked like after a night-gaunt had caught them.

But he couldn't just leave—

The monster stepped back into the hallway. No screams. No destruction.

The night-gaunt wasn't here for them.

Sniff.

Its head turned toward his own room now. Clawed talons pushed the door open and followed inside.

Bravery deserted Shaw as he turned and hobbled through the door, descending the stairs as fast as he was able. Each step threatened to spill him headlong down the marble stairs. Halfway was a landing with a 180-degree turn, followed by more stairs.

Shaw looked behind him, praying he wasn't on some higher-up floor. He couldn't outrun the monster forever.

On the door he'd passed through was painted a number one. Soon he would be on the ground floor. One more set of—

Stepping onto the landing, his feet tangled and spilled him forward. With a barely controlled cry of agony he impacted against the floor. His side shrieked in protest while his cane skittered away from him. It rebounded off a wall and started down the next set of stairs without him.

"Damn it!"

No time for this. No time. No time.

Shaw crawled to the next stairs, then started down on his bottom, the way a child might. It was undignified, embarrassing, and painful. It was also faster than he could manage on two legs. As he reached the bottom steps and retrieved his cane, the door above slammed open. Shaw forced his feet under him and started forward.

Sniff! Sniff!

"No."

He hobbled to the stairwell door and yanked it toward him, no longer having the luxury of keeping silent. The night-gaunt would have no other rooms to distract it before reaching him. Passing through the door, Shaw stomped his cane against the entry floor, rushing toward the hospital exit. Behind him the click-clack of sharp claws chased him, coming closer. Closer.

To left and right were hallways, and an information desk beside the door. Briefly he wondered if the desk would hide him, but the idea of it finding him cowering and with no other option discounted that. His only hope was in outdistancing the monster ... Which was no hope at all.

He huffed and puffed with the exertion of it all, praying to any god who might hear him that he wouldn't die this way.

The main door of the hospital was heavy and took all his might to push open. A tug in his right side told him this was too much for his current state. He imagined he could hear the snap of stitches.

A minor worry at the moment.

Out the door, down the few steps and onto a sidewalk.

Where to go. Where?

Damn it! Where *could* he go?

A small park on the opposite side.

Forward then.

One hand on his cane and his entire attention behind him, Shaw staggered into the street, hospital gown flapping in the slight breeze. A great horn sounded from his right. He turned to find two round lights bearing down on him. Another horn blast.

He fell over.

CHAPTER 8

S haw!"

Singh sat bolt upright in bed, staring into the shadows of his room.

A nightmare.

More than that.

A premonition.

No. Not that either. A premonition was something that was to come. This had happened.

His friend was *alive*, but he was also in grave danger.

"Shaw," he whispered.

Three more days until the *Dauntless* arrived in New York. So much could happen in those few days. So much that could happen to Shaw.

Teeth gritted, Singh reclined into his pillow, sleep banished and wishing he could speed the ship forward through sheer will alone. He examined these familiar sensations of helplessness and frustration. So similar to the time Shaw had disappeared into the slums of Whitechapel. Cthulhu's idol. Ananya. The *Necronomicon*.

Those poor women. Even now it was unclear just what Shaw had been responsible for and what had been done by that lunatic Kosminski.

Singh, Inspector Abberline, and Prince Eddy had all searched, and finally found Shaw out of his mind, influenced by that evil idol.

Kosminski and Ananya had paid for playing with such evil. The first to an asylum, the latter to the depths with a hideous elder god named Dagon.

Singh shuddered and leaned further into his pillows.

Patience.

He closed his eyes searching for some sliver of inner peace.

CHAPTER 9

April 19, 1912
The Streets of New York: Morning

The lights bore down on him, like the eyes of some predator beast. He tried to retreat but had neither the leverage nor the strength to do so. His only recourse was to hold one hand out toward the vehicle. A paltry, last-ditch thing, more reflex than defence.

It stopped inches from his outstretched fingers. The word *Studebaker* predominant on the grill, close enough to touch. The tires, more visible now that they were so close, were like those on a bicycle, maybe twice as wide though.

A slam of the driver's door, a muttered curse. Then, "Doctor?"

He looked up into a semi-familiar face.

"Who?"

The investigator. Cassandra ... something.

She was no longer dressed as a nurse. Back to her slacks with suspenders, and a button-down shirt under the brown expedition jacket.

"What's going on?" she asked.

"Monster," he said, gesturing toward the hospital doors. "Monster."

Nothing moved.

Cassandra gently dragged him to his feet, one eye on the hospital, and helped him to the passenger side of her automobile. Door open, he was placed inside.

"Monster, hmm?" she asked, turning back toward the hospital doors.

Still nothing came.

No sniffing, no click-clack. Nothing.

"I swear ..." He shook his head.

Had it been real?

Delusion?

No he—

The heavy wooden door burst toward them, slamming against the outside wall. The night-gaunt leapt through to land with a click-clack of nails on cement, sniffing at the air. It spun toward them and let out a wailing screech. A noise fit to burst his skull.

"Tell me you see this," Shaw begged.

The investigator cursed again as she rushed around the car to jump into the driver's seat. She didn't bother closing the door but stomped the gas pedal while shifting into first.

"I see it," she said, the car lurching forward. "That's a night-gaunt."

Shaw scrambled to get his feet into the car, pulling his bad leg in with both hands. He managed to get his door closed before losing it to some passing obstacle. With effort he looked out the back window, gritting his teeth against a cry of pain as his stitches pulled once again. Each step brought the pursuing monster closer.

"It's gaining on us," he said.

Cassandra flipped the car into second gear, then third, gaining some speed. "How 'bout now?"

"Keeping ahead, just barely."

No other traffic existed on the road to hamper the thing's pursuit. Nothing to distract it. The night-gaunt unfurled its wings and screeched again.

How could they keep ahead of it once—

The monster leapt into the air.

"Above us!"

"Hold on!" Cassandra jerked the wheel left, the rest of the car following.

On Shaw's right the night-gaunt landed on the street, breaking concrete and tumbling flat. Cassandra pressed down on the gas again, forcing the car to its limits.

"Which way's east?"

Shaw considered it, looking left and right. "I … have no idea."

Cassandra glanced at a passing building and grimaced. "West! Grab on to something."

Shaw grabbed the door with his right hand and placed his left against the panel ahead of him. He spaced his legs apart for support. Even so he was jerked around as Cassandra took the next left at a speed which threatened to topple them. At the end of the next block she took another left. Shaw saw the night-gaunt behind them. They'd gained some distance, but each turn slowed them.

Another left and he recognized the street they were on to start with, headed back toward the hospital.

"What good will heading east do?"

"It still there?"

"Yes, and gaining on us. It looks ready to leap again."

"Tell me when it does."

The monster swiped at a parked car as it passed, rocking the vehicle on its wheels and turning it a quarter way around. Now that they headed along a straight road the car once again gained speed, but the night-gaunt had the same advantage.

"It is catching up again."

Cassandra nodded. "What time is it?"

"Time? What could—"

"Just tell me the time, Doctor."

"I don't know! My watch is on the ocean floor. Close to dawn I would guess."

Cassandra cursed, looking skyward. "This'll be close."

"Here it comes, in line with us."

The creature had gained on them and took to its wings, flying up behind them with claws extended. The night-gaunt slashed at the back of the car, sending razor sharp talons through the fabric and metal of the back seat.

Shaw let loose a shout, but was unsure if it came from pain or fear.

The beast landed on the car's back end, grabbing one side in its claw while rearing back for a follow-up blow with the other.

"Come on," Cassandra said. "Come on. Come on!"

A vicious slash of claw. The car swerved under the impact. Cassandra righted it and continued to drive.

East.

"What's east? Why are we—? Oh!"

He'd said it himself. Dawn.

The first rays of sun peaked over the edge of the horizon, washing the street in gentle yellow. The monster screeched, this time undeniably in pain and rage. Shaw spun around to see the night-gaunt holding one talon up, halted in mid-swing. The hand smoked where sunlight landed. Without another sound the night-gaunt leapt from the back of their vehicle and disappeared into the shadows of a dark alley.

CHAPTER 10

April 19, 1912
New York City: 5:45 am

Cassandra continued to look back every few seconds, even after it was obvious the night-gaunt had fled. Shaw held tight to his door.

"I believe we can slow down now."

Cassandra glanced at him, then took another look behind. Still the car hurtled down the street at an unsafe speed. An embarrassed nod and she eased her foot from the accelerator, rolling to a stop at the border of street and sidewalk. She placed her forehead against the steering wheel and took several deep breaths.

With effort Shaw forced the hand gripping his door back into his lap, curling fingers around his cane in a desire to find some calm and control. Remembering the meditation tricks that Singh had taught him, he breathed in with his mouth then let it out slowly through his nose. Again. He tried to focus his thoughts anywhere but at their close escape and failed. That monster had only been seen at night in London. At the museum. In Limehouse. Now he knew why.

"Sun destroys the night-gaunt." He marveled at the simple solution.

"No. Sun will *hurt* a night-gaunt but won't destroy one. Luckily it has a short life outside the dream world."

"You've seen one before."

"I've seen a lot." It was almost a whisper.

Shaw turned his attention toward the investigator, considering her, unsure of what to say next. She *had* obviously seen much, knew much. She leaned back in her seat, jacket falling open to reveal the concealed revolver. A quick glance back the way they'd come and Cassandra urged the vehicle back into gear, sliding into the early traffic at a somewhat more reasonable speed. Shaw clamped one hand on the door and the other on his cane.

"My driving makes you nervous?"

Shaw looked toward the investigator, noting a hint of smile at the corner of her mouth. "This is my first time traveling in one of these machines," Shaw admitted. "They go much faster than a horse."

"That's the point."

Shaw found it hard to imagine wanting to get anywhere in that much rush, except for fleeing from some danger like they just had. Perhaps if they'd had one of these contraptions at their home in Cambridge they would have arrived in Southampton quicker, caught the thieves before they'd boarded.

No point living in the world of maybes.

"Your vehicle is destroyed."

"Not mine. It's borrowed."

"Oh, your poor friend."

She looked at him out of the corner of her eye, and Shaw had a sudden realization. By "borrowed" she meant stolen. Considering all he had done to keep these elder gods at bay, it should not have shocked him that Cassandra would do the same.

"What do we do next?" he asked in an effort to change topic.

"We?" She glanced at him then back to the road. "There's no *we*, Shaw. I saved you from that thing, but that doesn't make us partners."

"Lucky coincidence you were passing."

"Coincidence." Cassandra mused on the word a moment before giving her head a shake. "Look, I'm sure in your prime you were something, Doctor, but now you'd slow me down."

Shaw looked away, at the passing city. She was right, of course.

When had he gotten old?

The automobile rolled on, its back end giving a clatter of metal as some piece fell to the street. Cloth flapped in the breeze with each movement. A block later Cassandra turned in a tight semicircle, then brought them to the hospital's front door once again.

"You didn't ask my advice, but I'll give it anyway." Cassandra's eyes were on him, earnest and well-meaning. "Go home. Let the shipping company show their compassion and send you back to England."

"I can't go home."

The response surprised Shaw. Hadn't he been considering this very thing just yesterday? A return home and a reopening of his medical practice. Recovering what was left of his life.

But between then and now someone had sent a night-gaunt after him. That was his problem, though, not Cassandra's. It was a problem he was hard-pressed to see a solution for at the moment.

Who sent it, and what did they want?

Shaw opened the door and planted his cane against the pavement, shifting his balance. "I doubt I could ever return to a normal life."

That admission had truth inside it. The unspoken thoughts that had been crawling around inside his mind, given voice. He'd seen too much, knew too much. He belonged in the darkness now. Cassandra's eyes remained on him, sad understanding in them. Shaw pulled himself from the vehicle, closing the door behind him. Outside the car looked even worse. Scratches and tears in cloth and metal. The right end sagged, free of the vehicle's frame. Any passing policeman would surely stop to inquire about it.

"Best of luck, Doctor." A sincere-sounding wish at least.

Cassandra jerked the automobile to the left, back into line among others of its sort. Shaw did not watch her go, instead turning and passing through the hospital's front door. It was still early, and few people were around to see him return in his hospital gown. A dampness spread at his side where his mindless attempt to flee the night-gaunt had pulled some stitches loose.

The ordeal of climbing the stairs was slower than his descent. Step by step by step. Once again Shaw was grateful for being on the first floor. On arriving he found a cart with the necessary bandaging and supplies, taking what was needed. Another quick retreat, this one to his room and bed.

A quick patch up, then he could—

"There you are!" The voice was accusing, a sharp whisper.

Shaw turned to find a nurse checking his sleeping roommates. She wore the dour, no-nonsense expression of a career woman who had seen much, if not all. Shaw tried for an innocent expression as she approached.

"Where have you been?"

Shaw continued toward his bed. "My apologies, I am prone to sleepwalking."

The nurse's eyes traveled to the hospital supplies in Shaw's hand, then back to his face. He tried for a sheepish grin.

"My walk seems to have loosened the doctor's administrations. I thought to correct that."

The nurse came over, making a *tsk*ing sound, and took the bandages. She helped him toward bed with a sudden gentleness. "Pull up your gown and I'll take a look."

The idea of being in that much state of undress, in front of this woman he'd known for two minutes, embarrassed him. The fact that his outlook was utterly ridiculous, and he was a doctor and should know better, frustrated and embarrassed Shaw all the more.

"Come now, Mr. Wilson. I've seen more in my life as a nurse than you could imagine."

"I can imagine quite a bit."

The humor and horror behind that statement cut through his modesty, and Shaw hiked the gown up. A sudden realization occurred to him, and he marveled at it for several moments. His disposition had completely changed. Gone was his tendency to be surly and snappish, to refuse any offer of aid. The removal of that book from his life was like the lighting of a candle, from darkness to light, in short time. The last time he'd felt so free had been many years ago in London, before Whitechapel.

Another *tsk* from the nurse as she examined him. "You've pulled these stitches loose. What were you doing?"

Shaw shrugged, a much better reply than the truth. The gown itself was filthy from his slide down the stairs and his tumble in the street.

They say doctors make the worst patients. Shaw did his best to not watch the nurse's action for fear he would start to tell her how to do her job. There would be no good ending to that, especially since he was not supposed to be a doctor himself at the moment.

"There," she said, retreating from her work to examine from a different vantage point. "That should do, but try to take it easy."

"I shall. Thank you."

"Hmm." It was noncommittal, neither believing nor disbelieving.

She marched to a closet where a new gown was pulled out, then placed on the end of Shaw's bed. Then the nurse was gone, out the door and off to help the next patient. Shaw changed gowns then leaned back against the pillows, considering everything which had happened.

The night-gaunt.

Who had sent it? Who knew he was here, other than Cassandra?

That tug was back.

It had faded into the background during his urge to escape that monster. Now that everything had calmed he could feel it once again, and the more he tried to ignore it the more insistent it became.

"No."

He categorically refused to follow this urge, no matter *how* insistent it became. What was needed now was to catch up on the broken sleep of last night. Indeed, his eyes already drooped as Shaw leaned further into his pillows, mind drifting.

Drifting.

His mind slowed to a crawl, tumbling down the banks of sleep and into the depths of that ocean.

Blackness. Silence. Calm.

A malevolent, odious presence surrounded him, like a great fist squeezing his brain.

Serve me!

"No," Shaw sobbed. "No."

The presence intensified, threatening to devour him. His sanity threatened to flee. Soon he would be a mindless lunatic howling at the moon.

The presence retreated, leaving annoyance in its wake. This was not anything used to practicing patience, and it left Shaw shaking and trembling. His feet kicked against the sheets.

A low growl of barely controlled fury.

"Arkham," a different voice said into his ear.

Shaw jerked in surprise, eyes shooting open while he hissed with the pain of tugging his stitches once again.

"Who the hell …?"

All was forgotten as he saw the owner of that voice.

"St … Stephen?" Shaw's voice trembled just as his body did.

The man he had murdered aboard the *Titanic* to secure passage, dressed in the same dark jacket with a bloodstained shirt underneath. The clothes Stephen had died in. In death this spirit had remained to haunt him, to torment him—or at least to try. Shaw had told the spirit that he would kill a thousand more like him if it meant keeping humanity safe. He'd meant it then and still would now. In the end the dead man had been assaulted by the presence of the *Necronomicon*.

"Your soul was destroyed."

"Sleep."

Eyes sliding closed against his will, Shaw's consciousness receded, like the tide.

Drifting.

Again.

Following the path from waking to dreams.

His mind soared across an unfamiliar countryside of trees and brush, following a single set of train tracks. Left and right, he banked with the air currents, as a bird would. The sensation was incredible. To fly! Then the world accelerated to a dizzying, nauseating speed, always following those tracks, until mercifully, coming to a train station. A building one step up from an over-large shack, made of weather-beaten boards. In front sat two benches for those waiting, looking as if they'd been created at the same time as the station, and from the same materials. Above the station's door was a black sign with wood less weathered than the rest. One word in white lettering: *Arkham.*

Arkham?

A path led to the left, continuing toward a town, and his consciousness sped forward. Through the quiet streets where young people traveled along the sidewalk. Two- and three-bedroom houses on either side, all detached with distinct colors and styles. A few cars here and there, mostly parked.

Again, the vague sound of flute, audible on the breeze.

Twisting and turning, he followed the streets until coming to an open metal gate, recently painted a deep green. The sign on top proclaimed this to be *Miskatonic University.* Beyond was the campus and quad with several buildings.

A fresh tug pulled him back, as if he had reached the extreme end on a rubber band. Now he hurtled backward. Faster and faster. The train station, the tracks, the countryside, he passed by all in a blur of speed.

Beware the six.

What did—

Shaw jerked awake in bed, eyes staring at the ceiling. He twisted his head left, looking for Stephen and finding only empty space. Had the ghost been there, or was that another facet of his dreaming? He couldn't tell.

Arkham.

Miskatonic.

Neither name was familiar, but he knew instinctively this was where the insistent urge directed him. This was where he was expected to go, commanded to.

And what did that warning mean? *Beware the six.*

His eyes drifted to the nightstand, Cassandra's cap still on top. Inside were what meager possessions had survived the ship's sinking. Shirt. Pants. Shoes. His jacket folded neatly on top. It would take perhaps ten minutes to dress and leave.

Why should he?

The thought to go was not his own. Who's influence then?

Was this some sort of trap?

Maybe.

Then he would stay. It was settled. Only, what of the night-gaunt? That monster may have a short life outside of the dream world, but that didn't mean it wouldn't have one more night. Should he be far from here come nightfall?

How though? Even if he did choose to leave, he didn't have a schilling to his name, or a nickel now that he was in New York. He wouldn't even be able to eat.

And yet, to stay could mean death.

"Enough!"

Sleep was needed most. Without it no good decisions would be made.

After that, food.

Then he could make logical decisions rather than ones which stemmed from dreams.

He would consider next steps when he woke.

CHAPTER 11

April 19, 1912
New York City: 7:35 am

Penn Station."

"Penn Station?" Shaw mumbled in response.

Movement. A shift to the right. Cane planted for balance, feet following.

A breeze.

A flap of his coat.

Dampness in the air. Rain was coming.

What—

Reason and consciousness began to part the fog of his mind, forcing that cozy dreamlike numbness back.

Eyes grudgingly fluttered opened.

The world was a blur, indistinct.

The scuff of a shoe as sound returned. A short toot of horn from a passing automobile. The breeze again, making sound against his ears.

What?

Now he forced the sleep and blurriness back, wiped at his eyes.

The hospital room was gone. In its place was the outside of a great building that looked like a museum. No, not a museum. What had the voice said?

"Penn Station," he muttered, turning.

Behind, the street was a mix of automobiles and horse-drawn vehicles headed in either direction. A cab—the one which had deposited him here?—continued to the right. Shaw turned back and looked at the building before him.

"A train station?"

Yes.

No! He'd been sleepwalking, and the last time he'd done terrible things while in a dream state. Inhuman things. Shaw examined himself, finding he was dressed in the clothes he'd worn aboard ship. They'd plummeted into the ocean with him, the only possessions he still had.

A quick search told him that wasn't entirely true. One inside pocket held his reading glasses, while the other had a clump of paper which turned out to be currency, a mix of American and British. Quickly he stuffed it back inside, not wishing to appear conspicuous.

Where had that come from?

He knew for a fact that there hadn't been a penny in those pockets yesterday.

Had he stolen it?

That had a ring of truth.

From who? His fellow patients? The hospital staff?

Did it matter?

It did not. More truth.

A deeper question: Why was he at the train station?

Arkham.

Miskatonic University.

Of course.

Now that his head was clear the tug had returned, urging him forward. Annoyance filled Shaw at the insistence he enter this building. Was this to be expected every time he closed his eyes?

"Damn." He wiped one open palm down his face.

Two options that he could see, one dangerous, the other

illogical. He could return to the hospital—which he had now disappeared from twice—and the people he'd apparently stolen from. Return to the potential night-gaunt, and questions on whether he was Shaw or Wilson … Or he could board the train and continue on to Arkham and this university, doing as he was told. Like a horse in harness.

Neither was appealing.

A third possibility was to enter this train station, find a secluded washroom, and count his ill-gotten currency. From there devise a better plan. Returning to England was tempting, but not until he dealt with whoever hunted him.

"Yes," he muttered to himself.

That will do for a first step.

Marveling at the sheer size of the train station, Shaw started forward, not missing the uncomfortable scratchiness of the hospital gown. Up the steps and through the large doors, thankfully not as heavy as those at the hospital. Inside, the spectacular architecture overwhelmed him once again. Calling the inside a room was like calling the ship he'd been on a boat. This was a train station for certain, but on a scale he'd never seen. On each side were stairs leading to a multitude of gates where travelers would board their trains. There were the obligatory benches of course, and many of them, as well as a giant hanging clock which only Big Ben could give competition. The ceiling was high and wide, enough so that he half expected a cloud to float past. Here and there were pockets of human beings, standing, waiting, checking watch or tickets. Some moved toward gates while others settled onto benches. Porters looked about for anyone needing a hand with baggage in exchange for a much-appreciated donation. At the far end were several booths with ticket agents, destinations and times written above them. In one corner a smaller booth with a sign above which stated: "Telegrams."

For a minute Shaw considered the idea, tongue darting to moisten his lips.

"No." A shake of his head. "Logic, Shaw."

If the first telegram he'd sent had reached Singh, then the lad was at home and knew he was safe. Any updated information on his actions would do Singh no good, even if Shaw could come to some decision on where he was headed. If Singh *wasn't* at home, being in London or somewhere else, then neither message would find him and would be equally useless.

Still, he worried for Singh. Between the theft of the book and the night-gaunt's visit, his private world had become far too busy. If these people who'd sent the night-gaunt knew him did they also know about Singh? Surely he was too far, out of reach. These people would continue to come after him, wouldn't they?

That was sensible.

He still needed to warn Singh, but not this way.

In all honesty what he wanted was to receive a message *from* Singh. Something to say he'd gotten the first message, that he was healthy and safe. A fruitless frustrating wish.

Shaw continued across the station, headed toward the men's washroom. Focused on that one tiny quest in an effort to banish all other worries from his mind. Inside he found a number of stalls, all with doors half open. Good, he was alone. An equal number of sinks pressed up against one wall, matching the white tile floors. Remarkably clean, for a train station.

Leaning against one sink, Shaw forced several slow breaths in through his nose and out his mouth—he never could get it straight which was for in and which was for out. Meditation and these calming exercises didn't work as well for him as they did for Singh, still they did *some*thing, returned some sense of order. Calmed and centered, or at least as much as he was likely to attain for the moment, he was able to take a better accounting of the money in his pocket. A half-dozen American bills of various denominations plus some British pounds. A mismatched handful of coins as well. Enough to buy a meal or two, but was it enough for a train ticket?

Again, the train?

"Arkham," he muttered.

"Yes."

Shaw spun, looking for the ghost. It was Stephen's voice, that same dreamlike tone he'd heard at the hospital. Stephen must be nearby.

But Shaw was alone.

Had he truly heard the voice or …

"Am I going mad?" he asked the empty room. "Again?"

No answer.

Arkham.

Would he truly have any choice but to head there? Or would his subconscious and this undeniable tug decide for him? Next time he slept would he once again work against himself? Would he wake on the train next time?

More worrying still, did his subconsciousness know best?

No answer to that either.

Shaw went to the nearest sink and ran the water. In the mirror he found a near stranger scowling back, face in immediate need of a shave. Thin scratches lined the underside of both eyes, but fainter than they had been a couple of days ago. He wet his hands and rubbed at his face, then dredged his fingers through thinning hair, trying to make one part of his body presentable and half succeeding.

With a grimace he examined himself, taking the full appearance in. The pants and shoes were presentable, though in need of some care. No rips at least. His jacket and underlying shirt had taken the worst of it. The straight, thin cut along his left forearm could be hidden by crossing his arms, but the slashes across his abdomen and left side were more noticeable in the shirt beneath. The fabric was bloodstained and torn, and little he could do about that other than keeping his jacket buttoned.

What else?

Gingerly he pulled his shirt open, inspecting his wounds. The stitching on his abdomen appeared intact, though he wouldn't want to put any more strain on them to test the durability. The wound on his side had been pulled back together by the nurse, and a fresh bandage covered it … That hadn't been there when he'd gone to sleep, had it? A light redness tinted the white bandage.

The entire aspect was of a man down on his luck, a hobo at best.

Was that far from the truth? He *was* homeless, or close enough with his home on the far side of the ocean. Little money. No papers. The one person he truly trusted and counted on likewise across the ocean. And once again he was being hunted and this time only had himself to rely on.

A sigh came from the center of his soul. Calm he may be, but that didn't mean he liked the circumstances any better.

"You've been in worse difficulties than this," he told his reflection.

The reflection looked back, doubtful.

Shaw stood more erect, pulled his jacket straight and fastened the button. Cane firmly against the floor, he turned a slow circle, taking in the full picture. Appearance likely as good as it would get, he gave the doubtful reflection a last look. No decision had been made on what to do next, and each option was as unappealing as the next. The pull toward Arkham continued to be most insistent. One decision he could make was to perform these same ruminations on one of the station benches, rather than in the washroom.

He passed through the door and back into the train station.

CHAPTER 12

April 19, 1912
Penn Station: 7:46 am

Seated casually at the closest bench was Cassandra, both legs stretched out and one arm across the back. A stuffed rucksack leaned beside her. The investigator's eyes, focused on the men's room door, now shifted to Shaw.

"You look like you've returned from war."

Shaw wondered if that was a step up from hobo. He crossed the short divide between them and looked down at the investigator. "What are you doing here?"

"Thought those exact words when you walked into the station."

Shaw glanced toward the entry doors then back again. Had he passed her on the way to the washroom?

"Are you following me, Doctor?"

"What? No, of course not." A scowl crossed his face.

The investigator narrowed her eyes, mouth working. After a moment she shrugged.

"To answer your question," Cassandra said, drawing her feet back in, "I was leaving my hotel, on my way to this train station, when I almost ran you over earlier." She leaned toward Shaw.

"Now, if you're not in fact following me, what exactly *are* you doing here?"

"I ..."

What *was* he doing here? It made no sense whatsoever and, given voice, it would sound like lunacy. A mysterious tug toward this train station, with an equally cryptic dream urging him toward some place he hadn't heard of before today.

He sat beside her.

Cassandra nodded, as if understanding his inner conflict. "You've ignored my advice on returning home."

"I can't."

"So you said."

Shaw looked at the floor a moment before speaking again. "If I go home now, I will bring this evil to my doorstep. I won't endanger Singh this way."

"Singh?"

"My son."

"Doesn't sound very British."

"I adopted him while serving in India. My son in everything except blood." Shaw considered the lad. "Singh is smart. Capable. Strong. If he were here, he would help in any way possible, but ... I can't draw him into this danger. Not again. No, I won't return until I know what this is all about. I have nothing left, so why am I being hounded?" He searched his mind for some piece of information he'd missed. Was it possible? Or was it revenge for keeping the book hidden for so long? "We were the keepers of that book, Singh and I."

"Until it was stolen from you."

Had he told her that earlier? He couldn't remember how much he'd said.

"I did awful things to take possession of it, to keep it hidden and away from people who shouldn't have to know about this other world."

"Noble sacrifice. Letting others live a normal life."

"By the time I made that sacrifice it was too late for me. I already knew far too much." Whatever else, the word "noble" did not apply to him. "For years we were successful, then Wilson, or his people, found us. They stole the book, and I did more terrible acts to get it back … or try to."

"Then your ship hit an iceberg."

Shaw scoffed. "There was no iceberg. Wilson came damn close to raising Cthulhu. The elder god sank my ship."

"What?!" Cassandra leapt to her feet, shock and horror warring for control of her features. She appeared ready to flee but instead retook her seat, raising one shaking hand to wipe her mouth with the back of it. "That madman!"

"I agree."

Her gaze returned to Shaw. "You saw … *it* … then."

Memories of that night wormed their way to the front of his mind, but Shaw forced them back. To remember, to examine the image of that towering nightmare, was to invite madness.

"I saw it," he breathed. "And once Wilson was in the ocean, I read from the damned book and sent Cthulhu back to sleep."

Cassandra flinched at the second mention of the god. The fact that the name did not assault him too was worrying. It was not something one wanted to become comfortable with.

He would be more careful.

The investigator looked off into the distance, digesting all that he'd said. It was a lot. Any other person, this information would be changing their entire view of the world, if they didn't simply think he were an old fool.

No. Cassandra knew. She had seen.

In a few moments her vision returned to the here and now, gaze refocusing on Shaw with a shake of her head. "Far as I'm concerned, this is an end of my affair with that book. It's resting on the ocean floor and good riddance. I hope to be dead when it resurfaces."

Yes, it *would* resurface, but how long would that be? It had no locomotion of its own. Could it return without the help of human beings? No one could dive down that far. There were … *others* … more suited to retrieve it though. The fishlike crossbred sailors of

Limehouse, followers of the aquatic god which had taken Ananya to the depths.

"I'm headed to my next case," she continued. "Best I can offer, Shaw, is to get you to a city with less excitement."

"Thank you, but no. As I said, I can't retreat now."

"Can't or won't?"

"A little of each, I suppose."

"Where will you go then?"

Shaw gritted his teeth, cursing at the realization that still no better possibility had presented itself. If he wasn't headed back to the hospital in hopes of returning home, then he knew where he *was* headed. The fact that the choice was not truly his own grated.

Damn it.

"Apparently," he said, "I am headed to Arkham."

A slight pause, a narrowing of the eyes. "Arkham? What's there for you?"

"The university. Miskatonic."

"I see. And at the university?"

"I have no idea."

Cassandra raised one eyebrow, fingernails tapping against the bench's wooden back.

"It came to me in a dream," Shaw explained. "I feel a … pull, toward this place."

There it was, the lunacy out in the open.

More fingernail tapping until Cassandra slapped her palm against the wood. "You believe in coincidence, Doctor?"

"Not particularly."

"No." Cassandra slid a paper from her jacket and unfolded it, holding it up between two fingers. "Shortly before our encounter with the night-gaunt, I received this telegram for my next case. Care to guess where?"

Shaw's eyes flicked to the paper and back. "Arkham?"

"Specifically the university."

"Why?"

"A professor has lost something he hopes I can find." She replaced the paper inside her jacket.

Lost item. Professor. Miskatonic University. Arkham. None of it meant anything to Shaw.

"We have about thirty minutes before the next train leaves."

Shaw turned toward the ticket booth, not sure how to word his concern over ticket prices, or his lack of funds. Embarrassment filled him. Shame. Again he felt like a vagrant with his hat out begging for coins.

Damn it. How had he fallen so far?

Belatedly he realized Cassandra's words.

"We—?"

But she was already on her feet, scanning the open area. "Wait here."

She crossed the station at a quick pace, making a detour around one family with two young children, then another around a man in a shabby suit. It became clear she was headed toward five men strolling away from the ticket booth. Dressed in obviously newer suits, they came to a stop in a loose circle, engaged in amiable conversation. Head down, Cassandra plowed straight into the backs of two, falling to the ground a moment later with an uncharacteristic cry. A couple of the group looked outraged, as if attacked, while the others helped Cassandra to her feet. She made a great show of apologizing while backing away, the perfect picture of embarrassment. The men returned to their conversation while Cassandra went around them, headed toward the ticket window. There she spent several minutes before returning to Shaw, waving two tickets.

"Direct route to Boston, then a transfer to the smaller Arkham train."

"You bumped into those men on purpose."

She sat, pulled a billfold from inside her jacket and removed all the money—a dozen bills of various denominations—then threw it onto the opposite bench.

"You pick-pocketed them?"

"One in any case. Train tickets aren't free you know."

Cassandra apparently had a gray area where morality was concerned, but he was hardly one to judge. Stephen's enraged, dying expression jumped to mind. Stephen, who had been murdered by Shaw for clothing and passage aboard the ship. No, he was no better than Cassandra, and a great deal worse.

Shaw glanced toward the men, then back. Judging by the quality of their suits they could afford a few dollars of donation. "Thank you for the train ticket."

Cassandra gave a quick nod.

Across the station one man looked at his watch and said something. As a group they headed toward the gate which promised a train to Baltimore. On their way, they passed the telegram office where Shaw's eyes lingered once again.

"They charge by the word," Cassandra warned.

"I don't know where he is anyway."

"Your son?"

"I hope he's safe at home, but Singh isn't the sort to sit still."

London, Shaw decided. That's where the lad would most likely still be, meeting with Albert Victor's son, trying to pass on the message of danger for a book now on the ocean floor.

Cassandra got to her feet, eyes on Shaw. "We can board now."

With some little struggle Shaw also stood. He held one hand out. "Doctor Archibald Shaw."

"I think we've met."

"A proper introduction if we're traveling together."

"Hmm." Cassandra took his hand. "Cassandra Pickman."

Traveling. That sounded like a chance encounter. Two like-minded souls who happened to be taking the same train. It was more than that though. The coincidence. Fleeing from the night-gaunt. He and this investigator were connected, like it or not.

"Don't slow me down, Doctor. I will leave you behind."

Cassandra grabbed her bag and headed toward the gate for Boston, as the five men had done for Baltimore. It was fortunate they hadn't boarded the same train. When the one man found his billfold missing, they were bound to remember the woman who'd bumped into them.

CHAPTER 13

April 19, 1912
Train from New York City to Boston: 8:32 am

On either side of the train cabin were benches which could seat three comfortably, covered in green leather, yet they had the room to themselves. Whether this was because of luck or because Shaw's physical appearance convinced passengers to look elsewhere, he neither knew nor cared. Above was a rack for storage of bags. One window, set into the door, looked out on the hallway beyond.

Shaw unbuttoned his jacket and eased into the seat. Soon they were in motion and once the conductor had come by to punch their tickets, they watched the scenery go by for several miles in silence. Shaw leaned his head back, eyes drooping against the insistence of exhaustion. Cassandra leaned forward, speaking in a conspiratorial tone though no one could have heard.

"Want me to look at that before you sleep?" Cassandra nodded at his left side.

He returned a confused expression before glancing down. The bandage over his stitching had a spot of red the size of a penny, larger than it had been in the washroom. *Damn it!* He'd exerted himself too much again, twisted carelessly in his sleep travels. He cursed under his breath, sure that he would never be allowed to fully heal.

"You're a doctor too, then?" Even as he said it, he could hear the bite of sarcasm to his words, fueled by frustration.

Eyes narrowed. "I know a fair amount of first aid, but if you'd rather restitch the wound yourself, I won't get in the way."

Shaw closed his eyes, embarrassed and ashamed. This woman was obviously capable of much, and even if she wasn't it didn't excuse his response to an offer of assistance. He remained silent, trying to gather the words to say.

"I apologize for my boorish attitude, Cassandra. I would like to blame a lack of sleep, but truthfully I've spent too many years away from civilization."

In some ways Cassandra reminded him of Ananya. Tough. Capable. A leader. She had that fluid sense of morals but, unlike Ananya, seemed to be on the right side of good and evil. The investigator rose to her feet, any insult seemingly forgotten.

"Wait here, Doctor. Try not to bleed to death before I return."

A grim joke, and Shaw's mouth opened at the shock. He forced it closed, refusing to rise to that bait. Without further word she opened the door and disappeared into the train's passage.

Shaw leaned his head back and closed his eyes. The rocking of the train and the steady clackety-clack of the wheels were soothing, lulling him into a doze.

"You will kill her too," a dreamily calm voice said.

Shaw's eyes shot open as he swiveled toward the sound.

Stephen.

Again.

"You bring death wherever you go," the ghost said without emotion.

The words were true. Shaw had long felt like a harbinger of death.

"Your soul was destroyed."

"No." Stephen's voice was soft, wondering. "My soul was devoured."

"Devoured?"

Stephen turned his ghostly face toward him. "I am one with great Cthulhu now."

For a moment his expression changed to one of tragedy and sorrow, then it was gone.

Shaw shook his head. Back on the *Titanic* he'd taken this man's life, and that had been bad enough. Later, when he watched Stephen's soul torn apart by the presence of the book, it had been terrible, monstrous. Now, Shaw knew there were still worse fates.

"How—?" Shaw began.

"I am in hell, Doctor. Madness. Torture. I retain a fragment of who I was."

Stephen spoke as if describing a dream he'd once had.

"Why are you here, Stephen?"

"Arkham."

"Yes. I am headed toward Arkham."

Should he be? Stephen had mentioned it at the hospital, then Shaw had the dream. If Stephen was part of Cthulhu now, that meant the elder god was directing him to Arkham. Why should he do that blasphemy's bidding? Shaw objected to the manipulation.

"Why does Cthulhu care where I go?"

"You are a tool to command. A pawn."

"And why should I go to Ark—"

The cabin door opening brought Shaw's focus back. His eyes snapped open.

Dreaming again?

Cassandra stood in the open doorway, several items in her arms, including a white towel and one bandage that should cover the entire wound.

"Where—"

"Ask me no questions, and I'll tell you no lies."

He was about to ask where Stephen had gone, rather than where she had gotten the items, but allowed the original thought to drop away. Instead he focused on his companion and her armful of undoubtedly ill-gotten gains.

She dropped her items onto the seat and returned to the door between their cabin and the passage. She lowered the blinds over the windows then flipped the lock. Once again she crossed the room, smiling briefly.

"There's a cabinet of basic medical supplies," she explained, "in case anyone gets hurt on the train." She perched on the seat across from him. "Take your coat and shirt off Doctor."

"My …?" He looked at the clothing in question. "Of course."

Determined to be a better patient than he had been at the hospital, Shaw did as told, uncomfortably aware of his state of undress and what this would look like for anyone who entered.

Which, of course, was why she locked the door.

The bandage's bloodstain had spread slightly since Cassandra left. She leaned closer to examine the wound.

Slowly she removed the existing bandage and looked at the stitching underneath. Shaw sighed at the sight of blood around the wound. It was no more than a slight ooze, nothing life- threatening. The days of not moving aboard the *Carpathia* had given some time to heal, but this still needed attention.

She dabbed at the wound with the towel, coming away with a slight reddish tint. Mostly dry then. Perhaps they could just leave it—

"This is going to hurt."

"I'm not—"

Cassandra grabbed the stitching ends and pulled.

"GAH!"

"Keep it down, Doctor." She tied the ends together nimbly.

Shaw hissed while Cassandra placed the fresh bandage over the wound, making it tighter than the previous one. It was more secure, but Shaw was aware of it with each breath he took.

"That should hold," she said, "unless we have to run."

"Considering last night, I wouldn't bet against it."

Cassandra half smiled and leaned back in her seat.

"Thank you."

It seemed the pain of the stitching being pulled together had chased his fatigue away, at least for the moment. The seats were comfortable, and Shaw knew sleep would come again in short order. He leaned forward to retrieve his clothing from the floor, but Cassandra held out another prize. Dark brown and thick fabric. Shaw took it, letting it unfurl into …

"A jacket?"

"Hope it's your size."

Shaw shrugged into his destroyed shirt, pulling the borrowed jacket over it. "Where did you … No. Never mind."

Cassandra gave him a wink.

The jacket was a bit roomy. The previous owner had been twenty pounds heavier than he was. Shaw was grateful to replace the current one and pulled his few belongings from the pockets, slipping them into the new jacket. Feeling much fresher than he had a minute ago, Shaw leaned back into the seat. "How long is this train ride?"

Cassandra consulted her ticket. "Four hours to Boston, give or take. You have time to sleep."

The pain of those stitches being pulled had woken him just enough. "What has this professor lost that you mean to find?"

"His nephew."

"His …?"

How does one lose a person?

No. He could imagine several ways, most did not end well for the nephew. Was this why he was being pushed toward Arkham? It felt small, insignificant. Not the battle against relentless evil he expected.

"How is this relevant to our current circumstance?"

"Our current circumstance," Cassandra repeated, speaking slowly as if to a somewhat dim child, "is that both you and I are being guided toward Arkham—not to mention each other it would seem—and you do not believe in coincidence."

"No, but—"

"As for relevance, this is my job, if nothing else. It's what I do to eat, which I find somewhat relevant to my personal well-being."

Shaw wondered how much of her money came from cases, and how much came from relieving people of their wallets … Truly irrelevant and an attempt to justify his words. He'd been too long out of civilization, and day-to-day life bewildered him. Money. Jobs. Travel. Food. It was all so mundane.

"Besides," Cassandra added, glancing out the window as if all answers were written across the glass, "darkness and evil tend to find me rather than having to search them out. Something to do with …" A quick shake of the head. "There's times I just know I'm headed in the correct direction."

"This feels right?"

Cassandra was silent, staring through the window. "Feels as if we're headed toward danger and darkness and death."

"Comforting."

She had left it for him to decide whether danger and darkness and death was the correct direction. So many questions bounced inside his head, but each got in the way of another so none would come forward, like too many people trying to get through the same door at once. His thoughts were muddled. Perhaps after he slept.

Darkness and evil tend to find me.

Shaw understood that. For too many years he had slipped deeper into this insanity. Even in Cambridge where they'd lived like hermits, keeping the book safe.

Now this night-gaunt.

Yes, that monster qualified as darkness and evil.

On the edge of sleep his subconscious mind continued to sift through stray facts and ideas, making connections he couldn't while awake. Images floated across his near-dreaming mind. Cassandra. The night-gaunt. St. Vincent's Hospital.

It had come down the hallway, sniffing at the air, going into the room before his.

Darkness and evil tend to find me.

Shaw jerked, eyes open and entirely awake. "The night-gaunt wasn't after me."

CHAPTER 14

April 19, 1912

Train from New York City to Boston: 8:55 am

Cassandra raised one eyebrow, no other change of expression.

"It was sniffing at the air, following a trail, but that trail started around the corner. It went into the room before mine where I'd never been."

A mental picture of Cassandra stalking the halls, checking each room for the bed with Wilson in it.

"It was following you!" he said. "I was just on the path you'd taken out of the hospital."

She considered a moment. "Possible."

"Possible—?"

"I told you, darkness is drawn to me, and vice versa."

Gritting his teeth, he stared out the window again, annoyed that he was headed to Arkham on the strength of some vague dream and an incorrect assumption. The night-gaunt was no danger to him after all.

All coincidence.

Coincidence?

Only, as he'd told Cassandra, he didn't believe in coincidence.

A creature he'd encountered once before and barely escaped just happened to be in the same hospital as him? A thing from the nightmare world which had killed the museum director and a guard before battering great doors open and making its escape. *That* had just happened to be in the same place as him?

No.

That wasn't all though.

"The ghost," he muttered.

"What?"

A shake of his head. The voices had woken him, and Mrs. Hooper had urged him to get out of that room, to flee. Would she have done so if he hadn't been in danger?

Again. No.

"Do *you* believe in coincidence, Cassandra?"

"No."

No hesitation, no consideration. Just as he hadn't needed to think on it when she'd asked the same question.

"That night-gaunt may have been there for us both."

Cassandra gave a grunt of acknowledgment and leaned back, away from Shaw and the conversation.

"At least we are safe from it during the day," Shaw added.

"There's many other creatures which can skulk in the sunlight."

Several more miles passed with sleep continuing to elude him. Too many thoughts. Too many questions.

"How did you come to be looking for the book?" he asked.

A cock of her head and the attention shifted back. Once again that appraising stare, as if considering how much Shaw could endure.

"Before coming to New York I was investigating the disappearance of a salesman in the town of Innsmouth."

"Never heard of it."

"No reason you should have. They've isolated themselves by choice. One ramshackle bus passes through on its route of these small towns and this salesman, looking for fresh opportunities ..." She shrugged. "No one arrives there by happenstance, and anyone who should visit is treated as the unwelcome stranger that they are."

Shaw could recall hearing of places back home that were off the beaten track. Places where people wanted to be left alone and it was best not to push that. He gestured for Cassandra to continue.

"The buildings are dilapidated, and the *people*." An emphasis on the word as if she considered them anything but. "Backward's the way many would describe them, but it's more than that. They've crossbred with another race, something from the ocean, creating perverted monstrosities." She shuddered at the memory. "They worship a god called—"

"Dagon."

Cassandra started, eyes narrowed. "You *do* have knowledge, Shaw."

"An encounter years ago."

"With these fish people?"

"Yes, but with Father Dagon as well."

"You've … seen Dagon?"

Shaw realized how insane it was for anyone to encounter one of these gods, much less two. By all rights he should be gibbering in a madhouse. "He … it … was called accidentally by the holder of the book. An accident. She'd intended to call up Cthulhu."

Another jump. Both of Cassandra's hands came down on the arm of her seat, gripping tightly before letting loose again.

"Madness!" she said.

Shaw could still see the expression on Ananya's face, the fervor in her eyes. She had honestly thought she could call one of these gods and be rewarded, be placed by their side as a favored one. No, Ananya was guilty of ignorance for certain, but her eyes when Dagon dragged her back to the deep were not mad.

Cassandra looked forward again, lips working against these facts. When her gaze came back around it held a bit more respect for Shaw. He may not keep up physically, but there was nothing wrong with his mind. Not with his memory and knowledge in any case.

"What happened in Innsmouth?" he asked.

"I left suddenly. Locals took offence to my questions and broke into my hotel room. Close call. I found James Wilson was arriving in New York with the book. He was to bring it to Innsmouth and someone named Marsh."

"Marsh?" The name was unfamiliar. "Why bring it there at all?"

"Wilson was born and raised in Innsmouth."

"I see." Shaw considered it and realized he *didn't* see, not entirely. Oh, it explained the destination of Innsmouth, but … No. "Why not raise Dagon instead of … the other one?"

It seemed Dagon was easier for her to hear than Cthulhu.

"I've been wondering on that myself. Could the book have influenced Wilson and steered him toward certain actions?"

Shaw remembered the looks of Wilson's accomplices and could believe that. The book, or maybe Cthulhu itself … Shaw shuddered at the memory of his dream aboard the *Titanic*, navigating through the depths until in the presence of that malevolent being. The idol alone had influenced Shaw to do some particularly heinous acts years ago.

"Yes," Shaw agreed. "It's possible that James Wilson was not in control of his own mind, not entirely."

"I'd intended on intercepting the book, to keep it out of Wilson or Marsh's hands."

"Be glad it's on the bottom of the Atlantic instead."

"For now."

Yes. For now.

Where did it all end? More worshippers of Dagon on this side of the ocean. This Marsh person looking to possess the *Necronomicon*. For every step forward, two steps back. Now someone had conjured another night-gaunt to chase one or both of them.

"You recognized the night-gaunt. You'd seen one before."

Cassandra nodded.

Shaw lowered his voice, added a gentler edge to it. The voice he would use for a patient. "Innsmouth was not your introduction to this world of darkness."

Cassandra shook her head, jaw set, and looked away. That

seemed the end of it. Shaw also looked aside. If Cassandra didn't want to talk, then it was none of his business. Memories of Lassiter and his fixation with the idol, the Maut, Cult of Kali, and a trail of death that spanned years, forced themselves into his mind. Incidents from before this woman had ever been born. Yes, he could appreciate not wanting to relive the past. Cassandra removed her jacket, hanging it from a hook before retaking her seat. The holster on her left and the long knife moved in unison, extensions of her body. She glanced around, as if someone might have snuck through the locked door, then with one hand unbuttoned the cuff of her shirt and dragged the sleeve up toward her shoulder.

Repositioning to lean forward she held the bare arm out toward Shaw, who obligingly leaned forward as well. What was he expected to see? He pulled his reading glasses from the inside jacket pocket and placed them on his face.

"No," he whispered, taking in the faint lines etched into her skin. "My God!"

Tattooed into the flesh of Cassandra's arm, starting an inch above her wrist, were words in the same horrible script Shaw recognized from the *Necronomicon*.

"So faint," he muttered, the voice of a scholar before some long-lost text. "Faded."

"They're darker at night," she said.

Line after line which his mind immediately started to translate. Even now his lips moved in a parody of speaking, mouthing the words.

"I keep these hidden. Always."

"Yessss." Shaw forced his mouth shut, tore his gaze from the writing, back to Cassandra's eyes. "You must!"

Her eyes widened. "Impressive, Doctor."

"Years of practice, and bitter experience."

This had been a test of his resolve, as much as a revealing of her secret. Had she expected him to lose his mind, even temporarily?

"Only two people've seen these tattoos before you. First jumped from a window."

"And the second?"

"Tried to cut my arm off."

"What if I'd similarly lost control?"

Cassandra didn't answer, didn't need to. Her revolver was prominently displayed, but he doubted she would have used it. A push would topple him, giving enough time to leave the cabin. Shaw would have raved in this furnished cell until someone found him.

"I took a chance showing you." She rolled her shirt sleeve down and refastened the cuffs.

His heart still raced inside his chest, his breathing shallow. Shaw closed his eyes and went through a short process for clearing and centering his mind. When he opened his eyes he found Cassandra staring at him, muscles tensed. Ready to defend herself?

Shaw shook his head. "I'm fine."

"You're about as fine as I am."

A short bark of laughter, not entirely devoid of humor. "Perhaps *fine* is optimistic."

"I'm impressed you could look at all."

Another deep breath and his focus had shifted further from the covered markings, his calm returning. "This tattoo was surely not by choice."

"No more than paper consents to be written on. As I said, there's more than one way to print a book."

The *Necronomicon* had been printed on leather. Dead flesh. It hadn't occurred to him that it would be printed on living leather too. Incredible! Horrible! To live with such a thing.

"You … have others?"

Cassandra nodded several times, as if unable to find the words. She breathed out a slow breath, looking back with haunted eyes. "Don't know why I showed this to you."

"Maybe because we are both survivors," Shaw suggested. "Victims of the same horror."

"Victim?" she spat. "I'm no victim, Doctor, so save your pity."

Shaw spread his hands in a placating gesture. "Perhaps then you wanted to tell your story to someone who would understand. It helps to share such trauma."

Cassandra stared out the window, lost in her own thoughts while Shaw kept his eyes on her, studying this remarkable woman. The burden of those tattoos would have broken most people. He'd struggled under the weight of that book, and it was something he could leave in another room or escape for periods by leaving the house. He couldn't imagine carrying it everywhere he went.

"They cover most of my body," she said, not turning from the window. "Everywhere except my hands and from the neck up." Now she refocused on him. "I was a child, seven years old at most, when I received these."

"What kind of parent would allow such a thing?"

"My …" Cassandra broke off, shook her head. "I remember other children, though we didn't play together. The house was huge, a mansion in fact. Lots of people."

"Who were they?"

Another shake of the head. "No idea. They dressed in dark robes, held … rituals in the basement."

"A cult?"

"Cult always brings to mind people trying to call the devil and ultimately dissolving into orgies. These people called real monsters which shuffled through the corridors."

"More lunatics worshipping monsters." Shaw found the inclusion of children in this the most heinous, as the cult in India had with Singh. "Did the other children also have tattoos?"

"No. They might have in time but … One night I woke to a lot of noise. Shouts. Gunshots. The house was under attack. A fire. My mother came for me and we escaped. I never found out who had attacked. Another cult? Police? Something worse? Anyway, no one came looking for us that I know. My mother raised me—least she said she was my mother. She looked nothing like me."

"Where is she now?"

"Died when I was sixteen."

Shaw wondered on how great a tragedy that was.

"I know I have a destiny but refuse for it to be these tattoos."

"Why did they do this? What was their goal?"

"Mother told me these were special. Don't understand the

writing and can only see it in a mirror. Can't look at them for any length without feeling like I'm losing myself. Sinking. I keep them covered, change in the dark."

Shaw considered all this woman had been through, and at such a young age. His eyes slid to the arm she had shown, as if he could look through the fabric and read the words there.

"Mgahnnn nglui."

"What?"

The train compartment was suddenly hot, like being in a room with a fireplace much too large for it. Dizziness passed over him, and a fog in his mind. His head throbbed and the words she'd shown danced before his eyes.

He leaned back, eyes closed.

Still the words assaulted his mind, demanding attention.

"A portal."

Had *he* said that?

Yes.

"A portal?" she asked.

"The words. They open a portal."

"A portal where?"

"Hmm?" he muttered.

"Shaw!" The voice was firm, more steel in it than in her knife.

His eyes refocused.

"What did you mean they open a portal?"

"A portal?"

"That's what you said."

That *was* what he'd said. He could hear himself speaking. A shake of his head, fighting to clear it.

"The tattoo on your arm. It ..." The words no longer clogged his mind. "I ... No, sorry. It's gone now."

"Hmph!" Cassandra leaned back, arms crossed.

Hard to focus through the sudden fatigue. Shaw felt his eyes drooping.

Cassandra repeated to herself, "A portal."

Sleep took Shaw.

CHAPTER 15

April 19, 1912
Arkham, Massachusetts: 2:17 pm

Arkham gave Shaw a sense of apprehension from several miles distant. His palms sweat and he was restless, wanting to flee, lame leg and other injuries be damned. The train station was a slight surprise, looking exactly like the one from his dream and adding to his disquiet. Even down to the benches and station name plate. By this point prophetic dreams should be less of a surprise to him, but he doubted that would ever be the case.

A battered green bus waited for passengers from the train. Cassandra shook her head.

"It's heading the wrong way," she said, starting in the opposite direction.

Shaw fell into step beside her, the investigator slowing her pace to allow him to keep up. He wouldn't complain, but hoped for a shorter walk. At least his leg was rested. They followed a straight course up Garrison Street from Arkham station. After one bridge and three blocks they arrived at the gate to Miskatonic University. Not too long a trek after all. There they followed a path until arriving at the center of an inner lawn. Miskatonic covered more area than expected. A U-shaped collection of buildings gathered around an inner quad, with the open end pointing toward Garrison and the gate. A total of nine buildings surrounded them with paths between each, allowing students multiple ways in and out of the campus, and perhaps to other buildings not part of the main grouping.

Shaw found himself looking over his shoulder, half expecting something to be there. "Where do we find this Professor Watkins?"

Cassandra looked at him, a quizzical expression on her face. "I never told you his name."

"I saw it on the telegram earlier."

"You would have made a fair investigator, Doctor."

An investigator. Yes, he'd done his share over the years, none of it ending well. In Bandagar his bumbling efforts had resulted in the deaths of Walsh and several other soldiers. London had seen the death of the museum director and guard. Whitechapel… No, better to leave those memories dormant. On the *Titanic* his investigations led to the deaths of more than a thousand of his fellow passengers. He hadn't seen the exact amount yet and didn't want to.

"Professor Watkins teaches linguistics. I imagine we'll need to find that department."

Only no building was clearly labeled as Linguistics. Literature was perhaps the closest. Then again it could just as easily be in the building marked as Science.

Shaw turned a slow circle, hoping to find some student or staff member to ask directions. No one. Thinking back to his college days there was always something going on, people on the move from one place to another, groups of friends standing about talking.

This place was dead.

They'd made great time from Boston to Arkham, arriving as their connecting train had been in the process of boarding. Missing that train would have meant a six hour delay for the next. Now it looked as if they would lose all the time they'd gained.

"Administration?"

"I suppose." She let out a sigh. "Watkins could be on his way home by the time we find his office."

Administration would point them in the right direction but also would cost them time getting there and answering questions.

"Hey!" Cassandra yelled.

Shaw turned toward the object of her attention. A thin boy, frozen in place, protruding eyes behind thick glasses aimed in their direction. He looked skittish, a deer in the sudden presence of predators.

"What building has the Linguistics department?"

The boy made no movement for a moment before pointing behind them. Two buildings cast a shadow in their direction, another path between them.

"The Science building?" Cassandra replied.

The boy shook his head, and Cassandra muttered under her breath, "This'd go quicker if you'd speak." Then louder, "Literature then?"

The boy nodded. Cassandra and Shaw both looked toward the other building, and when they turned back to give thanks the boy had disappeared.

"What the hell was that about?" she said. "Think he's never seen a woman before?"

"Maybe just not ones who are so … outgoing."

Cassandra grunted and started toward the building. Inside was a board with the layout, put there for new students and the uninitiated like themselves. Watkins's office was labeled. The going was necessarily slower for Shaw's sake. He could see it frustrated his companion, but he wasn't about to apologize for it. They traveled at a fair pace, but he wouldn't be able to run.

He wished he could, but if wishes were fishes, and all that.

As it turned out, Watkins's office was in that building but he had a class in session in yet another building. After finding the correct lecture hall, they let themselves in at the back. The room was built with seating at an angle, much like a theatre, with the lecturer at the bottom. Smells of chalk and paper, wood and polish. It reminded Shaw of his own university days. Simpler times.

They took two empty seats and directed their attention to the speaker, Professor Watkins. The man's voice carried across the open area without effort, such were the acoustics of the hall. He paced from one side to the other, animated, engaging, his focus continually shifting from one student to another. The man himself was somewhat overweight, pushing the edges of his brown jacket open to settle on either side of his belly. A simple striped tie down the center to meet pants which matched his jacket. Wire-rimmed glasses under thinning brown hair rounded out the picture of university professor. Shaw placed his age as somewhere in his late forties to early fifties.

Engaging as Watkins was to his students, the subject of Speculations About the Origin of Language held no real fascination for Shaw. Perhaps if he'd come in at the beginning of the lesson. In no time at all his mind had well and truly wandered.

Cassandra was more attentive, though she seemed to be measuring the man more than listening. Out of habit Shaw patted the pocket where his watch should have been but found nothing. Like the *Necronomicon*, it rested on the ocean floor. A glance around confirmed no clocks existed here either. A place out of time. Without knowing when the class had begun or when it ended the point was moot in any case. He glanced at Cassandra, who nodded without changing focus. She held up two fingers, then a closed fist. Two and zero? He hoped that meant twenty minutes and not two hours.

Was his inability to stay still caused by doing nothing else the last couple of decades? No. He was an academic not an adventurer, not by choice. This was where he should be most at home.

"Oh!" he said. It wasn't a shout, but certainly above the whispers students were exchanging. If Watkins noticed he gave no sign. Shaw turned toward Cassandra and continued in a lower tone, "The pull is gone."

Cassandra shifted her eyes toward him, taking him in, then raised both eyebrows in acknowledgment before returning her focus to the professor. Shaw wondered when the last time he'd felt it had been. It had been present at the train station in New York.

Once they were on the train? Between the fatigue and tattoos and their conversation, he couldn't recall.

Watkins's lecture wound down twenty minutes later. Cassandra remained seated until the majority of students had filed out, and those few who stopped to speak with the professor had gone through their motions. The final student asked Professor Watkins a question in a low murmured tone and Cassandra rose to her feet, descending the hall's steps. Shaw followed, managing one step for every two of Cassandra's. She waited at the bottom for them to meet the professor together.

"Professor Watkins?" Cassandra asked as the final student jogged up the steps toward waiting friends.

The man's attention swiveled around, eyes narrowing at Cassandra—quite obviously not one of his students—before returning to normal. A curious expression returned to his face. "Yes?"

"Cassandra Pickman," she introduced herself, halting a few steps from the man. "My associate, Doctor Archibald Shaw. You sent for me."

"Oh! Yes, of course." He extended one hand and shook both of theirs in turn. "I expected you would send a message first."

"We left New York in a hurry."

"Ah, I see." Watkins waved one hand. "Not that I am critical, mind you. Time is of the essence."

His gaze lingered on Shaw, a quizzical cock to his head. Was it the attire? Had Watkins observed his too-large coat, or the bloody shirt beneath, and judged him as out of place? Or was it the fact he was here at all? Shaw kept his face bland, unthreatening. The doctor's face.

"You're missing a nephew?" Cassandra prompted.

"Please, come to my office."

Cassandra waited for the man to gather his papers and lead the way. They exited through a door at the bottom of the lecture hall into a short hallway. That led to another and another until Shaw was unsure which direction he was facing.

"The buildings are all connected underground?" he asked.

Watkins glanced over one shoulder. "We're under one corner of the quad at the moment."

More technological marvels. Each one made Shaw feel more and more like a dinosaur. Gigantic ships. Automobiles. Buildings connected through underground passages that were not dank caves, but well-lit corridors.

"Out of curiosity," Cassandra said. "Where did you get my name?"

"Ah ... that was ... Oh yes, the school librarian. Doctor Armitage."

"Armitage?" Cassandra mused a moment before giving a shake of the head.

It would be impossible for someone in Cassandra's line of work to remember the hundreds, perhaps thousands, of people she came into contact with during each case. She waved it off as unimportant and refocused on the professor while Shaw's eyes narrowed a moment, replaced just as quick with his best doctor expression. Watkins, for whatever reason, was lying ... or at the very least holding something back.

Why?

Their host stopped to pass through a door which proclaimed, "Professor Reginald Watkins," his name sandwiched between two others. "Professor Warren Rice" just above, and "Professor Ferdinand Ashley" below. Inside three desks waited, all unoccupied. A small area was arranged at the center for students taking advantage of office hours.

"My officemates are currently giving lectures."

Watkins gestured toward two chairs, and Cassandra pulled each closer to the professor's desk.

"Tell us about your nephew."

The professor leaned forward, elbows on his desk, lips working. His eyes shifted toward the floor then back, as if unsure of where to start. The professor's fingers tapped against his desk's blotter. "I have two nephews, Matthew and David. They've been with me since the age of four."

"Which one's missing?"

"Matthew, older by twenty minutes. They're both adults now, in their twenties. Matthew left home as soon as he was able, to see the world. What he's truly searching for is a life of wild hedonism."

The professor had gritted his teeth and took a deep breath. An emotional topic it would seem.

"If Matthew is an adult, he can't exactly be dragged home by one ear," Cassandra said. "Not if he doesn't want to come."

Watkins raised one hand in a *hold on* gesture. "My other nephew is more level-headed and responsible. He lives with me still." The professor once again tapped his fingers against the desk. "I get a letter from Matthew every couple of months. Sporadic communication. Matthew knows I don't approve of his lifestyle, but he is still my nephew and I care deeply for him. Still, he is in touch with David on a more regular basis."

Cassandra leaned forward in her seat, a voiceless encouragement to continue.

"David came to me with a letter from Matthew, or part of it in any case. One page of strange text, copied by hand from some other source. David hoped with my expertise in linguistics I could identify it."

"Did you?" Shaw asked.

A slow shake of the head. The man's eyes slid aside for a moment, and he shuddered. Cassandra glanced to Shaw, who raised one eyebrow.

"No," Watkins continued. "It was all gibberish. No pattern at all. If those were indeed words, then the language worked like none I've ever seen. I would need a Rosetta Stone type of discovery to understand it."

Again his eyes slid away, discomfort in a memory.

"And?" Cassandra prompted.

"What?" Watkins refocused on them. "Oh. Nothing. Imagination."

"You felt uneasy," Shaw suggested. "Any time your eyes landed on the words."

Watkins's gaze flickered between Shaw and Cassandra. A lick of the lips and a nod. One brief humorless laugh. "Yes. Ridiculous as that sounds. I couldn't stand to look at those letters for any length of time." He pushed both hands through his thinning hair. When he returned them to the desk, one gave the slightest of tremors. "I took the page to a friend in the Archaeology department. Doctor Bell. He has a second degree in ancient languages."

"Did he have anything to add?"

"Bell took one glance and refused to look again. Told me to leave it alone. When I explained it was to do with my nephew, he was silent for quite some time. All he would say was it came from a very dark, ancient text."

"Oh, yes," Shaw agreed in a whisper.

Very dark.

He glanced at Cassandra. Agreement on this text's origin flashed between them. Yes, as she claimed, she was drawn to the darkness.

"Do you have the letter?" she asked.

Watkins shook his head. "In my study at home, locked in my desk. I was ... uncomfortable carrying it."

"I'd like to see this letter for myself." Cassandra stood. "I'd also like to speak with David."

CHAPTER 16

April 19, 1912
Professor Watkins's Home: 3:32 pm

The professor's house was a ten-minute walk from Miskatonic, less if Watkins and Cassandra hadn't been slowed by Shaw. They'd crossed Garrison Street, traveled a block along Lich Street to turn onto Parsonage. Cassandra showed some impatience, glancing back at him, then toward the way they traveled. Every so often she would loose a low sigh. Watkins gave no sign he noticed, falling into step beside Shaw and matching his pace.

"I hope you'll forgive the observation, Doctor," Watkins said, looking ahead. "But your clothes are ... umm ..."

"Showing signs of wear?"

"Yes. That's it."

In London it would be unthinkable to mention this directly to a person. Instead, he would be ignored while others *tsked* behind his back. Which was truly preferable?

"I have had some ... misadventures lately," Shaw said. "I lost much of my belongings that were with me."

"The doctor's ship from England sunk."

"Good lord!" Watkins came to a halt. "Not the *Titanic*."

Shaw grimaced. "The same."

"I see. I see."

That seemed the end of it. The three of them continued on in the mild spring air. Buds of maple trees announced the banishment of winter. Squirrels chittered and birds chattered. It could almost make Shaw forget for a moment the secret evil only he and select others knew of.

Almost.

"Here we are," Watkins announced.

The professor's house was so much larger than what one man and his nephew needed. It reminded Shaw of his home in Cambridge. Would he ever see it again? Would he even be allowed back now that he'd failed in his task to keep the book safe?

"David?" Watkins called as the three passed into the entry hall.

No answer.

Off to their right was a sitting room. Blue fabric covered sofas facing toward a fireplace. Cozy. To the left another room with closed doors, and something about those doors said "knock before entering." Ahead, curving stairs led to a second floor while the hallway continued on, passing the stairs and leading to a doorway and rooms beyond. Judging by the size, the house would have four or five bedrooms at least.

"David?" A little louder.

Growing up in England it would have been boorish for a person to enter the house and call out in such a manner. Different society. Different time. Different standards.

A clash of cultures. Yes, he liked the sound of that.

"I suppose he's gone out," Watkins concluded. "This way."

He opened the door on their left and passed into what had to be the man's study. A desk covered in books and papers beneath a window, giving a view of an outside garden. More books crammed shelves around the room with still others in stacks on the floor. Classics. Textbooks. Reference. All here and there among each other with no evident organization. A wooden globe in its frame, elegant and well crafted.

"It's in my desk drawer," he said, sitting in the desk's accompanying wooden chair which looked less comfortable than two padded chairs nearby. Watkins pulled the center drawer toward him and retrieved a letter. Without a glance he handed it to Cassandra.

She moved toward another window for better light before looking at it. Shaw came up beside her and peered over one shoulder. Cassandra grunted with pain, as if punched, on seeing the text. She held it to her left, allowing Shaw a clearer view. "Hmm?"

"Surely from the *Necronomicon*," he said, shaking his head to clear it. His heart hammered. "Not familiar, not … I've seen only a page or two."

All this in low mutters between them. He took hold of the letter from one corner.

"I …" he started. "I …"

A headache had sprung between his eyes. By the look on Cassandra's face, she was experiencing the same. She staggered back a step, retreating from the letter and dropping her hand from it.

"Are you well?" Watkins asked, rising to his feet. When no answer came he crossed the room and placed his hand over the text, breaking the line of sight. "I warned you it was hard to look at. I had thought perhaps I was being weak-minded, influenced by my archaeologist friend's warning, but the proof is here with your reactions."

Cassandra tore her eyes from the letter. "We've seen similar writing before, both of us."

"You have?" The professor ushered her toward the two padded armchairs facing each other across a chessboard on a table. "What does it say?"

"I can't read it," she admitted, "but the doctor—"

Shaw remained in the same spot, letter in hand, words no longer obscured. His lips worked, a low mumble issuing from them, the way a child would while learning to read. Only here the words coaxed him, encouraged him, demanded that he speak them.

"Az … Azathoth," he said, not knowing what the word meant

but not liking the sound at all. He looked toward Cassandra. "I … I …"

"Shaw?"

His gaze was dragged back to the text. "Throdog Azathoth."

"Shaw!" Cassandra yelled. "Drop it!"

Shaw heard the words and agreed with them to the center of his soul … but he couldn't. The words pulled from his throat, voice rising to a near shout in moments. "Mgepogog ot mgepogor. Ah'n'ghft legeth'drn r'luhhor. Ah'n'gha'drn ot shuggogg!"

The scrape of wood on floor. A chair tipping. Shaw could not shift his focus though he desperately wanted to. The next line. The next line. It sucked his consciousness downward. A spiral. A whirlpool.

"Mgahnnn nglui."

In the next moment Cassandra was at his side, snatching the letter from his hand and holding it away from him. Without looking she folded it once again.

"Doctor?"

Tears coursed down his cheeks, though he was hardly aware of anything within the room.

"Shaw?"

With effort he focused on the source of that word. Cassandra. For the first time since fleeing the night-gaunt he saw fear in her eyes, mouth agape but no words to say other than his name. Shaw stepped back with one shake of his head. He wiped the tears from his face, realizing a sweat had broken across his body as well. A swipe across his forehead with one sleeve.

"What …? What did I …?"

"I have no idea."

"You read the words?" Watkins said, incredulous. "How?"

The professor stepped back, collapsing into the remaining upright chair. Not just incredulous but frightened. Sick. Hearing those words for the first time had been an assault on the man's mind.

Cassandra led Shaw to the tipped chair, uprighted it and guided him into the seat. He collapsed like a sack of flour, all strength gone from his limbs. Embarrassed, he wouldn't make eye contact with Watkins or Cassandra. How had he resisted the unexpected words tattooed on Cassandra, but had lost himself when seeing these?

They sat in silence, each lost in thoughts.

"Cognac."

Shaw and Cassandra looked at the professor, who was weakly getting to his feet.

"Yes, yes. That is what we need. A good stiff shot."

The man crossed the room and busied himself at the globe, which opened to reveal a hidden bar. The clink of glasses.

"When the six are gathered," Shaw whispered, "the portal shall open."

"What does that mean?"

Shaw shook his head. He'd heard part of it in dreams and now … He had no idea where the rest had come from.

A moment later Watkins was back with three glasses. Shaw didn't want the drink, had never been any sort of drinker, but he downed it at a gulp. The liquid burned, filling him with heat through his extremities, shocking his senses. He gasped. Watkins had only been looking for something normal, controllable to do in the face of the terrifying, but it had done the trick. Those horrible words danced at the edge of Shaw's mind but came no closer, like wolves outside the firelight.

"The words you spoke," Cassandra said, leaning forward, her own drink untouched.

Shaw shook his head. "What did I say?"

"I recognized one word. Azathoth."

Both her and Watkins looked uneasy at the sound of the name.

"Azathoth?" His eyes came up to meet hers. "What does it mean?"

"It's the name of another god. An older one."

"Older?"

"Older than Dagon or … Cthulhu." She shuddered at mentioning the names and downed her drink. "Older than Yog-Sothoth, who was worshipped by the cult I was raised in."

Shaw wasn't sure which one to ask about.

"Azathoth is the god that other gods fear."

A cold sweat broke across Shaw's body. Hands clammy. "Why?"

Watkins cleared his throat, making Shaw jump. He'd forgotten the man was there.

"Perhaps we should put the letter away," Watkins suggested. "At least for now?"

"I'm fine," Shaw said.

Watkins shook his head. "I'm not."

Cassandra held the letter out and Watkins took it as if the paper might bite him. He returned it to his desk and closed the drawer.

Azathoth.

That one word danced at the edge of Shaw's mind, greater than the others.

Azathoth.

Cassandra still leaned toward him, eyes on his. "There was—"

"Uncle?"

CHAPTER 17

April 19, 1912
Professor Watkins's Home: 3:57 pm

The voice calling from the entry was soon followed by a figure. It appeared in the doorway, taking the scene in. Shaw and Cassandra. The open globe bar. Watkins's expression.

"David," the professor breathed. "Come in."

David was a thin, tall boy in his twenties, blond hair meticulously combed back straight. He wore glasses similar to his uncle and indeed looked to be following in the man's footsteps in terms of fashion as well. A simple suit, a blue striped tie. The attire of a professor, or of someone who wished to be.

"This is my nephew David," Watkins said needlessly. "David, this is Cassandra Pickman and Doctor Archibald Shaw."

"Pleased to meet you." David shook hands with each of them.

"They're here to find Matthew."

"Oh! Of course. Thank you for coming."

Cassandra glanced at Shaw, who raised one eyebrow.

"As I told your uncle," Cassandra said, while David rolled the wooden chair over from the desk, "I can find him, but that doesn't mean I'll bring him back. Matthew's an adult and can make his own decisions."

"That's fine." David held up both hands. "I just want to know that my brother is safe and healthy. His letters since he returned have been … well, increasingly odd."

"Odd how?"

"They started out fine, his usual self. Matthew has always been someone who did what he wanted and looked to consequences afterward."

"Unfortunately true," Watkins confirmed.

"And now?"

"Now? He's gotten mixed in with some group." A wave of one hand as he climbed back to his feet. "Better to see the letters for yourself."

"Please."

David was gone five minutes before returning with a handful of envelopes, holding them toward Cassandra. She shuffled through the letters, four in all, then returned to David with a questioning look. "When was the last letter?"

"Three weeks."

"Not particularly long."

"No."

"He's been out of contact for longer in the past?"

"Yes, but … Well, read the letters."

Cassandra stared at David a moment longer, then over to Watkins, and once again back to the envelopes. She tapped at the postmark of the first. "Ipswich."

"He was working with the loggers," Watkins added.

"Shouldn't be too hard to find," Cassandra said.

Shaw looked from uncle to nephew, not believing that neither could have made the trip to Ipswich to look for themselves. If it had been Singh, he would have been on the next train to look in on the lad.

"Yes, well," Watkins said, breaking in on Shaw's thoughts. "Beware. Ipswich is uncomfortably close to Innsmouth. Practically neighbors. And Innsmouth is not a place where strangers are welcome. The people there are uneducated, superstitious, and isolated."

David made a sound of agreement, and Shaw remembered all that Cassandra had said about Innsmouth herself.

"And Ipswich?" Cassandra asked.

David and the professor looked to each other. The younger man shrugged.

Cassandra pulled the first letter from the envelope without further comment. She began reading aloud while Shaw leaned forward, resting both hands on the head of his cane.

February 27, 1912

David,

A quick note to let you know I am back on this side of the continent once again. I'm close to home and have taken up residence in Ipswich, for the time being at least. California was beautiful, and the weather was nice —No snow there in the winters. Some of the people were certainly those who enjoy life, but not to the extent that I do unfortunately. This led to a quick departure after I tried to introduce the local sheriff's daughters to my way of thinking. I know what you're thinking, why didn't I simply move on to one of the other states. Texas perhaps. Well, the strange truth is I found myself missing Massachusetts. I wanted to see the Miskatonic again. That sounds ridiculous after all I'd said last time I left, and it came as a shock to me as well. I am sure after being home for a week or two this madness will have passed, and I can move on to a place with more excitement.

For now I have a job doing logging with some company here. I hate the necessity of working but at least it is outside, and I am working with my hands. Please don't tell uncle I'm back just yet, I am unsure how long I am staying and wouldn't want to get his hopes up. In addition there is always a quiet judgement which comes from him that I just don't want to endure at the moment. Besides, I know how he feels about Ipswich and any of the towns close to the coast. I must say that the people here seem nice enough, though Ipswich rolls up the streets at night and there isn't much to do. I continue to look for some like-minded people who want to enjoy life to its fullest. Time will tell.

Your brother, Matthew

Cassandra flipped the letter over, as if there must be more on the back side. Finding nothing, she looked at David who gestured for her to carry on. She replaced the first letter into its envelope and pulled the second one free.

March 6, 1912

David,

I knew there must be people like me, and I found one in a coworker! This fellow I am working with, Richard, is indeed like minded. He hates the necessity of work and simply wants to enjoy life, and oh how he enjoys life. Richard is part of a larger group who meets in the evenings and on our days of rest. Not one of them wastes a Sunday morning going to church, and we are all generally still asleep when the church bells ring. I am extremely happy. You should come visit, it would do you some good.

I will spare you the details this time, though mostly because I am still tired from last night and need to work tomorrow. Why must we waste so many hours of the day toiling for someone else? In any case, these new friends of mine live life by their own definitions. If anything they push life to a greater excess than I ever have. I hope to learn some ideas from them.

Matthew

"Letter number three," Cassandra said, suppressing a sigh.

March 15, 1912

David,

My new friends have been somewhat hesitant to fully include me in their activities, which I can appreciate. Many of the things we do would have us charged for lewd behaviour, depravity, and a dozen other ridiculous laws created by puritans. Tonight there is a party at an abandoned farm outside of town. It is secluded and the perfect location for our group to cut loose without worrying about who is watching. I expect debauchery and hedonism at a high level. Wish me luck. Will write more tomorrow with details.

...

The party. Well, what to say ... It was different, to be sure. Not what I was expecting at all. These people have some strange beliefs, and they worship ... well, it's not the Christian god. That's for sure. The night started with us stripping naked and standing in a circle in the woods. I was ready for anything and excited for the same. Everyone started chanting in unison however. It was a strange melody which burrowed into my brain and made me dizzy. This morning I couldn't tell you one word that was said in all that chanting, but I remember how uneasy I felt. Afterward came the more physical activities I had been expecting. I've never experienced a time that flowed so easily. Every person there was ready for anything. I had trouble keeping up and at one point I must have blacked out because the next thing I knew it was morning.

There is another group ... a group within the group, I suppose. I met them briefly last night. All of my new friends hold these people in awe, like they are some kind of second coming. I don't know what they're all about, but I have every intention of making my way into this second group. These could be the people I've been searching for my entire life.

Matthew

March 28, 1912

David,

These people are, well, different to be sure, as I said. They walk their own path which is something I respect, and something which I've searched for. I'm not sure that the path these people follow is one I want to join ... In fact I know it isn't. It's impossible for me to leave though. I've seen too much. The simple act of sending this letter will be a process of secrecy.

The smaller group I told you about, remember them? Well they are much more secretive and they hold darker beliefs and goals. There is more to them than they say, and more to these gods they worship. These people aren't a group, or a club. They're a cult ... and a dangerous one. People have been disappearing around Ipswich. Mostly young girls. I know it's this cult's doing, though I have no proof. These people aren't just deluded. They can do the things they say in those chanting rituals.

I've seen things.

Their gods are real.

I'm including a sketch from one of their holy pages. It used to be part of a book but now they have only fragments. It's part of a ritual or spell? Something. I don't really know. Show it to uncle and see if he can figure it out. If not maybe someone at the university...?

I'm scared, David. This isn't what I wanted at all.

And now I can't leave.

Matthew

"That one arrived three weeks ago," David said.

"I see why you might be concerned."

Shaw looked at the investigator and shook his head. "Another damn cult."

Cassandra agreed then lapsed into thought for a moment. "Three weeks gone by. Trail may be cold. Still, I'll take the case and search for Matthew."

Both uncle and nephew looked relieved at the words. Shaw knew that Cassandra had decided to take the case before they'd even left New York.

"Expenses are payable in advance," Cassandra said. "Five dollars per day. Fees for my investigation are due upon completion of the case."

"Of course."

"You have a photo of Matthew?"

"Yeah," David said, crossing to the desk. He pulled a framed picture from the wall and returned, holding it toward Cassandra. Inside were two young men. One was David and the other a stockier version of the lad, an irreverent expression on his face.

Cassandra flipped it over and removed the back then looked to Watkins. "May I?"

"Of course."

Removing the photograph she slipped it inside her jacket. "I want to get to it as soon as possible. What time is the next train to Ipswich?"

"No train, only a bus. It leaves at eight from the train station."

"Eight?" Cassandra rolled her eyes.

"The bus does a meandering route twice a week," David added. "Heading first to Essex and Bolton before reaching Ipswich. On the way back it goes further east before returning through Manchester and Martin's Beach."

"I'm familiar with it," she said.

Shaw would need to find a map at some point and familiarize himself with the surrounding geography. None of it meant a thing to him.

"I suppose …" Watkins looked to David, then at the clock. "Well, why don't you stay the night. We'll make up a room for each of you and you can be on your way in the morning."

Cassandra looked toward the door, as if getting to Ipswich on foot was an option. After a few seconds she turned back. "Very generous of you."

"I'll make sure Amelia knows to make up the rooms," David said, "and to include two more for dinner."

"Amelia?" Shaw asked. He'd seen no other person than these two.

"Our housekeeper."

"Oh, of course."

A housekeeper. That was one luxury he and Singh couldn't have in their house. Prince Eddy had provided for their keeping a large home, but having a stranger around that book was something they couldn't allow.

Lost in the past again.

Watkins ushered them to the sitting room—which he called a parlour—across the hall, closing the door to his study behind him.

"When the rooms are ready David will let you know. There's time to freshen up or nap before dinner."

Left alone in the parlour, Shaw leaned toward Cassandra. "Is this why we were drawn here?"

"You were drawn here, Doctor. I came for a job."

Shaw leaned back in his seat, gaze locked on the investigator. "I thought you were drawn toward dark circumstances."

"Hmm, still not sure why I shared so much personal information with you, Shaw." She drummed her fingers against the arm of her chair.

"Kindred spirits?"

"Hmph! Well, fair point, that writing's the sort of darkness I am drawn toward."

"So we are headed to Ipswich tomorrow?"

"No. *I'm* headed to Ipswich tomorrow."

"But—"

"You were drawn to Arkham, specifically the university."

"Yes."

"Why?"

"I … I don't know."

"No." She leaned forward in her seat. "I've no doubt we're linked in this, but Ipswich is my part. The university is yours."

She was right. He had no impulse to leave, no awareness that he had accomplished what was needed.

"Do you feel a nudge in a particular direction here in Arkham?"

"No. That's all gone now."

"Hmm, maybe it'll return."

"I …" He wanted to protest, to go with her to Ipswich. Why though? The need to have a definite next step? Maybe. Or was he that foolish to believe this capable woman needed his protection? "I'll look around the university while you're gone."

"You'll need this." Cassandra pulled free a thin handful of folded money from her pocket, holding it toward Shaw.

"No, Cassandra. I couldn't. Thank you."

"Are you helping me on this case?"

"Well, yes. If I can."

"Then you have expenses too."

She didn't drop her arm and gave no indication that she would. Shaw stepped forward and took the money. Added to what he had from the hospital, it would give him some freedom. He nodded his thanks and pocketed the bills.

"Keep an eye on Watkins and his nephew too."

"You don't trust them?"

"I don't trust anyone."

Shaw raised an eyebrow at that.

"Present company excepted … mostly."

"I understand. Most of the people I trust are dead."

"Comforting."

CHAPTER 18

April 19, 1912
Professor Watkins's Home: 6:00 pm

Shaw was delighted to find a set of replacement clothes laid out for him on the bed of his room. Shirt, pants, and jacket. He and Professor Watkins were of roughly equal size and weight, and it all fit more or less perfectly. It was a pleasure to dispose of his ripped shirt, though the pants and too-large jacket Cassandra had gotten him on the train were worth keeping as spares. He laid these across the chair while dressing in his replacements, marveling at how a change in clothes could improve one's disposition. That plus a shave and a wash had made him a new man. Now all he needed were some spare socks and briefs.

Dinner was a simple affair, though delicious. Chicken with some roast vegetables and potatoes. Shaw tried to remember the last time he had eaten. His stomach had rumbled at the smells drifting from the lower floor for the hour prior. At dinner, after filling the void in his stomach, Shaw thanked Watkins more than once for the clothes.

"My pleasure, Doctor. Glad to help."

"You look the part of university professor yourself now," David added.

"Yes, I suppose I do."

"Your knowledge is impressive," Watkins said. "Between your medical education, and … um, well … the other stuff."

"Yes! Uncle says you were able to read those words."

Shaw didn't like the subject being dragged back around to the writing, but he knew the role of guest and stopped chewing, placing his knife and fork beside the plate. He gave a quick nod.

"It takes a toll on the mind," Cassandra interjected. "As you must know, Professor."

"Me?"

"You must have looked on the words more than once while trying to decipher them?"

Watkins considered this, shifting position. One hand clenched and unclenched. "True."

"I only looked at it the once before handing it to my uncle and that was enough."

"In regard to the toll on Shaw's mind," Cassandra said, "would it be possible to leave the doctor here while I went to Ipswich? Give him some time to rest."

"I am fine," Shaw protested. They had rehearsed this pantomime earlier and Shaw was playing his part. "A little muttering is hardly reason to leave me behind."

"Muttering? You were shouting," Cassandra reminded him.

Shaw waved the fact off, as if the words did not still linger, trying to come together in some full text that he could speak. He fought against it and so far he'd been successful, but that was due less to his ability to resist and more for the fact that some part of it seemed to be missing. What he fought more was his mind's insistence of trying to figure out what that was. It was exhausting mentally.

"Of course you can stay, Doctor Shaw," Watkins said. "More than welcome."

Shaw stared in Cassandra's direction a moment longer, not

wanting to agree too easily, then turned to Watkins. He gave a wave of defeat.

"Thank you. Perhaps some rest is in order."

"Amelia can have your other clothes cleaned while you stay."

"I'm afraid the shirt is beyond saving but the rest would be much appreciated." Shaw glanced at Cassandra then back. "Maybe I could find a place to purchase some new items."

"Church Street has some places," David suggested, "and more on Main Street."

"Ah, thank you," Shaw said. "Where are these streets?"

"Oh! Sorry, they are the two streets before the river."

"You would have crossed them coming from the train station," Watkins added.

"The better places are near town hall," David said. "Between Garrison and Parsonage. I have study group tomorrow, or I would take you."

"Quite all right," Shaw said. "You go to the university?"

"Studying anthropology."

"Perhaps I will take a closer look at the university while I am here," Shaw mused.

"Did your brother go to Miskatonic?" Cassandra asked.

"Oh, no! He barely made it through high school … Not that he was dumb. No, he just always preferred doing to listening."

"Like their mother," Watkins mumbled.

David turned toward his uncle, then back toward the guests. "I don't remember her much."

"What happened to her?" Cassandra asked. "If you don't mind me asking."

"My sister …" Watkins began, then let out a sigh. This was not something he enjoyed talking about. "David knows this whole story already. My sister arrived at my door one night with two nephews I didn't even know I had, not quite four years old. Twins, like Maria and I. She'd disappeared years earlier, a wild child that broke our mother's heart. Maria was in a state of distress when she arrived and took to bed for several days while I got the boys cleaned and fed."

"Then she left again?"

Shaw listened quietly to the back and forth between the two, watching the professor.

Watkins continued. "She was here about a week. The night she left, Maria came down the stairs and we spoke for some length. All memories of our childhood, friends we'd known, our parents and their final days. I couldn't get any illumination on where she'd been or what she'd been up to all that time. She changed topics quick the one time I asked, giving me instead every last bit of information about David and Matthew. In the morning she was gone again."

"And you raised the boys as your own?"

"I did. Don't judge Maria harshly for leaving them with me. She was never meant to be a mother, not in her own mind. That's why she came here, to leave her children with someone she trusted."

Throughout the story David continued to eat his food, apparently none the worse for hearing the story again.

"Matthew is much like his mother, I'm afraid. Wild. Anything for a good time. He left home as soon as he could, wanting to see the world. For all his hedonistic ideals I suspect he is searching for his mother, whether he consciously realizes it or not, and if he can't find her in body, he can adopt her spirit."

The room fell silent for several moments, the information needing to be digested as much as the food. In time Watkins spoke up, hesitantly.

"Doctor, can I ask you about your voyage? Aboard the *Titanic*."

"*Titanic*?" David said. "You were aboard the *Titanic*?"

Shaw mentally gritted his teeth and wished Cassandra had kept that piece of information to herself. He wondered just how much truth he should give to the two and decided the iceberg version was much more appropriate.

CHAPTER 19

April 19, 1912
Professor Watkins's Home: 9:20 pm

Shaw was exhausted. The small amount of sleep he'd managed on the train, and the brief nap before dinner, had done little to fill his internal reservoir. Cassandra would be off early in the morning, and he hoped to be awake to see her off.

Arriving at the top landing he looked to the right, at the open door to his room and the awaiting bed. To the left was Cassandra's, door ajar, light coming through the opening.

"Shaw?" A whisper, barely audible.

"Yes?"

No response.

Was Cassandra calling him, or had she merely mentioned his name? The voice was too soft to say for certain it was Cassandra at all. Watkins and his nephew were still downstairs so ...

Shaw moved closer to the partially open door.

"Beware the six!" Another whisper.

"What?"

All he knew for certain was it came from the other side of that door. He raised one fist to knock just as it opened before him.

Cassandra stood in the opening, jacket off, both staggering backward in surprise. The revolver in her hand half raised in defence before pointing back toward the floor.

"Shaw," she breathed, looking left and right. "Did you hear?"

He nodded, and they listened a moment.

"Gone now," Cassandra said.

She stepped backward into her room, leaving the door open behind her. Still without a direct invitation, Shaw stayed in the doorway, glancing around to confirm no one was inside. The queen-size bed occupied the center, sheets smooth except for where her jacket had been tossed, the revolver's holster and huge knife resting on top. A desk and chair were in the right-hand corner while a wardrobe loomed to his left, beside the door. It was a mirror image of his own room, and empty of people other than the two of them.

"I was just looking out the window," she said, "for the night-gaunt, when I heard someone say my name."

Thoughts of whispered voices were set aside at the mention of that monster. He'd come near to forgetting about it.

"You think it will follow us here?"

"No, though I can't say why."

"Then—"

"I don't believe in taking chances."

Shaw wondered if the night-gaunt had come from Arkham in the first place.

"I'm glad you're here," Cassandra said, changing the subject. She placed her revolver on the desk then turned, unbuttoning her shirt. She pulled it past her shoulders.

In his younger days he might have convinced himself something else was happening. "Cassandra?"

"I need your help, Shaw. Call it a doctor's examination if you like."

That shifted his perspective. "Of course."

Cassandra threw her shirt on top of the jacket, then dropped her trousers. In moments she was in brassiere and knickers, no hint of modesty in her demeanor.

"I can see most of the tattoos, but there's some I can only glimpse in the mirror, and it isn't the same. I need you to look at my back, and my legs."

Shaw hesitated, opening his mouth to speak but no words coming.

"Does this embarrass you?"

"Of course not. I'm a doctor. The sight of a human body does not affect me." Shaw considered a moment. "You are asking a lot of me, to look at these tattoos."

"I am." Her expression softened. "And I won't think any less if you refuse."

Another hesitation on his part. He did not want to see any more of that writing and wished he had gone straight to his room ... but Cassandra needed his help. Could he truly refuse?

"What am I looking for?"

"The words you saw downstairs."

"Right." Shaw took a deep breath and began to scan her tattoos, trying to keep it at a cursory glance, not get drawn in too deep.

They were indeed darker at night. Now they appeared to be freshly inked.

"Isn't that remarkable?" he said.

"Focus, Doctor."

"Yes ... yes ... of course."

It took little time for him to be dragged under. He realized that while they were darker at night they were also more dominant, more imposing.

"Insistent," he muttered.

He wanted to look away but was unable. He traced the line of one tattoo with his fingertip.

"No. We're done."

Cassandra grabbed her shirt and threw it on, holding it closed. Shaw's eyes continued to rove, following the flow of macabre artwork. The slap across his face a moment later brought his senses back. His eyes refocused on hers, then he turned away, stepping toward the window.

"Better dress quickly." He rubbed at his stinging cheek.

Now he knew why he was able to resist the markings on the train but not the ones in the letter. It was a matter of intensity. The sound of cloth rubbing against same as Cassandra redressed.

"It's safe now."

He turned back, eyes anywhere but on Cassandra. "I apologize."

"No, Shaw. I should have known better."

"They're not there," he said. "The words from the letter."

"You're sure?"

"I am."

"So I don't have a complete text."

"Of that … passage? Spell? Whatever it is. No."

"I see." She considered that. "Did Matthew send only a portion? Or do they also have an incomplete text."

CLICK!

An almost audible sound inside his mind, accompanied by the sound of …

"Do you hear a flute?"

Cassandra listened then shook her head.

"It's gone now, but …"

"But what?"

"But … No. I don't know. It's on the edge of my mind but … Maybe I need to sleep on it."

"That is a possibility. You haven't had that much sleep over the past day."

Shaw agreed and started toward the door, putting more weight on the cane than usual.

"Oh!" Cassandra said, snapping her finger. "One last thing, Doctor."

He turned back. "Yes?"

"There was a word. You said it on the train when you first looked at my tattoo, and again when you read the letter."

"A word?"

"Nglui."

"Nglui?"

"Does it mean anything to you?"

After a moment's thought Shaw shook his head. "No, sorry. I …"

Two related pieces slid together as something he didn't know a moment earlier suddenly became evident.

"Gateway," he said, unsure where that knowledge came from. "Portal."

"Portal again." She tapped her lower lip with one finger. "Was that what you were trying to remember?"

Was it?

"No. I don't think so."

He tapped his cane against the floor similar to the way Cassandra tapped her fingernails against objects. There *was* more, but to consciously know what that "more" was—

Wait.

"They're related."

"What is?"

"The words on your arm, and the ones in the letter."

"How?"

"They … One precedes the other."

"A full page together?"

"No, it is still incomplete, the end is missing."

That's what was missing, what his mind was looking for.

"Interesting. See, you are earning that money."

"Yes, well … just what do we do with that information?"

Cassandra gave a grunt then perched on the edge of her bed. What indeed. She was not able to decipher the words herself, and if he tried then he could very well lose his mind.

"Something to sleep on," she said.

***

Back in his own room Shaw watched at the window, clearing his mind and looking for a trace of the night-gaunt. Now that he'd realized Cassandra's tattoos and Matthew's letter were connected, the words lingered at the edge of his mind, wanting to flow over him, drive him down, incomplete text or not. He couldn't allow it. Giving in to those without Singh or Cassandra nearby to help could be a disaster.

Deep breath in through the nose. Long release through his pursed lips.

Repeat.

If only Singh were here.

Another breath.

Not that Cassandra was not an agreeable and capable companion, but Shaw missed the lad. As much as he was glad that Singh was outside of danger on this one, he also wished to see him again.

Another breath.

Conflicting desires. Shaw's next exhale encompassed a ragged sigh. Eyes half lidded, he caught a quick glimpse of movement in the darkness, sure it was a night-gaunt, but it was only two dogs. They were lit by the wan moonlight as they passed between houses.

Large dogs.

One bayed, a decidedly un-canine sound. The other joined a moment later with some yipping-growling noises unlike anything he'd ever heard.

Not dogs then, but not a night-gaunt either.

These were not the sounds of wolves or coyotes either. In moments both the sounds and creatures were gone, disappearing into the blackness.

What were they?

He watched the spot where they'd disappeared, waiting for them to return, but all was still and quiet now.

His eyes drooped more. Had he imagined them? A product of fatigue?

A shake of his head. Those were real.

If nothing else the brief sighting had cleared his mind, distracted him.

With that he crossed the room to his bed and undressed. With no pyjamas he made do, the sensation of sheets against bare skin comforting. Moments after his head sank into the pillow Shaw had drifted into sleep.

CHAPTER 20

April 20, 1912
The Dreamlands: 2:47 am

Mental defences crumbled under the weight of exhaustion. The words which lingered at the edge of his consciousness were there, waiting for an opening. One word led to others, coming together like tumblers in a lock. What he'd read in Matthew's letter, what he'd seen on Cassandra's body.

They battered at his mind.

In his dream he slipped both feet from beneath the sheets, crossing to the roll-top desk. A sheet of paper. A half-sharpened pencil. He started to write.

"Nglui," he muttered. "Azathoth."

More *CLICKS* as pieces came together in his mind.

"Throdog Azathoth."

Vaguely, from a distance, Shaw was aware of his ramblings, the way a sleeping person can hear their own snoring from within a dream. His writing became more frantic, words which bordered on drawings.

"Mgahnnn shuggnglui!"

In the distance a flute played.

CLICK! CLICK! CLICK!

The room was gone. The desk. The bed.

In his dream something approached, something horrifying and without description. Though aware he was dreaming, this lumbering unknown terrified him. Dark and fearsome. Gloom closed in, suffocating him in a hot blanket of fear. Somewhere a creature bayed, answered by others which yipped with manic enthusiasm.

One ahead.

One to the left.

Another on his right.

One final howl, from behind.

Surrounded.

"Escape," he mumbled.

Yes. Escape. Escape!

He muttered the words, putting all he'd seen together. Matthew's letter. Cassandra's tattoos. He had the missing part now, what completed the spell. In his sleeping mind he arranged all into a proper order.

A pinpoint of silver appeared, expanding to an oval the size of a coin. Size of a plate. Then, finally, size of a man. It glowed silvery-white at the center, shifting toward green at the edges.

"Nglui?" Shaw asked.

Yes, exactly. Nglui. A portal.

The music of flutes grew, coming from the far side, changing each moment. Discordant and jarring, then calm, melodious. Still others, playing one after another, taking turns. The music had distracted him from the bays and yips and howls. Now they grew so close that he would see them in the glow of the portal. If he died here, torn apart by these things, would he die in the waking world as well?

In the logic of dreams, Shaw was sure this was true.

With a mad scramble he passed through the portal, leaving the beastly noises behind. They would not follow him through, he knew that, not here.

Where was here though?

The flutes played on. One nearby, then another far away.

He'd escaped the monsters, but had he fallen into a worse danger? He was pulled in every direction, his sleeping soul being wrenched like taffy. Would he be devoured like Stephen had? Madness pressed in on him, hot, fetid, and dizzying.

No.

The hollow voice was near and when it spoke Shaw's mind was his own again. The madness had been pushed aside and his soul was no longer being pulled apart.

Watch.

It spoke directly into his mind. Vision cleared and before him, both feet and miles away, floated an horrific creature. Immense to a point that he had no ready frame of reference. Dwarfing the Earth, and still the comparison meant nothing. The concept was staggering. This ... thing had a long misshapen form stretching away into forever, covered in random tentacles.

Cthulhu! he thought.

No, the voice answered. It sounded faintly amused. *Dread Cthulhu lies dreaming yet.*

Of course it does. Shaw had sent that elder god back to the depths.

This thing looked like it lay dreaming as well, but other than tentacles and monstrousness, it did not look like Cthulhu. A huge maw at the center opened in a slack circle great enough to swallow planets. Surrounding the opening were many half-lidded eyes, and inside wicked teeth that were closer to swords.

Shaw was struck numb at the sight, his mind too incapable of processing this. Madness knocked at the door of his mind once again.

This creature made no movement toward him. Was he beneath its notice? Years passed as he goggled. Time and distance meant nothing here, nor did direction. The logic of dreams once again.

But ... if this is a dream, and he knew it was, why couldn't he wake?

You must witness, the same voice spoke.

"Oh. I see."

In time Shaw became aware of an entire reality around him. This lumbering beast merely floated at its center, surrounded by the black of night filled with a million stars. Shaw's own position was on a boulder the size of a house, flat at the point where he stood. This rock floated in harmony with the beast, in orbit.

"Is this real?"

Define real?

Now the deep, hollow voice came from closer at hand, a step behind him. The same voice which had told him Cthulhu lay sleeping. The one which commanded him to watch.

Shaw turned to find a hooded, robed … being, behind him. This was no man. The speaker towered, eight feet in height, and where its face should be was more blackness, more pinpoints of stars. It waited patiently. At one side, gripped in a withered talon, was a flute, long and wooden, shaped like a tentacle with each sucker being one of the holes.

"You're the musician."

One of many.

Once more the music became audible. First from one side, played in a particular style, then from the other in a contrasting manner. Shaw turned, seeing the other players. Some were positioned on boulders much like his own, while others floated in space around this monstrous creature of teeth and eyes.

Each of those musicians exuded an untold sense of power. The power he'd felt in Cthulhu's presence. The power he'd felt in Dagon's. All of them were dwarfed in power as much as size by the one at the center. Uselessly he tried to focus on one of them, but each time he did his gaze slid aside, unable or unwilling to look on their full aspect. Even the one behind him. Humanoid in shape, but so much more. Its appearance continually shifted. A defence of his own mind, or a mercy of these beings?

The being behind him chuckled, the sound of planets dying.

No, this one had no mercy in them.

"Elder gods."

Hmm.

Had Dagon and Cthulhu also shifted their appearance and size? Was it just his perception, his mind finding some way to interpret the monstrous. Is that why people went mad at a glance of them?

"Please," Shaw begged. "Where am I?"

Your time is limited. Do not ask questions you already know.

Of course. The dream world, and his body lay dreaming back in Watkins's guest room. That should have given him comfort, but did not.

"And this …?" Shaw glanced at the slumbering god before him. He wanted to say this monster. This abomination. This nightmare.

You are in the presence of Azathoth. The blind idiot god.

With its free hand, the being gestured toward the floating monstrosity.

Blind? With so many eyes?

"I've heard that name," Shaw said. "Azathoth."

Quietly.

Shaw thought he had been quiet, but nodded respectfully.

You have called his name several times in the waking world. This is unwise.

The being did not shift its stance, but Shaw felt the reproach, the warning. He cast about for something to say, anything to change the subject.

"Why do you play that music?"

The being raised its flute and piped a tune for several seconds. When it lowered its hand an answering song came from the distance.

We play in turn, to keep the blind god sleeping.

"Sleeping? Like Cthulhu."

Another chuckle, longer. *If Cthulhu should wake, humans would suffer like never before.*

"And if Az …" He stopped himself and gestured toward the hulking beast. "If this wakes?"

Again no change of expression, no movement, but still a distinct sense of dread was conveyed. *If blind Azathoth awakes, even for an instant, everything will end.*

"Everything …?"

All reality. Everything you know, and all that you do not.

"Even you?"

Everything.

A memory of Cassandra: *Azathoth is the god that other gods fear.*

"Why was I led to Arkham? What am I—"

It is time for you to leave. Your presence upsets the balance.

"I—"

When the six are gathered, the portal shall open.

"I've heard that before. What does that mean?"

Fhtagn shugnahh.

The being raised one hand and pointed a gnarled finger at Shaw, pushing him. Though the portal lay off to his left and the push should have sent him backward, still Shaw hurtled toward it.

Never return, Archibald Shaw.

The warning was punctuated by one extended flute note.

He did not fall among the howling beasts as he feared, nor into his bedroom as he hoped. He found himself in another bedroom instead. Much smaller than the room he now occupied, or his bedroom in Cambridge, but familiar. This reminded him of Stephen's cabin aboard the *Titanic*. A bed and wardrobe. One reading chair near a side table. A porthole allowed moonlight to illuminate the room in a soft, wan glow. Beneath his feet the floor had the slightest motion, a gentle sway.

Another ship then.

Movement in the bed, a shape beneath the sheets. Someone shifting from their back to side position. Shaw froze, unsure what to do. To move backward, to open the door, would create enough noise to wake the sleeper. Forward then? His eyes scanned the room, looking for some course of action, some reason he'd been sent here.

On the nightstand, within easy reach of the sleeper, waited a familiar dagger and an unraveled turban.

"Singh?"

The sleeper rolled from bed and onto his feet, grabbing the knife. In that one quick movement Singh braced, ready for attack.

The focus of the lad bored into him in the dim moonlight, accusing. Then his eyes widened, his fighting stance eased.

"Doctor Shaw?"

"Hello, my friend."

"How is this possible?" With his free hand Singh brought the light up in the cabin. "Are you dead?"

"No … I don't think so." Shaw held one hand before his face and realized he could see Singh through it, and with each second he became more transparent. He spoke in a rush. "Singh. I'm in a town called Arkham, Massachusetts."

Singh mouthed the words, but no sound came from him. Then the word "Shaw." A moment later all was gone.

Heart pounding Shaw bolted upright in bed, gasping.

Was that real?

Define real. He heard the flute player's response inside his head.

Was Singh truly on a ship heading toward New York? Or was that wishful thinking in dream form? It was believable, something Singh would certainly do … But the longer Shaw was awake, the less realistic that appeared to be. More questions added to the list and no real answers. The only thing Shaw knew for certain was he would not return to sleep for some time. With a low groan he shuffled out of bed and crossed to the desk, determined that if he couldn't speak to Singh, he could at least write a letter. Partway across the room he stopped. The roll-top was up, a sheet of paper on the desk already.

No.

But he knew already what that paper held. The writing and sketching he'd started in his dream. A glance over his shoulder. Back to bed? Pretend he'd never seen it? Too late for that. Defeated, he continued his journey toward the desk where he retrieved the paper, folding it quickly, but not so quick that he didn't catch some of the words. So much like those on Cassandra's body, and the ones in Matthew's letter.

The missing piece.

No. He couldn't look at that. Not after what he'd seen tonight.

Shaw set the folded page aside and took a fresh sheet, starting his letter to Singh.

CHAPTER 21

Singh stared at the spot where his friend had been standing only moments earlier.

"Arkham, Massachusetts."

He moved to the desk and wrote the town name, not that he was likely to forget … though come morning he might convince himself it had been a dream.

No.

No chance of that.

Shaw was alive!

For the first time Singh became aware of a pull on him, on his soul, urging him forward.

CHAPTER 22

etween restless dreams and the sleepless hours which came after, Shaw found himself rising much later than usual, though what was "usual" he had no idea. Too late to see Cassandra off in any case. He dressed in the professor's loaned clothing, promising himself a trip to Main Street to at least purchase a change of socks and boxers. He rested on the bed's edge, slipping into his shoes.

Never return, the entity had said last night. The unspoken completion being. *If you return, you will not leave again.*

"Are you mad?"

Shaw looked up from his shoes to find Stephen in the corner of one room, well out of the sunlight. The visitation came during waking hours this time … at least Shaw thought he was awake.

"Mad?"

"Your visit to Azathoth could have doomed us all."

"Azathoth is the god that other gods fear," Shaw quoted. "Is that why I am here in Arkham?"

"No!" Stephen practically shrieked it. "The complete opposite."

"Opposite? What is—"

"When the six are gathered, the portal shall open."

"Yes, yes, I've heard that, more than once. What does—"

"You must find it."

"It? What is it?"

Stephen was gone again. This time Shaw was sure the ghost had been there, unless he was mad … Not outside the realm of possibility, but he'd had enough experience with ghosts to know they were not all in his mind.

The house was quiet as he descended. Cassandra would be long gone if she hoped to catch the eight o'clock bus. Not one to remain still when she knew her next step, she'd been itching to get on with the investigation. Rounding the bottom post, Shaw headed toward the dining room and kitchen beyond, intent on finding something for his breakfast. He was surprised to find Professor Watkins at the table, reading a newspaper. The man had said he had office drop-in hours this morning. On seeing Shaw, he folded the paper and set it aside on the white linen tablecloth. Shaw caught a glimpse of the masthead proclaiming the paper as the *Arkham Gazette*.

"Sleep well, Doctor?"

Not particularly. No. "As well as any night lately." Shaw slid into the seat across from the professor.

"I take it that has not been too well?"

Shaw gave the man a half-smile and helped himself to toast from a basket. His eyebrows shot up in surprise. Still warm.

"Amelia heard you moving about and brought something fresh. Coffee too." He gestured at a carafe on the table.

No tea. Ah well, beggars can't be choosers.

"I thought you would be at the university."

The professor glanced at the wall clock and shook his head. "Hours start at ten. I'll leave in a few minutes but wanted to be here when you woke."

"Thank you. I appreciate that."

"Is there anything you need?" The professor finished what was left in his cup.

"No, I don't think … Oh!" An idea rushed to mind, demanding

attention. After last night's dream he wanted to contact Singh more than ever. "Yes. Is there a place I can send a telegram?"

"There's a booth in the post office, on Main Street."

"Thank you."

"If there's nothing else, I should get going." Watkins got to his feet. "Amelia will provide anything else you might need."

Amelia. He knew Watkins had a housekeeper who also cooked the meals, but he'd yet to see the woman. Dinner had been brought to the table by David last night, and the dishes cleared by both uncle and nephew. Shaw felt he should at least introduce himself. After Watkins left, he shuffled back to an immaculate but empty kitchen. Stove and icebox. More cabinets than *he* would ever have need for. A back door led into a yard, while another—partially open —led to a basement. An open doorway continued into a passage which would lead back to the foyer. No sign or sound of Amelia anywhere.

Introductions would have to wait.

The time was just after ten, and Shaw contemplated what to do first. The university was at least part of his reason for being in Arkham, but he also needed to visit Main Street. In the end the university won for the simple reason that he didn't want to return to the house in between, and the thought of carting parcels about with him while he explored the school was less than appealing.

In the light of day Shaw thought Cassandra's wariness toward Watkins was unfounded. The professor and his nephew had shown nothing but hospitality since they'd arrived. These were the people they'd come to help after all. True, he had thought the man was lying at one point yesterday, but that could have been his imagination, or a hesitancy to share all details with people he'd just met. Still, he had kept his desire to visit Miskatonic from the professor. If they should bump into each other, he would explain it as passing by.

CHAPTER 23

April 20, 1912
Miskatonic University: 10:22 am

Once again Shaw stood on the U-shaped quad, turning in a circle, reading the names of each building. Archaeology was in one of these, but which? Not Medieval Metaphysics, whatever that might be. Ancient Studies? That sounded most likely. He would start there.

If anything, the campus was even more quiet than yesterday. He'd never seen anything like it. No noise. No students out and about. He had meant to ask Watkins about that but had forgotten.

A mystery for later.

Like the literature building, the entry held a board with the layout. Archaeology was located in the basement, which seemed appropriate. In the list of professor's offices there were two Doctor Bells. One Francis and the other Edward. No way around it but to speak with each until he could determine which was Watkins's friend.

Stairs, his old enemy, led down into the Archaeology department. Most stairs didn't give him trouble, but ones made of marble which could be slick under his feet made him nervous. Add to that the fresher wounds, and the fact he had walked longer and further, and gone up and down several stairs in recent days. That left his legs a bit more wobbly than usual. At least there were no crowds bustling past to make him jostle and make him less steady.

No one but the occasional person, seen in the distance.

Step by step he descended, grasping the handrail with his hand while his cane kept him balanced. Shaw reached the bottom, relieved, and headed to the right, wondering how much time professors spent in their offices anyway.

Shaw rapped on the door of Edward Bell and three other professors. It seemed Watkins was lucky to only share with two.

"Come in."

Shaw opened the door to find two of the four desks inside were occupied.

"Yeah?" a burly man to the right demanded, scowl on his face. A name plate on the desk identified him as Professor Silas Miller. His hands looked like they could easily crack walnuts. "What do you want?"

"Doctor Bell?"

The man grunted and returned to the book in front of him.

"Over here."

Shaw turned toward another man, thin to the point of undernourished. Round wire-rimmed glasses perched on his nose. A tan jacket rounded out the presentation.

"You're not one of my students."

Shaw gave him his usual, unthreatening expression and stepped forward. "No. Are you the Doctor Bell who is a friend of Professor Watkins?"

The man shook his head. "Sorry, you want Francis."

"Ah."

"Next door," the burly man grumbled.

"Thank you."

"Won't do you any good though," Edward Bell said. "Francis isn't in today."

"Ah," Shaw said. "No classes?"

Miller laughed. "You are aware it's Saturday, aren't you?"

"Oh!" Shaw said. "No I … I'm afraid I …"

"Some of us are here for office hours, but not Francis."

Explaining how he'd lost track of days would take more time than either professor would have interest in giving.

"Thank you, gentlemen." Shaw backed out of the office and closed the door behind him.

The laughter of the burly man carried into the hallway. He said something to Doctor Bell, but mercifully it was muffled by the door.

Saturday!

That threw a spanner into the works. Five minutes passed, Shaw tapping his cane against the tiled floor. The other person to speak with, the librarian, was just as likely not here … still, he would pass that building on his way out and may as well try it. First building on the far side of the quad. He exited Ancient Studies and made a straight line to the library. Two doors, twice his height at least, at the top of five stone steps. He may have to wait for Monday morning to do anything.

He mounted the steps and pulled on one door, almost losing balance in surprise when it opened. The door was thick oak and should have required more strength, but it swung as if weighing nothing. A well-designed piece of architecture.

Inside he stood in the dimness that filled all libraries. The scuff of his shoes against marble echoed off walls and windows before dissipating. Shaw drew a breath, the word "hello" on his tongue. He bit it back, unable to commit the faux pas of talking above a whisper in a library, even on a Saturday.

No one studied at the many hardwood tables, polished to a shine, and recently judging by the smell of wood polish. No one browsed the stacks that he could see. The check out desk was similarly deserted. For all appearances, the library could have been accidentally left unlocked. It appeared he would have as much luck finding the librarian as he did Doctor Bell.

A moment's hesitation, standing in the entry, wondering if he should come back Monday. No, he was here now, might as well try.

Shaw started forward, enjoying the silence until, two steps from the desk, a sensation hit him like a closed fist. He staggered.

"No." It came as a whisper.

Something was here.

Something malevolent.

Eyes closed, he went through the steps to clear his mind and prevent evil from entering. Deep breaths until he had control, then step by step he pursued that sensation. Following one path between the shelves, across to the next, until reaching the farthest corner. A set of iron stairs led down, the sensation pulling him forward. The same which had pulled him to Arkham? Maybe. Whatever it was resided in the basement.

What he wouldn't give for his lost sword cane.

And Singh, or even Cassandra.

Feet and cane rang against the metal steps until he reached the basement. This level of the library was lit, but more dimly, as if no one was expected to come here, or no one was welcome.

Shaw pressed onward, the apprehension covering him in a hot nauseous cloud. Several times he needed to lean against the nearest shelf for balance and support.

"Deep breath," he told himself. "Inhale. Exhale."

Mind cleared as much as was possible, Shaw looked back the way he'd come. Stairs waited at the far end for an escape.

"Escape?"

Did he truly think something would potentially attack him? The path ahead continued into dimness, visibility only good for twenty feet or so. He considered the question. If he *was* attacked here no one would ever know, unless his corpse was left behind.

He retreated a step back.

"No."

He'd been chased by monsters, faced cults and elder gods, survived the sinking of a ship. He would *not* be frightened off by this, not without knowing what it was.

Again he started forward, following the pull while making as little noise as possible. The basement was larger than the upper floor and he wondered if it connected with the rest of the university like other buildings did.

Shuffled step after shuffled step he kept his eyes on the darkness ahead … when he wasn't looking behind him. All the shelves full of musty books were ignored, barely aware of that old paper smell. Shaw made it down the basement's entire length until the pull, the calling, was more immediate. On his left. It must be close. If this sensation grew any stronger, he feared he would lose his mind.

A locked gate came into view, floor to ceiling. On the other side was a cramped room smaller than the ship's cabin he'd dreamed Singh occupied. Maybe eight feet deep and six wide.

It was in there, whatever *it* was, demanding to be free, for him to take it from here.

Not a monster then. Another book? A copy of the *Necronomicon*? Here?

No answer.

Please, no.

These were restricted books. Restricted for age and value, or for the safety of library patrons?

Something in there held untold evil power.

He wrapped the fingers of one hand around the bars and rattled them. They clanged and echoed through the basement. Far too solid to break in, and the lock was similarly serious about its function.

Is this why he'd been brought to Arkham? Still no definite answer. Perhaps not the *only* reason he'd come here then? Miskatonic University had been shown in his dream, but there was something else. Was this some dark serendipity?

"My God! How do I keep chancing upon these things?"

He remembered Cassandra saying how she was drawn to the mysterious, and vice versa. Cut from the same cloth.

"Damn—"

"Can I help you?"

Shaw jumped at the sudden voice, almost throwing himself to the floor. He turned as gracefully as possible to find a scowling man four feet distant, tall and thin, jaw that jutted forward in a near point. The man's dour expression appeared to be his one and only face. Round glasses magnified his eyes, making them bulge outward.

"You are no student, and I know all of the staff."

Gathering his wits Shaw threw his amiable expression on. "Are you the librarian? Doctor Armitage?"

"I am."

"I believe we have an acquaintance in common, Cassandra Pickman."

"Pickman? No one I know of."

"Oh." Shaw was taken aback, unsure how to proceed. "I … She is a private investigator and—"

"What of it? I said I don't know the woman."

"Of course. My apologies. I must have gotten confused."

Had *Watkins* gotten confused on how he'd gotten Cassandra's name? Or was this man lying? Shaw had to admit the librarian was unlikeable, but that didn't make him a liar. The man's eyes shifted from Shaw toward the sealed room and back again.

"If there is nothing else, the library closes at noon on Saturdays."

Shaw did not move, and Armitage raised one eyebrow to emphasize his last words. Taking the hint, Shaw started back toward the stairs. Behind him the librarian rattled the door, a reverberating metal clang filling the area once again. A moment later the man came into step behind Shaw, saying nothing but undeniably providing escort.

CHAPTER 24

April 20, 1912
Arkham, Massachusetts: 12:04 pm

A few minutes later Shaw found himself on the sidewalk of Garrison Street, Miskatonic University at his back. Cane tapping against the cement, he wondered on his next goal. Doctor Bell and the librarian had both turned out to be a bust.

While he'd been in the library the pull had been strong, but he wasn't sure that it was the same pull which had dragged him from New York to Arkham. A clear impression of danger, of evil certainly, but not a confidence that he'd reached his goal. As with last night, and indeed with his trip to the university this morning, there was an awareness of … something. A sensation of oddness, something out of place, something off. The pull which had drawn him here had been replaced by a more general one, as if all of Arkham was worthy of attention.

Had he seen what he was supposed to at the university?

No answer. No great onrush on knowledge.

"Fine."

He would return on Monday then.

Church Street was one block up, and Main Street the block

after, assuming David's directions were accurate. In fact, he could see what must be the town hall from where he stood. With a groan he started his slow trek to the post office. In truth, the journey from here to Main Street was no more than the one from the professor's house to Miskatonic, but his leg was starting to complain on the amount of exercise it was getting today.

Shaw promised himself a rest on reaching Main Street.

The last ten steps were the greatest effort and, as promised, he found a wooden bench outside of the town hall to rest his leg while taking in the surroundings.

Across the street and halfway along the block was the post office. As easy to find as Watkins had promised. In the other direction was a restaurant, *The Miskatonic Café*. They certainly did like naming things after the river. His stomach rumbled at the thought of food, that one piece of toast and cup of coffee worn off an hour ago. Just up from the restaurant was a place which declared itself as *Odds & Ends*. Shaw wasn't sure what that was about, but it sounded enticing. He would stroll past after lunch.

A quick plan made the post office first on the list; communication with Singh had been put off long enough. After that the thought of food was most appealing. There he could rest his leg more while filling his belly. Then this *Odds & Ends* place and finally some much needed clothing shopping.

Shaw leaned forward, ready to move on, when a rusted green bus came to a halt before him. The final foot of the bus's journey was accompanied by a rattling lurch where it waited, shuddering. The door opened and the driver stared at him. He wore a cap on his head, tilted to the one side. His left eye was hidden behind an eyepatch, and Shaw had to wonder on the safety of a one-eyed driver.

"Well?" the driver asked through a nasal voice.

"What …? Oh!" Shaw realized he'd been resting at a bus stop. He shook his head. "No, sorry. I was—"

The door closed on his sentence, and the bus rolled forward with another shudder.

"Rude," Shaw muttered.

However, it was good to have found a mode of transportation around Arkham. He would use it tomorrow to take a tour. Or was this the same bus which traveled on to Ipswich? No, the professor said that one stopped at the train station.

Another slow walk, coupled with a self-conscious crossing of the street as a car waited for him. At the post office he rethought the sense of a telegram. Once again he didn't know where Singh was, and he had far too much to say for a telegram. In the end, he headed to the booth for outgoing post instead.

"Yes, sir?" a boy of perhaps seventeen asked enthusiastically.

"Could I purchase an envelope and postage to Cambridge, England?"

"England?"

"Is that a problem?"

"No, sir. We just don't get many letters going further than Boston."

The boy slid an envelope across the counter to Shaw, then consulted a chart for postage rates, scratching his head. Inside Shaw's jacket was the letter he'd written the previous night. He'd thought he might continue it at some point and was glad to have brought it with him.

"Could I borrow a pen, please?"

"Yes, sir."

Shaw made sure he finished the letter stating exactly where he was, though it had been mentioned more than once already. Adding signature to the letter and address to the envelope, he handed it and payment over, a sense of completion at one task accomplished. Now that he had told Singh all he could, a heaviness lifted from him, a heaviness he hadn't realized he was carrying. Eventually, given enough time, that letter would find its way to Singh. If nothing else, the lad would be aware of what had come of him.

What had come of him? Shaw shook his head. *What exactly am I expecting?*

Forcing that train of thought from his mind, Shaw made his way toward *The Miskatonic Café*, delighted at the lightness in his step. It had been years since he'd felt this carefree, decades even, since those early days in India. Yes! The damned book rested at the bottom of the ocean, and whatever had drawn him to Arkham had not yet reared its head.

A deep breath, taking in the smells of spring. Not the sweet perfume of an English field perhaps, but still lovely today. A full circle, relishing the energy of Main Street, so much more lively than the university. On the far side of the street people traveled in each direction. Singles. Families. Workers. Children. On this side a family of four entered the restaurant, father holding the door for wife and children. Between Shaw and the family another man lingered a step into the alley, glancing at his pocket watch, fedora pulled low and obscuring his features.

Waiting for a lunch companion perhaps? Shaw closed the distance between them. Three paces. Two. The man suddenly jerked his head up. Shaw faltered a step. Came to a halt. A prickle of cold sweat trickling along his spine. Fear sweat.

The man had no face.

It was impossible, but he had no face!

Where his features should have been was smooth skin, and yet he still managed to glare at Shaw, taking his full measure. A moment later the man backed into the alley's dimness and was gone. No rush. No worry.

No face.

Shaw continued to watch the open alley where the man had disappeared, unsure he wanted to get any closer. His mind tried to convince him he hadn't seen it. Imagination. A trick of the light. There was no denying it, though. Moving to the sidewalk's outside edge, almost onto the street, Shaw inched forward, going around one lamp post, using it for balance.

Nothing.

The man was gone.

The lightness in Shaw's step was gone, the smell of spring covered with decay. At the restaurant's door Shaw paused, glancing behind him, up and down the street. Each of the Saturday pedestrians had become suspect.

Bizarre and grotesque! Was that man any direct threat to Shaw though? The man could have rushed him instead of fleeing. Shaw should be wary, of course, but what was he to do? Return to Watkins's house and sequester himself inside until Cassandra returned? The idea of giving in to that fear was more loathsome than the faceless man.

Inside he found a long, thin room with a single row of tables and chairs, plus a counter with several stools. All stools and chairs were covered in the same red and white fabric, while the table tops were draped in simple white cloths. He made his way to a table at one end where his back could be toward the wall, waiting for a waitress to take his order. While he waited he examined the other patrons. The family of four that had entered shortly before him occupied a spot two tables away. The children, a boy and girl of maybe six and eight, sat calmly and well-behaved. No fidgeting. No kicking each other covertly under the table. They each drank a glass of milk while the parents drank coffee and looked at the menu.

They *appeared* normal.

Further up was a rougher-looking man, disheveled clothing and cloth cap, the look of someone who worked with his hands. He also drank from a coffee mug, no sign of a meal before him. At the counter were several others, all individuals and unremarkable. Most had a stool between themselves and their nearest neighbor. On the other end from Shaw was another man. He wore a fedora, like the man in the alley, keeping his head at an angle to obscure his features. Shaw's gaze stayed on the man, waiting to see his mouth, sure that when he did his lips would be missing. Why would anyone lacking a functioning mouth be in a restaurant? How could they eat? They couldn't. He was being ridiculous, jumping at shadows. The man lifted a piece of toast from his plate and slid it toward his obscured mouth, coming back with a significant bite out of it.

Shaw didn't realize he'd been holding his breath until that moment.

"What can I get you?"

He jumped. The waitress had moved up next to him without his even realizing. She gave a quick laugh, lowering her order pad and pencil. Her mousy brown hair was pulled back into a bun.

"Sorry about that."

Shaw waved it off. "Quite all right. I was in the moon."

"Ooh, British are you?"

Shaw nodded, infected by the woman's natural enthusiasm. Most people made no mention of his accent, or hadn't yet. Of course, he'd only spoken to a handful of people, and perhaps British accents were not so uncommon.

"Do you have tea?"

"Sure do."

"I would love a cup, please."

"Anything to eat?"

"Soup?"

"Chicken noodle or vegetable?"

"Hmm, vegetable. Please."

She disappeared back toward the kitchen without further comment, and Shaw was left with his contemplations. The fedora man continued to eat his food without looking up. Strange for a man to not remove his hat indoors, especially when eating.

Enough! he told himself. *Don't descend into paranoia.*

He can't very well be eating toast without a mouth.

The man finished what was left, withdrawing money from his pocket and placing it on the table. He didn't look at it, didn't count to ensure he had the correct amount. Reaching out he grasped his chair, then slid his hand along the back to grab something. A cane? Different from his own. This one was thin, and instead of being held for balance, it was held forward at an angle.

Blind! Shaw realized, feeling guilty for ever suspecting the man.

The blind man made it to the door and outside, turning left to travel along the walk. He passed the window closest to Shaw and looked up, smiling, revealing his face for the first time. The man did indeed have a mouth, much to Shaw's relief. *Of course he did!* Further tilt to his head revealed the eyes, covered by dark glasses. An unremarkable picture of a blind man ... except ...

How could the man be smiling at him?

Shaw's calm slipped further as the man turned. His eyes! Or at least the left one … Nothing there. Only smooth skin.

"Your tea."

This time Shaw managed to not jump at the words, not outwardly at least. "Thank you."

When he turned back to the window, the blind man was gone.

The soup arrived shortly after, and Shaw enjoyed it and the tea. Both eased outward from his stomach, providing warmth through his body and a sense of calm.

The man at the alley had been a fact, no getting around that, but that was hardly the first strange thing he'd seen in Arkham, and he had the impression it wouldn't be the last. Compared to what he'd seen in his life, they were not even at the top of the weird scale for him.

Paying for his meal, he exited onto the street. People still wandered here and there, going in and out of the various establishments. One man made eye contact as he passed, giving Shaw a quick nod. All normal, unremarkable, day-to-day. With a brief huff he turned right and headed up a few doors.

Odds & Ends.

It was definitely a shop of sorts, but with a name like that they could sell anything.

A bell tinkled as he entered, and behind the counter a man glanced up from his book, considered Shaw a moment, then returned to reading. He wore a thick moustache, reminding Shaw of the one Inspector Abberline had years ago in London. His hair was thinning but still retained the original black color.

No greeting. No offer of help.

Had basic service changed so much since the last time Shaw had entered a store to browse? How long had it been? Vaguely he remembered wandering the market in Bandagar, looking at spices. Singh had been just a boy then.

The shop was comprised of three packed aisles in total, shelves on either side. Items hung on the walls and even from the ceiling. A bear trap. Snowshoes. A long saw for felling trees. In the first aisle it became evident that some organization had been attempted.

Similar or related items had been placed in boxes together. Pencils with chalk. One box full of marbles, some the size of his eye. Another held assorted buttons. Books. Utensils. Tools. Articles of clothing. With genuine joy, he came across a Union Jack flag, folded with care and respect, placed on a shelf. Shaw's fingers brushed against this unexpected bit of home.

Not the fascinating place he'd imagined. More of a junk store. The place was clean and well organized, without any dust on the items and no dirt on the floor, but nothing was of any particular interest. Nothing he couldn't find elsewhere.

He did find a copper-colored, rusty flashlight. A tube with a lens at one end. Two handles on top would prevent the holder from burning their hands. There were more efficient versions these days, but this was still better than the lights Bobbies on patrol carried years ago. He could see him skulking about Whitechapel with one of these.

Skulking about … tracking …

No. Before his mind traveled further down that road, Shaw turned from the tool and moved along.

Rounding one set of shelves he came upon a massive dog on the border between shopping area and back storage. Eyes flitted to Shaw, appraising him. The gaze lingered past the point of comfort, a warning to not do anything ill-advised. Shaw had always liked dogs, but this was not the petting kind. This was the attack and protect kind.

"Is your dog friendly?" Shaw called toward the shopkeeper. He turned to see the man staring back, the front counter in a straight line to him and the dog.

"Usually." The man returned to his book.

Shaw returned his gaze to the dog, who gave a snort and looked away.

Had he been declared as no threat? And was he relieved or insulted?

"Just move on, Shaw," he muttered.

Between dog and shopkeeper, the place held a less than friendly atmosphere. Not hostile exactly, but not welcoming either. Not wishing to appear rude, he would peruse the next aisle then keep going out the door. He continued scanning left and right but, as he'd already concluded, the store didn't hold anything he hadn't seen elsewhere. Maybe not those exact marbles, or books, but similar enough to decide he should have gone directly to the clothing store. Better to—

Shaw came to a stop.

His attention was caught by one particular item, something he wouldn't have expected to see outside of a dream. Was he dreaming *now*? Or hallucinating? It wouldn't be the first time. He moved forward again, wary, as if this item would bite him as surely as the dog.

A flute.

It was crafted in the shape of a tentacle, each of the finger holes carved to look like one of the suckers. For a full minute he hesitated before the flute, not touching it until he felt ridiculous. His finger ran along the smooth wood, slipping around it. He brought it up before his eyes, turning it in the light.

Dizziness.

He staggered and placed more weight on his cane. After a moment it receded, leaving a sense of bewilderment and wonder. The workmanship was exquisite, more so than in his dream—if indeed it *had been* a dream. If not for touching it and confirming he held a piece of wood, he could convince himself this was an actual tentacle. The coloring, a mixture of purples, blues, and tans, caught the light and almost absorbed it, like a piece of night. One end of the tentacle tapered into a mouthpiece. Shaw hesitated to blow into it, and he could hardly pretend it wasn't because he was afraid of what effect that breath might have.

Afraid. Yes. Absolutely.

Caution was key.

What coincidence to find this here though.

"Coincidence," he scoffed.

The word had no ring of truth. As he had told Cassandra, he did not believe in coincidence. What then? This flute had been placed here for him to find? That sounded more believable but …

"For what purpose?" he whispered.

More manipulation, and he would have none of it. Shaw held the flute above the spot it had come from, willing his fingers to let go. He couldn't do it. The flute was important in some way. Would it open a portal to Azathoth? Shaw was afraid that was exactly the case, though he'd reached there on his own. Purchasing this instrument did not mean he had to play it, but it was better in his hands than whoever else may find it.

Without more convincing argument than that, he worked his way back to the front counter and placed the bizarre instrument down. The shopkeeper's brow furrowed a moment, then told Shaw it cost fifty cents. Shaw placed two American quarters—as he'd learned they were called—in front of the man and slipped his newfound treasure into one jacket pocket. Chuckling at the silliness of purchasing the flute, he continued on.

"It will look good on a shelf. A conversation piece."

The clothing store was less eventful though about as impressive. He managed to purchase underwear, socks, pyjamas, and a change of shirt without anything strange happening. In addition, he found a leather satchel for carrying everything. Slinging it over one shoulder, he paid and started back toward the professor's house.

CHAPTER 25

April 20, 1912
Professor Watkins's Home: 4:32 pm

t had been a busy day and he would need to rest his leg tonight. Still, he felt energized again, and the few blocks back did not bother him at all. The sky had gotten darker, like dish water, in the few minutes since leaving the last store, looking as if it might rain.

"Oh! There you are," David exclaimed, sounding relieved. He wore a jacket and looked ready to leave. With Shaw's appearance, he shrugged off the coat. "Uncle, he's here."

Watkins came from the back of the house. "Doctor. I was worried."

Shaw, taken aback, greeted the two. "Is anything wrong?"

Uncle and nephew glanced at each other, but David spoke first. "It's just that, you don't know Arkham. Certain streets are dangerous after dark. It's best not to wander if you are unfamiliar."

"Why?"

"Well … It's …"

"Arkham is a strange town, Doctor," Watkins finished.

Shaw's mind jumped to the man with the missing face. Then

that locked room in the library. Yes, this was a strange city. If he'd seen this, then what was out there that he hadn't seen? He apologized for worrying the two men. Both waved it off and guided him through to the sitting room.

To his joy, a tea pot with steam escaping awaited him, with three cups.

"My apologies for not thinking of this at breakfast," Watkins said.

"Quite all right, quite all right."

The three enjoyed some tea, or at least Shaw did. He wasn't sure if the other two drank because they wanted to, or if it was to be inclusive. Shaw leaned forward in his seat, replacing his cup to the saucer.

"I visited the university today. Didn't realize it was Saturday."

Watkins chuckled at this, and Shaw joined him.

"The librarian was there," Shaw added, "but he'd never heard of Cassandra."

Watkins's brow furrowed, and he gave his head a quick shake. "Odd. It was certainly Armitage who recommended her ... though he didn't mention how he knew her."

Shaw kept his relaxed expression on. Armitage was an unpleasant fellow for certain, but which of them was telling the truth?

That night, when Shaw retired to his room, he locked the door. Watkins and his nephew gave every indication that they were exactly what they appeared, but he'd known others in the past who had seemed the same. If he was overreacting, then no one would be the wiser. If not ...

Slipping between the sheets wearing his new pyjamas, Shaw was physically comfortable but mentally uncertain. Everything whirled around his mind. Watkins. David. The faceless man. Armitage the librarian. Whatever was hidden behind that metal gate. As an afterthought, he realized the words from Cassandra's tattoos had faded in his mind, in much the way the tattoos faded in the daylight. They lingered on the outskirts of his consciousness but came no closer.

There would be no portal dreams tonight.

Thinking of Singh, he drifted off to sleep.

Darkness, like wading through liquid night.

Where was he now?

He wandered, surroundings not changing for his efforts, but he knew it was somehow wiser than remaining still. In the distance, movement. Strong-muscled legs thumping against the ground. A thud such as might be produced by punching a slab of meat. No yips. No growls. Nothing to say what these monsters were.

Shaw kept moving.

Breathing.

Why would dream creatures need to breathe? Then again, why would he need to breathe while here either? Were these monsters dreaming just as he was?

A flash of movement. Something tan in color.

He veered in the opposite direction, hurrying away.

Another movement, this one coming toward him. One of the creatures from the darkness …? Yes, it must be. The creature slowed, gaze landing on Shaw. The thing was vaguely humanoid, in that it had arms and legs, with a misshapen head at the top of a long neck. Two beady eyes and bare slit of mouth. No ears or nose. Thin arms, little more than sticks, were held before its chest while the legs, heavily muscled with two bends, gave the impression of great jumping ability. The feet ended in hooves.

It hopped toward him.

For all that it should appear comical it wasn't. This thing would have no problem jumping to intercept him then kicking him to death. Maybe one against his cane could be held at bay, for a time, but a second now joined the first.

Shaw backed away. For every step he retreated they took one forward. Still more came from behind the first two. A pair, then a quartet. Soon twenty of these leaping beasts had congregated before him. The group continued to grow, past the point where he could say how many there were.

Hop. Hop. Hop.

If they charged he was finished.

Their mouths opened to show rows of wickedly sharp teeth. The teeth of a carnivore.

Preceding them was a sensation of malevolence. This was not like being caught by a wolf or a bear that would kill for protection or food. These would kill for the sport of it.

No portal would save him.

No flute.

Flute? Yes! The flute he'd bought.

Where had he …?

Oh! Of course. That was in the waking world.

A steady, repeating noise approached.

Clop. Clop. Clop.

A horse?

CRASH!

Shaw struggled upright, eyes opening. Awake now, he rubbed one shaky hand down his face and gave thanks for the interruption to his sleep. He may not have opened a portal to Azathoth, but that didn't mean his dreams were any less dangerous. No desire to return to sleep, Shaw wandered to the window and watched a horse-drawn delivery truck with *Milk* written on the side in simple block script.

At the moment the driver stood cursing at the bottles which had smashed against the ground. The man picked up the shards of glass and tossed them into the back of his wagon before taking fresh bottles up to the nearest house. He left them at the door and returned to the wagon, urging the horse forward to the next customer.

Eventually they turned the corner, the street outside recovering its quiet, pre-dawn life. After that Shaw crept across his room and opened the satchel, pulling the flute free. On the edge of his bed, he studied this instrument while avoiding the inevitable return to sleep. He couldn't bring himself to blow into the mouthpiece.

What might be called if he did?

CHAPTER 26

Watkins and his nephew were both gone by the time he awoke the next morning. Neither had awaited him for breakfast, but once again food and coffee were on the table, hot and waiting. He ate quickly, wanting to catch the bus and see Arkham in its entirety, hoping this would expose the reason he'd been drawn here.

The book in the library was a danger, but only one part of a larger puzzle. What was the rest? Some future occurrence? That would explain why he had such a vague sensation about all of Arkham. All of the necessary pieces had not come together yet. Shaw placed it in his mind as something to consider.

In the meantime, he would gather information.

After the reaction from Watkins and his nephew yesterday, Shaw was more wary on his walk from house to bus stop. They had warned against being out after dark, but he still felt an unease at the thought of poking further into Arkham.

The same driver, with cap askew and eyepatch obscuring one eye, stopped for Shaw at town hall.

"Good morning," Shaw said.

No response. The man watched with his one functioning eye until Shaw was seated in the front row, next to the entry door. The seat leather was well worn, and the metal sides were dented as if from a hammer. Four other riders occupied the bus, empty seats between themselves and the next closest person. Each glanced at Shaw with suspicion before returning their gaze toward the outside world. The driver pressed the gas and jumped the bus forward onto the street.

Downtown Arkham was a ghost town, especially compared to the liveliness of Saturday. Gone were the people bustling back and forth. All of the businesses were closed.

"Is this usual for a Sunday?" Shaw asked.

The bus driver glanced in his direction without expression, then returned his attention to the road. Not friendly, but not exactly hostile either. Like the faceless man in the alley, this one contributed to his general unease while not giving any direct threat. Was this what living in Arkham was like?

The bus continued at its slow pace along Main Street with Shaw keeping an eye for any other places of interest he might visit tomorrow. Of course he would need to return to the university and meet the archaeologist friend of Watkins, Doctor Bell. Hopefully the man would share his information with Shaw where he refused with Watkins.

They took a left turn, went a block until meeting the Miskatonic River, then another left. This street called, appropriately enough, River Street, had the Miskatonic on his right, spanned by several bridges, while on his left were a series of squat warehouses. They crossed the Miskatonic on the second bridge, the same one they'd crossed after first arriving.

"I'm new in Arkham," Shaw tried again.

This time the man didn't even glance in his direction.

At the water's edge on the opposite side a barge bobbed in the water. Once painted white, the boat now had more peeled away than had been left behind. Muscular men unloaded crates and boxes from the barge to a waiting flat-bed wagon drawn by two scrawny horses. The animals scuffed the dirt with their hooves and stared at the water with distrust. A slap on the wagon's side as the workers jumped into the back. It drove off.

At the train station the bus stopped and waited. The driver didn't look toward the platform or even appear as if he were expecting anything and, after a few minutes, he drove on without anyone boarding.

They entered a more industrial area. Dark factories producing unknown products amid several warehouses. The flat-bed wagon had beat them there; the same muscled men were in the process of unloading crates with barely any effort. No grunting or gritting of teeth. It was, quite frankly, impressive.

Next came the part of town where well-to-do people lived. They passed several homes which bordered on being mansions. Porches started in the front and traveled around either side in many cases, while in others thick columns framed the front doors. Ancient trees claimed several lawns, the leaves of spring reaching toward the sky. Everywhere the windows had drawn curtains.

Even here were the signs of decay. The deeper they moved into the area, the more decrepit the houses became. Boarded windows and roofs missing tiles. Crumbling porches and trees which drooped toward the ground in defeat. One huge house had the roof entirely caved inward.

A great, aged church perched at the top of a low hill. The outside walls were dirt streaked and yellowed with age. Many people, stooped and wearing jackets and hats, headed in through the door. More people than the place should comfortably fit. A bell in the top belfry sat unmoving and silent.

"What denomination church is that?"

The driver stayed silent of course, no surprise by now. The bus rolled to a stop, with one middle-aged lady and a boy leaving. On the way out she gave Shaw a penetrating glare, judging. Shaw tried to muster a smile for her but found himself unable. He was happy when they rolled on. Whatever sort of church that was, it didn't give any indication of being Christian, or even Jewish. There were no religious symbols on the outside walls. No name of the church above the door. No sign stating when services were held.

They circled the hill and came around on a road facing back the way they'd come. More shuttered, less impressive houses on this side of the hill. One person left the bus at this point while others boarded. Another block or two brought them to what must be the entertainment district. One grand old theatre that wouldn't have been out of place in London occupied the city block closest to him. On the marquis above the entry were the words: The King in Yellow. For a moment Shaw considered this and the posters to either side of the doors. An evocative title that sent shivers down his spine for some reason. He felt a cold certainty that he did not want to sit through this show. Other buildings across from the theatre were less identifiable but equally well maintained. In marked contrast, the next block turned to run-down, dirty places. One of these was a rough-looking bar, reeking of desperation and violence as much as alcohol. Like the theatre, Shaw could see this place in London, but in Whitechapel or Limehouse. The area was two blocks in all and behind them as quick as it came.

A town library.

A clock tower.

A graveyard.

All of the sights one might see in any other town, but somehow sinister. As if each held some insidious secret.

"You are wasting time."

Shaw jerked at the words in his ear, turning to find Stephen on the seat next to him.

"What?" he answered in a low whisper, hoping no one would hear. He looked over one shoulder and found an older lady toward the back staring in his direction instead of out the window. Her purse rested on her lap, fingers gripping the handles tight.

"This is all a waste of time," Stephen waved his hands. "You were shown where to go."

"Miskatonic University."

"Yes."

"It's Sunday, no one is there."

Stephen made a noise of disgust, then a giggle. He went silent but didn't fade away.

"What else can I do? Why am I here?"

Add to that an unspoken question of why he should do anything Stephen suggested, as it all came through the influence of Cthulhu. Logically, Shaw should be doing the opposite of what was desired. And yet …

Stephen turned toward him, deep cosmic madness in his eyes. The gaze of someone who had seen far too much, more than Shaw had ever seen and that was a lot.

"The basement."

Shaw shook his head. "What basement?"

"THE BASEMENT!" Stephen shouted. The voice deeper, more ancient. Forceful. Demanding.

The older woman at the back screamed and demanded to be let off.

Stephen was gone.

CHAPTER 27

April 21, 1912
Professor Watkins's Home: 11:24 am

Once again the bus was faced toward the river, heading toward the more familiar side. Passing the train yard, he saw the tell-tale sign of a hobo's fire and several people gathered around it. They crossed the Miskatonic over a third bridge; the barge which had been there earlier was gone. In the distance he saw a ripple in the water and wondered what fish might exist there.

The town's edge rose toward the surrounding woods. Like the water, Shaw wondered what lived among those trees. Whatever inhabited either place was something to be avoided.

The bus passed a modern-looking hospital, clean and white, then skirted the university where a couple of people got off. Shaw was pleasantly surprised to find the bus passing close to the professor's home.

"Could I get out here?" he asked, leaning forward.

The driver glanced at him and pulled aside, opening the door. Shaw gave a thank you, which got as much response as anything else, and departed; the bus was on its way again a moment later.

The round trip had taken an hour and imparted no greater knowledge on what he was here in Arkham for.

He trudged through the door of Watkins's house, the weight of the world on him … No, the weight of Arkham. The entire city had an aura about it. Odd. Menacing. Evil. More was happening in Arkham than what he and Cassandra had come for. No tug in any specific direction, other than the university library. The entire town seemed of interest.

Which way should he go? Cassandra would be back soon, and he had nothing to show for his time here.

"Hello?" he called, waiting for a few seconds before heading deeper into the house. "Professor Watkins? David?"

No answer.

The house was silent.

Was he alone?

The memory of Cassandra's suspicions came back, followed by the contradiction between Watkins's and the librarian's stories. He listened for the slightest sound and still found nothing. Shaw headed upstairs. It was the perfect chance to look around and see if anything could either prove or disprove the suspicions he was starting to have. He wanted to trust the man, and David as well. Both had treated him well, but he had been tricked before.

The bedrooms were what they appeared to be. He took a cursory glance into each, not truly knowing what it was he searched for. After looking into each, including another guest room, he returned to Watkins's room and scanned the contents from the door.

Nothing of interest. Nothing at all.

A glance over his shoulder and he entered the room, feeling like the intruder that he was. Still, he had done much worse in his aim to protect humanity. The room held much the same furniture as his own temporary accommodations. Bed. Bureau. Wardrobe. Desk.

He scanned the desk, but this was obviously not as important to

Watkins as the one in his study. The drawers slid open without a sound, and without any content.

Shaw closed the last drawer and exited the room. Without knowing what he was looking for, it was difficult to find. Was the absence of anything catching his attention a positive sign? He assumed so. Another five minutes were passed in David's room with as much to show for his efforts.

Shaw stood in the hallway tapping his cane against the side of one foot, considering. After a moment he continued on to his own bedroom and almost collided with a woman coming out. She was somewhat older, maybe Shaw's age, with some white streaks in her black hair. In her arms was a bundle of bed linens which showed her eyes over the top edge.

"Oh!" she said, taking a step backward. "I'm sorry."

She kept her face hidden.

Recovering from his own fright Shaw said. "You must be Amelia."

The woman nodded, not moving.

"How is your day, Amelia?"

"I … My day is fine." She was taken aback, as if no one ever asked how she was doing. Perhaps that was true. "Thank you."

Her eyes were distinct, somewhat protruding. They reminded him of the fishlike people he'd met in London's east end decades ago. The followers of Dagon.

"The professor and David are out?"

"Yes."

"Ah, I suspected as much."

Amelia offered no extra information and Shaw stepped aside, not wanting to be the one to delay her. She took a step forward then turned toward him.

"Did you find what you needed?"

"Ah …" He assumed she had seen him snooping around and started formulating some explanation.

"In town," she added. "Shopping."

"Oh! Yes, I did. Thank you. I managed to buy some clothes yesterday."

"If you have any wash, you can set it outside your door."

He gave her a smile and thanked her for her kindness. She turned to leave again. Shaw felt he'd made a superficial connection, but wanted Amelia to be more at ease and searched for something else to say.

"You don't have to hide your face," Shaw said. "Not with me."

Now he felt like an ass. The poor woman was possibly self-conscious about her looks. She turned back with those huge, unblinking eyes. After a moment she lowered the linens and exposed her nose, wide and flat, and a mouth which was blubbery, lips loose.

Shaw gave her the most accepting expression he could, keeping his eyes on her the entire time.

"This doesn't ... repulse you?"

"We all look different in some way. It's what's inside that truly counts."

She considered that. "What's inside. I like that."

"I met several people like yourself in London years ago."

"Like me? Truly?"

"Oh, yes."

"I ... did not think there were others, not outside of ..."

Her eyes averted but a warmth lurked in them. Shaw decided to change topics. "Do they treat you well here?"

"Oh, yes. Better than others I've worked for."

"You've been with the professor long?"

"Since he came to Arkham, years ago, with the boys."

"With the boys?"

"Yes, sir."

Watkins had told them his sister had brought the boys. Had that happened at another place before they'd come here? Possible.

"Does the professor not own this house?"

"No. Miskatonic University owns all of the houses the teachers live in."

"It's such a large house."

"There have been many who have lived here. It has many secrets."

"Secrets?"

Amelia's eyes grew wider and she took a step back, shaking her head. Shaw understood, she had said too much.

"Between us," he said, waving a dismissing gesture toward the words.

Amelia thanked him and turned back toward her tasks. Shaw watched until she had started down the stairs to the ground floor. Nothing was left up here to look at, nothing in the first place it seemed. Once Amelia had reached the floor below, Shaw followed, arriving at the bottom of the stairs in time to hear her in the kitchen.

The professor's office. As when they had first arrived, the door was closed but not locked. Still, it wouldn't do to be caught inside this room. He closed the door and headed for the desk. Would it be locked? The drawer pulled easily, exposing the usual, bland contents. Matthew's letter was gone. Shaw hadn't consciously realized that was what he was looking for in here. For the best it being gone. He had a job to do and couldn't waste time raving in the office until someone came along. But why would Watkins have moved it? Because of his reaction? Possible.

The sitting room held no interest to him. He'd been in there more than once and had even been left alone there. Nothing would be hidden in that room. Likewise, the dining room and kitchen would be without anything of value.

THE BASEMENT, Stephen had wailed.

He'd seen a door in the kitchen which must lead there. He felt a moment of distress. He didn't want to go down there. A sure sign that he should.

With as much stealth as he could muster, he headed for the back of the house and the kitchen. At the open doorway he slowed, watching for signs of Amelia. He'd made a friend there, he was sure of that, but getting caught sneaking around wouldn't do that friendship much good.

Luckily she was outside, hanging wash, and Shaw was able to ease into the kitchen and down the basement steps without her noticing. Lucky thing she was outside too, since each step creaked like a boat in a storm.

Rather than the expected dirt floor, he found cement, giving the room a roughness while still being clean. Singh would have had a problem standing upright, but the ceiling gave ample space for Shaw's lower height. There were no windows to allow in natural light, and if there had been they would have been unnecessary. Even the bare bulbs with their pull chains hung unused. On each of the four walls were glowing five-pointed stars, each line of which had a slight curve rather than the exact straightness of a pentagram. The glow provided enough light to see clearly in the basement.

Shaw shuffled toward the nearest star.

Some bioluminescence, like certain algae, was his first guess. A paint made using such a material?

The closer he came, the more he knew it was no such thing. These symbols were carved deep into the foundation of the house, the glow unearthly. He looked over one shoulder at the next star which appeared no further away than when he'd first arrived at the bottom on the stairs.

These were ... otherworldly, but the symbol gave him no impression of dread. They were not evil. Shaw traced the symbol with his free hand. Flakes of mortar crumbled and fell to the floor, losing their glow. The star remained.

Free me!

Shaw spun toward the voice. It came from his left, near one of the house supports. He started forward.

"Hello?" He didn't want to call too loudly and get Amelia's attention.

Help me!

Another step. Two. Three. He arrived at the nearest support—one of six as far as he could see—and passed it. Nowhere to hide here, no dark corners.

"Where are you?" he called.

A knock from behind him. Something sharp against glass.

Break the mirror!

Shaw spun to find a mirror hung from the nearest pillar. His reflection did not stare back. Instead, a swirling mist played within.

"Who are you?"

Who would you like me to be?

A face appeared before him, the final of Jack the Ripper's victims. Mary Jane Kelly. He knew that face well. Kelly had haunted him for more than a year.

Help us, Shaw!

He took a step away, not fooled for a moment. Mirrors were gateways, but they wouldn't bring back the dead woman, not without some other sacrifice in any case. He shook his head. That meant whatever was inside the mirror could read his thoughts. More precaution was needed, and he used Singh's teachings to close all avenues into his mind.

Mary Jane Kelly disappeared, replaced by the swirling mist.

Free me! the voice said again, weaker this time. Pleading.

He backed away one step, eyes still on the mirror. Inside a horrible vision appeared and charged him. Inside was a monster of eyes and beaks and horns. One mouth full of teeth. Shaw backpedaled, colliding with the next wall. The mirror snickered to itself.

"What are you?"

Prisoners, the mirror said.

Prisoners. Plural. Shaw opened his mouth, ready to ask more, but shook his head. These caged things were minor evils and not the reason he was here. He looked around, wondering why he *was* here. What was in the basement he needed to see?

The mirror? The star?

Further across the basement was another support with a second mirror hung from it. On seeing it, this one cursed him and told what horrible things it would do if freed. The mirror on the third support wept continuously. He felt empathy toward this last trapped creature, but not so much that he would be so foolish as to break the glass. The final mirror he came to held nothing, but gave no reflection either.

Watkins knew about these mirrors, and if he did then

Matthew's letter was not his introduction to the nightmarish hidden world.

The weeping and curses and howling continued as he moved on.

Release us!

You will be rewarded.

The kind of reward these creatures offered would not be anything he could want. The best they would give was a quick death, and that was unlikely. Another circuit of the basement and Shaw was satisfied he'd seen it all, but still had no idea why he should come down here.

He listened for Amelia's footsteps, and when he heard nothing from the floor above he started his climb.

CHAPTER 28

April 21, 1912
RMS Dauntless

Singh stood on deck staring into the distance. Around him stood a few groups of crewmen, also staring until an officer came along and shooed them back to duty. They'd been muttering to each other, shaking their heads.

Singh didn't blame them.

The apprehension of seasoned sailors confirmed what he already suspected. The storm ahead did not seem normal. The day had been clear until nearing dinnertime, then the skies had darkened, closing in from each side.

Still they continued forward.

Good. If he was to die, he would not want it to be while fleeing.

The wind picked up, trying to blow his turban aside. The air smelled strongly of ocean and fish, and the temperature had dipped several degrees.

Another couple of passengers made from sterner stuff leaned against the railing nearby. Singh heard snatches of their conversation, what the wind would allow. *Titanic. Sunk.*

One man pointed into the distance.

So this was where the ship had gone down.

What still remained here?

The ship diverted to one side, perhaps trying to avoid sailing directly over the *Titanic*'s final resting place.

Sliding one hand inside his jacket, Singh wrapped his fingers around the ceremonial dagger there. It would do little good against any supernatural horror, but it gave him comfort.

CHAPTER 29

April 21, 1912
Professor Watkins's Home: 6:02 pm

rode the bus around Arkham today."

Watkins looked up from his dinner. "And what did you think of our town?"

"Confusion," Shaw admitted.

Both of his dinner companions agreed. No surprise there.

"I saw a church on a hill with many people entering."

"That is no Christian church," David said. "Very popular though."

"You do not want to go there," Watkins added.

Popular church, not Christian and doubtful it was any other religion he was acquainted with. Which god did it serve? There had been no particular pull for Shaw to the church, and he had no intention of taking a closer look at this point.

For a moment he considered mentioning the mirrors and the symbol in the basement, but decided to bide his time. He wavered between trust and suspicion, and at the moment his impression was over onto the wary side.

"I saw a play coming soon to the playhouse."

Watkins nodded. "The King in Yellow."

"That's it. I've never heard of it before."

Neither of his dinner companions had either. Another curiosity, but not the reason he'd been pulled here. In his dream he'd been shown Miskatonic University, but a stroll around the campus had yielded nothing except a sense of something dangerous from the library. Tomorrow was Monday, and the staff and students would be back. Perhaps that would yield a more definite result.

That night, turning in early again, he was visited by nightmares. Not the same as that first night, but frightening nonetheless. A ship rocked in the ocean, buffeted by waves and rough seas. Shaw watched the scene from further out, as if flying a few feet higher than the ship, close enough to see the name. RMS *Dauntless*.

Singh's ship. In his dream he knew this.

The water continued to rock the ship until a horrible, familiar creature rose from the waves. Father Dagon! The monster stood in the water, so much larger than it had been when Shaw had seen that god in London years ago. There it had grabbed the cult leader, Ananya, and taken her back to the undersea kingdom.

On the far side of the ship a second figure rose, more horrible than Dagon. Somehow he knew this to be Mother Hydra. Dagon's mate.

"No," he howled. "Leave that ship alone!"

Dagon howled with laughter.

Shaw tried to move forward, using only his own mental urges. Nothing. Not an inch of progress. Between blinks the tableau reset itself. In the distance dread Cthulhu towered, gaze toward the nearest shore, ignoring the ship. Shaw was unclear if this was still the *Dauntless* or if he was looking at the *Titanic* now.

Another reset.

The lights within the ship flickered.

Gunshots. Shouts. Screams.

People walked on the ship's deck. Slowly. Dreamlike. They climbed the surrounding barrier and plunged into the water. Wave after wave of passengers and crew. The ship went dark, and only a sliver of moon showed them continuing to plunge to their deaths in the icy waters.

Shaw awoke, a sea of sweat soaking his sheets and bedclothes.

Was it real, or just a nightmare?

So many dreams. Prophetic ones. Warnings. Nightmares. Seeing things actually happening. No way to know which was which. These nightly visitations were enough to drive him absolutely mad.

And, once again, he feared for Singh.

CHAPTER 30

Shaw perched on the edge of his bed, head in hands, waiting to hear Watkins and David leave. He was not prepared for chitchat this morning. Last night's dream was a particularly vivid attack on his mind. He was sure the ship Singh had boarded—and he believed now Singh was indeed on a ship—had not been attacked by Dagon, Mother Hydra, and Cthulhu. He could not, however, convince himself that a madness had not taken hold of them as they neared the spot where the *Necronomicon* lay on the ocean floor.

Once uncle and nephew had gone, he eased the bedroom door open. He would rather not even see Amelia at this point. Shaw arrived in the dining room to find the same toast and jam waiting for him. This morning tea instead of coffee, and the *Arkham Gazette* lay on the table, folded.

Newspaper spread on the table, he skimmed through the headlines. It didn't take long. With the *Titanic* sinking, anything about ships was an interesting topic now. One told him that the RMS *Dauntless* had lost contact with shore. Their final message had come as they'd approached the area near where the *Titanic* had sunk. The search continues.

RMS *Dauntless*. The ship from his dream.

Singh's ship.

He leaned back in the dining room chair. Was it possible for the *Necronomicon* to reach from the depths and affect people on a ship?

Powerless! No way to find out with any certainty what had happened to the *Dauntless*. Damn it to the depths! Where was his son?

A choice danced before him. Linger in morose silence for some confirmation … or do what he can to destroy these monsters or prevent their return. With a renewed focus and the anger to back it up, he headed for the front door. Outside was a rainy, blustery day. Shaw borrowed an umbrella from the hallway and headed for the university. The weather was wet and miserable, matching his mood perfectly.

Once again he reached the university and headed for Doctor Bell's office, knocking on the correct door this time. After a moment of no response, he knocked again.

The other Doctor Bell's door opened, and burly man looked out. "You again."

"Yes, back on a week day this time."

The man grunted an acknowledgment. "Bell doesn't come to office before class."

"When is his class?"

Burly man stuck his head back into his own office and spoke, met with a responding murmur. The man returned. "He's in class now. Should be over in an hour."

"Thank you."

Without any reply, burly man closed his office door again. More low voices which Shaw could not pick out and couldn't care less about anyway. An hour to kill. Shaw started along the basement passage, following signs which directed him to the library. He wanted another look at that book, or at least a sense of it from the metal doors.

A much more circuitous route getting there, following the

underground passages to avoid the rain. Fifteen minutes of twists and turns until he stood outside of the library. To enter he needed to climb the stairs back to main level.

The librarian was nowhere to be seen, and Shaw followed the sensation of the evil tome until once again his fingers wrapped around the locked gate's bars. This time there were students at tables, in the stacks. Reading. Studying. Searching for books. Each looked up for brief moments as he passed, eyes following.

Whatever occupied that locked room was at least part of the reason he was in Arkham. Whether some small or major part of the reason he had no idea, but whatever the case this wasn't something that should go uninvestigated. Once again he felt the presence of … something. An evil behind these bars.

"I knew you'd return."

Shaw started, hand gripping the head of his cane, as if the sword were still hidden there. He turned, knowing the unsettling librarian, Armitage, lurked behind him. The man quirked a humorless smile, glancing at the cane as if guessing what was missing.

"Yes," Shaw said, not hiding his annoyance. "I'm back."

"There is something of interest inside that room." It was a statement, not a question.

Shaw nodded.

"Something dangerous?"

"Yes."

"It calls to you."

Shaw thought about that but didn't honestly know. He kept his eyes locked on the librarian. "What book is this?"

The man grinned, the most life he'd shown so far, then it was gone. Armitage stepped forward and retrieved a key from his pocket. With a thrust and twist he opened the gate, stepping inside and not looking to see if Shaw followed or not.

Of course he followed.

The librarian acted different today. Last visit he couldn't wait to get Shaw out of there, this time he was more welcoming … No. Luring. Coercing. There was something he wanted Shaw to see.

Armitage turned, eyes burrowing while Shaw performed a half-circle, following the sensation. *There!* Before he could retrieve the book in question the librarian stepped forward, gloves already on his hands, and pulled it from the shelf. The man turned back, book held gently with both hands.

"We are two of a kind, I think. Cut from the same cloth."

Shaw did not argue, all attention on the book. His breath caught. He wanted to name the book but was afraid to give it voice.

"You've seen such forbidden tomes before." Another statement, but Shaw agreed in any case. "This is *De Vermis Mysteriis.*"

Shaw released a pent-up breath he hadn't realized he'd been holding. *Not* the book he feared, but still … He held one hand out, but Armitage made no effort to relinquish it.

"This book calls to you," Armitage repeated.

Did it?

No.

Not more than any other evil item or artifact. He could sense it, could determine this is not something others should read, but this was not what had drawn him to this room. Other books occupied spots on the shelf and made his skin crawl. *Notes of the Marquis de Sade. Unaussprechlichen Kulten.* Others which didn't have identifying marks on their spine. He wanted to burn this book, this room, maybe the entire library.

Shaw shook his head. "No. Not this one."

Still he held one hand toward the librarian, who narrowed his eyes. Armitage replaced the book on the shelf. "I didn't say you could touch it, did I?"

Shaw dropped his hand.

Armitage scrutinized Shaw, jaw working. Shaw felt as if his soul were being weighed.

"Yes," the librarian said in a low whisper, and whatever Armitage had seen it was apparent the two were still considered kindred spirits. Shaw did nothing to contradict the sentiment.

Armitage returned to the gate and clanged it shut, then came back to crouch before the same shelf of books. He removed the books from the bottom, stacking these precious tomes carefully and with respect to one side. The bottom shelf had a white star shape etched into the wood, the same one he'd seen in Watkins's basement. Armitage traced the symbol before pulling the shelf free and exposing a hidden compartment.

The presence hit Shaw, like a wave of solid evil.

He stepped back, coming up against another set of shelves and jostling the books there.

"Be careful, you fool," Armitage warned. Shaw barely heard him.

Whatever rested inside that compartment assaulted his mind and soul. He struggled to get his mental barriers up. Armitage pulled out a rectangular shape draped in black satin. He placed it on a nearby table, pulling the cloth aside to reveal a leather-bound book of yellowed moldering paper.

Shaw knew this book.

"No," he whispered. "No!"

"Oh, yes," Armitage answered. "This one you know."

"I do."

"This one calls to you."

"It does."

"I've never shown another person this *Necronomicon*. In truth it hasn't been here long."

The book had been masked by the lesser evil of the other tomes, and by the symbol on the compartment. Oh, if only he'd known about that symbol all those years ago! The malevolent presence had still come through, but less. Now that it was free … now …

"I received this copy from a student two years ago. He'd escaped a cult and taken this treasure with him."

"Yes …"

"It was driving him mad, though. He couldn't keep it and donated it to the library. I've kept it hidden since then."

Shaw forced the book out, shut down all ways into his consciousness. He would *not* be seduced by this power. He'd lived with it for years and resisted, he could do it now. The suddenness had taken him by surprise, but that was over.

"This is evil," Shaw said, pointing. "Pure evil."

"It is."

Armitage reminded him of the director at the British Museum many years ago. Things had not ended well for that man, and he'd only held the statue of Cthulhu. It was likely Armitage would suffer a much worse end.

"You must allow me to take this away."

Armitage slapped his hand on the book and stepped between it and Shaw. "I thought you understood."

"I—"

"Get out!"

Armitage gestured toward the door. What could he do? He had no concealed sword. No Singh to back him up. Armitage was at least two decades younger and in better physical condition. For now Shaw would have to be content with the book staying hidden as it was.

Whether these other books were the reason he'd been drawn to Arkham or not, they needed to be removed from the temptation of those who don't know any better. For now they were not a present danger though. Like the *Necronomicon*, they remained under lock and key and had done so for some time apparently. They would keep for the time being, but he would return.

His next step was still to meet with Doctor Bell.

CHAPTER 31

"Do I know you?"

Professor Bell was in his early fifties, wild hair and beard. The man wore a neat suit complete with vest. He was stooped over a block of stone on his work table when Shaw knocked and entered. The man had not returned to his office after class but had instead headed for some sort of archaeology work room. Bell held a brush in one hand and a magnifying glass in the other.

In a few steps Shaw had closed the distance between them. "No, but we have a mutual friend. Professor Watkins?"

"Ah, Reggie. Yes." The man lowered both hands to rest against the table without releasing either of his tools. "What of him?"

A wary note to his voice, as if he suspected what might be the problem. Not just wary though, afraid. A look that whatever misfortune had hit Watkins might spill over onto him.

"I am looking into the letter he showed you."

Now Bell did put his tools down, dropped them in fact. The

stone before him had been forgotten as the man jumped up, knocking his stool backward to clatter against the floor.

"No," he said.

"No?" Shaw responded.

Bell shook his head.

"Professor Watkins says you warned him away from this inquiry."

"I did, and I give you the same warning."

"Why?"

Bell did not respond, staring back at him.

"Your warning comes too late for me," Shaw admitted, "by several decades."

A cock of the other man's head. "What do you mean?"

Shaw wondered how much detail he wanted to give but not seeing much choice. "I've seen the writing before. Not these exact words, but similar. In India, and in England. They come from a damned book called the *Necronomicon*."

The archaeologist took more steps back, shaking his head. "You … know."

"I've had many encounters with this dark, hidden world. Too many."

"My … condolences … is the word I want, I suppose." Bell came forward again. "I … have seen things as well. In Egypt."

"Oh?"

Once again Bell stared silently before looking away. "I encountered a different book. One I brought back and placed in the library under lock."

"I have seen it, I think."

"Not as malevolent as … as the one you named." Bell shook his head, unable or unwilling to say the name of the book. "Artifacts too."

"Artifacts?"

A quick agreement from Bell. The man glanced over his shoulder at a floor-to-ceiling cabinet. The door held a solid lock which would take a shotgun to remove without the key. His gaze returned to Shaw, a defeated look, but more. An expression which Shaw recognized. A desire to share his story, a need.

"We were … on a dig, years ago. A sudden sandstorm covered our excavation while exposing a city nearby."

"A city? In the desert?"

"We investigated, of course. I … I … Don't recall everything that happened. Some of us disappeared along the way. A chase … I lost all of my party, my friends, that day."

Bell recounted the story as if unsure of the details himself.

"I'm sorry."

"The desert took the city back with another storm, as it had taken our dig site."

"Did you look for the city again?"

Bell shook his head. "We went into that city as a group. Later, an entire *year* later, I was found wandering in the desert alone, out of my mind. I have no idea where that time went."

Shaw looked at his leg, a constant reminder of what happened when one delved too far into these things. No wonder Bell warned people away from all of this. The man also glanced at Shaw's leg with understanding.

"From one of these things?"

"A cult of their followers," he explained, doubting Bell truly wanted to hear the details. It was his intention to remove weight from Bell's world, not add more.

The archaeologist turned and headed to the cabinet, pulling a key from his pocket. He opened the thick doors and looked over one shoulder in invitation. Five shelves occupied the interior with a foot and a half or so between each. On the shelves were various artifacts. A thin dagger. A blood red jewel. Assorted gold coins. An amulet with a symbol engraved into the metal.

"I've seen that before." Shaw gestured toward the amulet.

"The amulet?"

"No, the symbol."

"Where?"

A five-pointed star with a swoop to each of the lines, a faint glow to it. Bell took the amulet in his hand, flipping it over to show a blank back. It was supported by a thick chain. Shaw looked into the other man's eyes.

"Carved into a basement wall. That one was glowing brighter though."

"The spell must be charged to work. It will corrupt certain substances, but not others."

Bell held the amulet up again and allowed the light to glint off the metal. As far as Shaw could see, it didn't have so much as a blemish to it.

"What is it?" Shaw asked.

"A symbol of protection."

A sensation, like a chime inside his own mind. *This* was why he'd come to the university, or at least another part of the reason. He needed to know about this symbol. Annoyance shot through him at the realization that he had no idea of what to do with this information.

"Protection from what?"

Shaw realized his gaze was still locked on the amulet. His fingers flexed with the desire to hold it. With effort he forced himself to look into the archaeologist's eyes. The archaeologist took a step back, his eyes wary, his stance ready. Shaw leaned back against a table.

"I have no desire to take it from you," Shaw lied. "Not without your permission."

"A permission I cannot give." Bell returned the artifact to its spot in the cabinet and closed his cabinet, locking it. "It's protection from *them*, you see."

"Them?"

Bell raised one eyebrow. They both knew who *they* were.

Shaw changed his question. "Protection? The amulet or the symbol."

"Both? I don't know exactly."

It must be the symbol. Here, in the library, in Watkins's basement.

"The one I saw glowed a faint blue."

"I don't know what your circumstances are Doctor Shaw, but

you should head in the opposite direction."

"If you know as much as I think, then you're aware of how effective running would be."

"True." The man sounded genuinely sorry. "I wish you luck." Bell opened his mouth, then closed it, shaking his head.

"What is it?"

"It's … I had a dream last night."

"Yes."

Bell looked into his eyes and saw no judgement. "All I remember is some words. I woke in a panic, sweating as if I were trying to run away."

"What were the words?"

"Does 'when the six are gathered, the portal will open' mean anything to you?"

Shaw jerked as if poked with a pin. "Yes, but I don't know what. Can you tell me anything else?"

Bell shook his head. "Sorry. It seemed like something I should tell you."

"I see. Anything else?"

"Yes. Please don't come back."

CHAPTER 32

April 22, 1912
Professor Watkins's Home: Noon

O n the way back to Watkins's home Shaw replayed the conversation with Doctor Bell. He'd shown far too much interest in the amulet. If he should need to return to take the amulet, Bell would certainly remember his interest. Question was, did he need the amulet itself or just the knowledge of it?

No. The real question was would he actually take the amulet before breaking into the library for that damned book?

Another *Necronomicon*! Unbelievable.

At the professor's house he rested one hand on the knob, considering several conclusions. Armitage was not a person to be trusted, and he held an incredibly dangerous book. The book itself was not their only goal, but they needed to consider the best way to retrieve it. Bell's mind was definitely cracked but not broken. He had managed to continue his teaching position, so he couldn't be completely deranged. His encounter with the hidden world had affected him, but he was more to be pitied than feared. And Watkins? What Shaw had seen in the basement did not match with the personality the professor showed. That needed to be explored and rectified.

There. He did have one last avenue to explore while waiting for Cassandra to return. One last thing to distract him from the presence of a book he hoped to never see again. At least this one was decomposing, though that didn't make it any less dangerous.

Mind lost in contemplating the existence of that damned book, Shaw stepped through the door and stood silent, head lowered. Watkins called from the kitchen, something unintelligible from Shaw's position. Another voice responded. Not David.

Shaw planted cane against floor and stumped forward, every second step a hollow thud. In moments he'd arrived at the dining room and found Cassandra had returned. She leaned, both elbows against the table, while sipping black coffee from a mug. Watkins came in from the kitchen with a tray of snack items. Cheese, bread, and meats.

"This should keep us until dinner." The professor glanced up. "Hello, Doctor."

Cassandra turned and gave a weary smile.

"When did you return?"

"Just now. Barely had time to drop my bag upstairs."

Shaw joined them at the table and poured a cup of coffee with hands that shook. The knowledge affected him deeper than he'd known, and as he prepared to say the words aloud he realized how close to crumbling he was.

"There is a copy of the book. At Miskatonic."

"The book?" Cassandra started. "*The* book?"

Watkins placed the coffee pot directly on the table, missing the trivet. His eyes were suddenly miles away, lips working. "At the university? Hidden?"

Shaw agreed but decided against blurting exactly where it was hidden. There was still the matter of those mirrors and symbols downstairs. "Safe enough for now."

"Safe," Watkins mused. "Good. Good."

Shaw turned to Cassandra. "What did you discover?"

"Straight to it, hmm?" Cassandra drained the contents of her cup and placed it on the table before her, twisting in her seat to retrieve a notebook from her bag. While she prepared, Watkins refilled her cup, hands shaking in anticipation.

"Ipswich is nice enough. Not unfriendly," she began. "Only a few thousand people, so I was able to find where Matthew worked easily enough, and from there traced it back to where he was staying. Boston or New York would have been more difficult. Matthew and a couple of friends lodged at a boarding house. They were quiet and well-mannered, only interacting with others during dinner. Most nights they were out and only returned in time for curfew."

Cassandra paused, taking a drink from her cup before continuing.

"One day Matthew and his friends took dinner like usual, only they didn't come back. The boarding house owner didn't see them again. Not much left behind in personal effects. Change of clothes, but no letters."

"No forwarding address?" Watkins asked.

Cassandra shook her head.

"So we have no idea where he's gone then."

"Not yet. I—"

"Kingsport."

All three turned toward the open doorway and David. The young man had a letter in one hand.

"This just arrived, and I'm only going by the postmark on the envelope."

"Kingsport?" The disgust in Watkins's voice was plain. He turned to Shaw and Cassandra. "An inbred town of uneducated and superstitious people."

"That was your opinion of Innsmouth," Cassandra said.

"It's no better."

Watkins, it seemed, was not particularly tolerant of other people, at least not those who lived closer to the ocean.

"You've read the letter?" Cassandra asked, turning back to the nephew.

"I thought it best if we all heard it together." With that he pulled the folded paper from the envelope and cleared his throat.

April 12, 1912

David,

We remain in Ipswich, though not for much longer. The inner circle of this cult say we are to move on but won't say where. The local police are taking too much interest in the goings on of our group. My friends within the larger group—no, they are not friends and never were. I know that now. For whatever reason they lured me into this cult. In any case, these people I once assumed to be friends have quit their jobs, given up lodgings, and packed what belongings they had. They insist I go with them, as if I truly had any choice in the matter.

I hear someone coming. I'll continue this letter shortly.

April 17, 1912

We arrived a few days ago. This is the first I've been able to get some time without prying eyes and continue this letter. We're in Kingsport now, in a great house on the outskirts of town, on top of a bluff. The ocean view would be magnificent if not for the circumstances.

These people believe insanity.

Gods, older than the Christian one. I would believe it was nonsense if I hadn't seen things with my own eyes. Heard things with my own ears. Something spoke to us from across worlds. The voice reverberated inside our minds. One girl screamed for two full days after that, and I can't blame her. The screams were enough to break my mind, much less what caused them.

The cult has other pages with that same insane writing I sent you, though these pages are of less importance than that partial one. I don't understand any of this. They are searching for the missing text and will stop at nothing. They thought an entire book would soon be in their hands, but when the possibility fell through a great anger filled the cult.

That's when they murdered the screaming girl.

If I could run I would, but they would chase me and bring me back. I know too much to be allowed to leave.

I hope to sneak this letter out today. There's a slight chance.

David, these people must be stopped, but I have no idea how.

Help me.

Matthew

"Looks like I'm headed for Kingsport," Cassandra said.

"Not alone," Shaw said. "Not this time."

She glanced his way but didn't argue. Watkins looked uncomfortable. He opened his mouth to start speaking a few times before finding the words.

"Look, don't think less of me for not going with you. In all honesty this is too much for me."

David placed one hand on his uncle's shoulder. "I'll go with them uncle."

Cassandra shook her head. "I can't guarantee your safety, David."

"I understand, but this is my brother. I'm going with you."

Shaw turned toward the professor, watching his expression. He appeared content that David was willingly placing himself in danger among inbred, superstitious people. Shaw cleared his throat.

"I wonder, Professor." All eyes turned his way. "Does this scare you because it is unfamiliar, or because you know more than you've let on?"

Watkins shook his head. "I … don't understand."

David looked much the same while Cassandra leaned forward.

"I've been in the basement," Shaw said.

Watkins sucked in a breath. His eyes shifted to David, then toward the other exit. "You shouldn't have, Doctor."

"Uncle? You said to never go down there. What is in the basement?"

The tone was questioning, not accusing like Shaw's. After a moment Watkins let out a sigh and settled back into his chair.

"I can see how what you found would look suspicious," Watkins said. He glanced at David then back again. "You've been in Arkham for three days. You've had a look around. You must realize this is not like other towns."

"I … Yes."

"Everyone living in Arkham has seen strange things. It's a daily occurrence. I've lived here my adult life, ever since college, and I've seen more than some, not as much as others. Flashes in the sky. Shapes gliding below the water. Strange items. Strange people. Strange buildings. Churches to gods we don't mention. Books in the library locked away for our protection." He breathed in deep and let it seep out. "Those mirrors in the basement came with the house and belong to the university. They hold … things. I don't go down there, haven't since I first moved in. I … don't trust myself to not listen to those voices."

Shaw regretted his questioning. He knew better than most what it was like to live with knowledge you didn't want. The professor looked embarrassed by the exposure of what lay downstairs.

"My apologies, Professor. I have not been a gracious house guest."

"If anyone has a right to wariness, it is you, Doctor." Watkins waved the apology off. "All I want is my nephew back." The room was quiet. Watkins's gaze shifted to David and back again. "Maria warned that one day someone may come looking for them. I am afraid that someone has."

"This is why you brought Cassandra specifically to Arkham?"

"Oh! No, no. I didn't know of her connection to the bizarre until you both were here. *Your* appearance and connection came as even more of a surprise."

"Then … if Armitage gave you Cassandra's name …"

Watkins considered. "Armitage knows then."

"Knows what?" David asked.

"Too much," Cassandra said. "He knows about me and my … connection to the hidden world. Maybe even about Shaw, and whatever makes you and your brother special."

"There's nothing special about us," David protested. "We're two normal people."

Cassandra let that part drop. "I think we should see Armitage tomorrow."

Shaw told them of his two encounters with the librarian, and of the hidden books in that locked room. Of *De Vermis Mysteriis* and *Unaussprechlichen Kulten*.

"The *Necronomicon*," he said, starting to tell of the copy Armitage kept hidden. "The ... The *Necro* ..."

A wave of dizziness assaulted Shaw's consciousness, making it difficult to speak. It enclosed his mind like fog drifting across a lake. His head throbbed in rhythm to his rising heartbeat. Once again the words were alive inside of his mind. Cassandra's tattoos, what was in Matthew's letter, and ...

CLICK!

It was all ... all ...

Again the soft tune of a flute.

Words pressed against the inside of his lips, demanding freedom.

No.

No.

"Shaw?" Cassandra placed one hand on his arm.

"I'm fine. I'm fine." He forced a calm expression to his face. "Too much excitement. I think I'll lie down before dinner though."

CHAPTER 33

April 22, 1912
Professor Watkins's Home: 11:27 pm

Something approached in the darkness. The soft clack of inhuman feet against tile. He stood in the university library, surrounded by books and shelves and murky darkness. How had he arrived here? Last he remembered was ... what? It was a struggle to think. Cassandra! Yes, she had returned and ...

That sound. A night-gaunt?

No.

The same creature which had haunted his dreams these past nights. The humanoid monster with powerful legs. It bared vicious teeth. Another came from behind the first. And still more. A swarm of the beasts.

One leapt.

"No!"

It was enough to wake him. He returned to the waking world, groggy and uncomfortable, only half sure he had in fact woken. The clock on his bedside table told him the time was well after eleven. Had no one come to wake him for dinner? No, of course they had, but he wouldn't be roused. They had assumed it best to let him rest.

Perhaps his meal had been left in the kitchen.

Shaw moved, groaning at the stiffness of muscles, as if waking from a long sickness. He still wore his day clothes, even his jacket. He'd come upstairs and collapsed onto the bed. That explained the discomfort. He lay on top of the sheets, head against one of the pillows, cane next to him.

Cautiously he probed for signs of the throbbing headache, the dizziness, and found them mercifully gone. Perhaps only until he moved, but even so, if that was all it took then he would lie still until morning.

What of the words?

Earlier they had been pressing against him, linking together. The writing in Matthew's letter, those tattooed on Cassandra, and … and … and the writings he had made while asleep that first night. These filled the gap. He held the complete spell.

It seemed that, having come together, the words were content to lay dormant.

For now.

Or had he been muttering them in his sleep again? Could he taste them on his tongue? His eyes flicked, taking in the parts of his room he was able to see without moving. No. No portal. No—

Something moved, near the window. Just enough moonlight through the glass to outline a shape. Whoever—or whatever—it was faced him, as if deciding what to do next.

Shaw grabbed his cane and struggled, gracelessly, to an upright position. The wounds he'd received on the *Titanic* creaked and protested at the suddenness of movement. He turned on his bedside lamp. The momentum nearly took him over onto the floor, but using the night stand he was able to halt himself.

"Impossible!" he whispered.

The monster from his dream. It crouched, beady eyes on him. The sight was enough to get him moving, feet onto the floor, back toward the wall. Shaw held the cane out, as if it were his lost sword rather than a polished stick. Switching hands, he leaned one leg against the bed for balance and stared the creature down … or tried to.

The creature lurched toward him and received the cane across its face. It backed away, more surprised than hurt, then shook its misshapen head and bared those teeth. In the dream, this thing had been terrifying; in reality, it was worse. Once again it came forward, more cautious. The thing feinted left, which Shaw followed, then came back from the right. Too late. Shaw was committed to the wrong direction. Best he could do was overcommit. Following through, putting all his weight behind the motion, Shaw continued to the left, increasing speed and falling to the floor with a cry. The beast snapped on empty space with the clack of meeting teeth. From the floor Shaw rolled over to meet the creature, cane once again out before him. No time to regain his feet.

Somewhere on this floor a shot rang out.

Cassandra?

Pay attention, you old fool!

The monster spun, coming forward, and the best Shaw could do was to backpedal, scoot himself along the floor one-legged until he reached a wall. This thing had other ideas. Muscular legs bent at both joints, like a coiled spring. The mouth opened again to display its carnivore teeth. If it should land on him, Shaw knew he was finished. He brought the cane around, pointing it toward his adversary. With luck he could brace the cane and impale this thing.

The bedroom door slammed open against the inside wall. Both Shaw and the monster's focus jerked in that direction. Cassandra stood in the doorway, lit by the upper hallway's light. She pointed her hand at the thing.

BANG!

It fell to his left, landing on the bedroom floor. A neat circle decorated the center of its forehead. Smoke curled from Cassandra's hand, and Shaw realized she held a gun. She rushed over to the monster on the floor, gun pointed.

"I think its dead," Shaw managed, using the desk and his strong leg to pull himself to a standing position.

"You're an expert on ghasts then?"

"Ghasts?"

She poked the ghast with one foot. "Dream monsters, like the night-gaunt. Smaller and less dangerous by themselves, but traveling in packs. One was in my room as well."

"I've been dreaming of them."

Cassandra nodded, as if this were expected. "They're fast, strong, and agile."

"Did I call them here?"

Cassandra looked at him oddly.

"I … have been muttering the words from your tattoos and Matthew's letter," he admitted. "And from this." He pulled out a folded piece of paper. "I wrote this our first night here. It joins yours and Matthew's writings."

"Possible, but I think someone else called these here."

Shaw looked at the dead creature. Already it had started to dissolve, like a nightmare on waking.

"You said these travel in packs, but we've only seen the two."

"Damn it!" She spun, already halfway to the hall. "Come on."

If these ghasts were as abundant here as in his dreams, he feared they would not get to the professor or David in time. Shaw exited the room a second behind Cassandra and collided with her back.

"What …?" Shaw said.

"Go back."

He followed Cassandra's gaze, back toward the stairs. The hallway was full of a dozen ghasts, making their way forward, legs crouched to leap. Behind were two humans dressed in dark robes, both with hoods up to conceal their features.

"Armitage!" Shaw spat. One had to be.

Behind the two were several others in various types of dress, all with the same smooth features of the faceless man he'd seen at the restaurant. They focused on him and Cassandra.

"Move, Shaw!"

The investigator aimed and shot a ghast as it leapt through the air toward them. Then a second one. She turned and pushed Shaw into his bedroom, almost knocking him over in the process. Once back inside the bedroom, she spun and slammed the door, twisting the useless lock.

"That won't hold," he said.

"I know."

Cassandra rushed to the wardrobe and pulled it. The furniture gave grudgingly. It was too heavy. Shaw put his shoulder into the other side, using his normal leg for balance and strength. Between them they managed to get it in front of the door as the first ghast assaulted it from the other side.

"Get ready," Cassandra said, going to the window.

Shaw gave no argument, grabbing his satchel. Most of his belongings were already inside, and the few that weren't could stay here. He threw the bag over head and shoulder, wearing it crosswise.

More pounding on the door.

"What's the plan?" he asked, joining her at the window.

"It's an impossible jump to the ground," she said, "but if I can make it to that tree ..."

She looked at him, then back to the tree, and shook her head. Shaw accepted the reality of their options before Cassandra. The professor and David were likely already captured, and now his inability to climb down a tree would result in Cassandra's capture as well. Even before acquiring the wounds from the ship's sinking, he couldn't have possibly made that escape.

"You need to go, Cassandra."

She looked in his direction. "No."

"I can't get to that tree," he said slowly, patiently, "much less climb down it. Soon those things will climb the outside wall and through that window. I doubt you have enough bullets for all of them."

"I'm not leaving you."

"Didn't you warn me you'd leave me behind if I slowed you down? Are you not good for your word?"

Cassandra's eyes narrowed. "My morals are fluid, Shaw. I do as it suits me in a given moment." She glanced out the window again. "Too late anyway."

A hooded man and several of the ghasts had gathered below. Some faceless people as well. If Cassandra had left immediately, would she have gotten away?

She reloaded her gun while Shaw sunk down onto his bed. Pounding against the blocked door was matched by frantic yips from below the window. It was only a matter of moments. Time for desperate measures. Shaw opened his satchel and retrieved the flute he'd found at *Odds & Ends*.

Cassandra raised an eyebrow at the sight of it. "What is—?"

"Maybe a way out."

Do not return!

"This flute will open a portal to Azathoth."

Cassandra staggered back a step. "No!"

"Do you have a better plan?"

"Any plan would be better." She looked around, revolver in her fist. "I … Maybe I can shoot the two wearing robes."

"And?"

"If they control the ghasts and those faceless things—"

"One is in the hall and the other is down below. How will you shoot them both?"

Cassandra shook her head. "I can't."

Shaw raised his hand, bringing the flute to his lips. Would he need a specific tune?

"Wait!" Cassandra pleaded.

Shaw didn't. It might be a terrible thing to cross to that other dimension, a permanent solution for him, but it would be equally terrible to be caught. What would these cultists do if they got their hand on it?

He blew a long discordant note and waited.

Nothing happened.

Another, trying his best to match the notes he'd heard in the dreamworld. And again.

Nothing. No portal.

Now he felt like a fool on top of them being trapped. "The spell then—"

A creaking, scuffing noise came from the far end of the room.

Both turned toward the sound, Cassandra aiming her revolver in that direction.

"They're digging through the wall," Shaw said.

Not quite.

A section of wall swung toward them, and in the opening a shape holding a lantern. The light gave a garish under-lighting to the person, making their expression menacing and monstrous. Cassandra aimed the gun at its center.

"Amelia?" Shaw said, placing one hand on Cassandra's shoulder. "The housekeeper?"

"Please," Amelia said. "Come quickly."

The pounding on the door continued, and the unmistakable sound of claws on brick from outside the window. Cassandra looked over one shoulder, then rushed through the hole in the wall Amelia had created. Shaw followed, with the housekeeper coming last. She pulled the wall and sealed them inside.

"A secret passage?" Shaw asked.

"I told you this house had many secrets. Not all are in the basement."

With that she squeezed past them and down a passage. Inside, all was plaster and wood, the unfinished side of the house no one ever saw. A set of rough, spiraling stairs took them to the floor below. Amelia gave a sign for quiet and pushed on the wall. She stepped forward, listening, then gestured for them to follow.

The kitchen.

At the back door, Amelia once again looked for danger. "Head for the train yard," she said, pointing in that direction. "Cross at a bridge, but stay out of the water."

Cassandra passed through the back door, revolver still in hand. Shaw stopped before the housekeeper. "Thank you, Amelia."

Her expression became more pained, more worried. "Go."

They made it a block before the first ghast crossed their path, from one side of the street to the other. It was half a block away but looked neither left nor right and continued on.

"They've realized we escaped the house," Cassandra said.

CHAPTER 34

April 23, 1912
Streets of Arkham, Massachusetts: 12:15 am

From behind came the sound of pursuit, yips and shouted commands, emphasizing her words. Their advantage had dissolved. They glanced around for some avenue of escape, then Cassandra rushed to the only car in sight. The back seat was slightly elevated from the driver, and a roof hung over both seats. It reminded Shaw of the horse-and-carriage taxis of London. The back door opened easily.

"Get in," she ordered.

With all other options worse, Shaw crawled into the back of the car. Every experience he'd had inside these things had been either a horror or a felony. He hoped this would only be the latter. A green plaid blanket was spread across the seat, and Cassandra tugged it free.

"Get down," she said.

Shaw lowered himself to the floor and looked at her expectantly. His leg and the stitching both screamed at him, and would likely scream louder still tonight. Once down, Cassandra jumped in and did the same, closing the door behind her. She spread the blanket to cover them both and leaned her head forward. The camouflage wouldn't do if someone took a close interest, but with luck it would be enough to stop those passing by.

"The ghasts can only survive at night," she explained in a low whisper. "Come sunrise there will be less pursuers."

"And more visibility."

She nodded, and Shaw had to agree that choosing one over the other made sense.

"Shh," she said needlessly.

Several bodies passed their hiding spot. Whether these were ghasts, the faceless, or the robed people, they couldn't know, and it didn't much matter. Both held their breath as capture or worse came within feet of them.

Minutes, which felt like hours, later the footsteps had moved on. Still they remained in silence, listening to the night.

"Tell me about the basement," Cassandra whispered.

In the warm darkness of the blanket, Shaw gathered his thoughts then told her everything that he'd seen since she'd left for Ipswich. His encounters with Armitage in the library. His visit with Doctor Bell. The first sighting of a faceless man and his ride on the Arkham bus. He ended with the mirrors in the basement and how they spoke to him, the symbol on the wall and what Bell had said about it being for protection.

"Why would Watkins have these mirrors?"

"He said—"

"Oh, I know what he said."

Shaw considered that in the dark, sifting through the facts. "The abductions and the mirrors seem unrelated."

"True. Do you still trust them?"

Shaw considered the professor and David. Comparing them to the cultists and monsters who'd attacked the house, Shaw's trust tended to land on the other side of the argument. "I don't know."

"I'd be surprised if you did."

"They treated us with hospitality."

A weak argument at best.

"Well, the professor paid me in advance," Cassandra sighed. "I suppose we owe them the benefit of the doubt."

"We'll rescue them?"

"Of course, first we need to rescue ourselves."

"I—"

The front door opened, someone getting behind the wheel. Both Cassandra and Shaw's eyes widened. The car started and pulled onto the street. Bracing herself against the door, Cassandra slowly rose to look at the driver. She lowered herself again, looking toward Shaw. The light from passing gas lamps showed her face in two-second intervals. She made a gesture in front of her with a flat palm, as if wiping her face away.

One of the faceless.

She drew her revolver then rose slowly again until steady enough to place the gun against the driver's head.

"Keep driving," she said. "Take us to the train station."

Shaw wondered on that logic. The late-night train would have come and gone, and it would be morning before another was available. In the space of a thought the car swerved right, followed by several bumps and a jarring collision. Cassandra was thrown forward, half of her crossing into the driver's area. Shaw was wedged in well, his head pressing against the seat and feeling the metal underneath against his ear and temple.

Cassandra groaned.

"Are you okay?" Shaw asked.

"Pull me back."

Shaw struggled out of the car's bottom, using the car door much as Cassandra had. He found the investigator was also wedged in, unable to get the leverage to push herself back. Out the front of the car, through the cracks in the car's windscreen, was a massive tree. The car's front had been pushed inward, its steering wheel crushing the driver back into his seat.

Shaw grabbed Cassandra by the legs and pulled, inch by inch, until she was free. They crawled from the wreckage, shaking their heads. No other vehicles passed, no other people. It wouldn't stay this way. Cassandra checked the driver and shook her head.

"Dead."

She considered the faceless man a moment, her fingers working, as if she wanted to tear something apart. "We should go."

"Where?"

"Away from this car to start." Cassandra headed back the way they'd come. "The trains will be expected though."

"You told him to take us to the trains."

"Sounded like a valid idea at the time. Suggestions?"

There was one place he felt they needed to go before leaving Arkham. "Miskatonic."

"The university?"

"We can't leave that book there."

Cassandra exhaled and veered to their left. "As good a place as any. We can sleep there tonight, if it looks safe."

A walk which should have taken minutes cost close to an hour. Each time they got as much as half a block, they needed to hide in the shadows once again. Ghasts. Faceless men. Each sent them scurrying for hiding more than once. Neither of the hooded men they'd seen were on the streets, and in the end getting to the university wasn't as difficult as their escape from the house.

The library door was ajar.

Cassandra took the lead, revolver in hand, while Shaw did his best to catch up. He closed the door behind them, knowing it may slow any escape but also not wanting to attract the attention of any security the university might have.

From behind, Shaw guided the investigator down the stairs and across a mostly dark room until they arrived at the gated room.

The metal door stood open as well.

"No!" Shaw said, pushing in front.

He entered the room and went to the shelf, intending to hurl books onto the floor and open the secret compartment. No need. Like the library door and the metal gate this was open. The hidden compartment was empty. The book was gone.

"Damn it!"

Cassandra placed one comforting hand on his shoulder.

"I should have taken it with me. I should have demanded Armitage hand it over."

"Would that have worked?"

"I …" He thought of the hooded man he was sure to be Armitage and shook his head. "No."

"Armitage needed the book. He wouldn't have just given it up."

"Why show it to me?"

"To taunt you? Maybe to see what you would do?"

Shaw looked around him at the other books of the library, none of which were at the malevolence level of the *Necronomicon*. They had masked the presence of that book, hidden it until it was needed. What was Armitage planning?

"We aren't safe here," he said. "If Armitage was taunting me, then he knows I would come here."

The revolver was up again. "Let's go."

Shaw clanged the gate shut again, hoping it would be enough to deter anyone from entering. Without the key, he had no way to secure it, and far more books than he could carry remained inside.

The further they traveled toward the front door, the more Shaw was convinced that this was some sort of trap. Memories of hiding in the British Museum while pursued by a night-gaunt came to mind. They had narrowly escaped then, due to the fact that it wasn't there for either him or Singh.

Step by step in the darkness. Across the basement. Up the stairs. Moonlight came in through the windows, lighting their path. He could see the shelves and tables and the—

"No."

"What is it?" Cassandra whispered.

"The door." It was open once again, the moonlit night outside framing the door. "I closed it."

Shaw found himself suddenly driven to the ground. A weight holding him there. At first he thought Cassandra had knocked him down for some reason, but the weight above wrapped its hands around his throat.

No!

He had no leverage to fight back, no air to call for help. The wound in his side howled in protest of the rough treatment. Sounds of struggle nearby. A punch. The sound of metal being drawn.

"Rah!" Cassandra exerting herself.

The weight eased a moment, though the hands remained around his throat.

"Let go!" Cassandra hissed.

Shaw gurgled a response.

"Fine."

A moment later the weight and the hands were gone. Cassandra rolled him over.

"You okay, Shaw?"

He nodded, not trusting his voice.

A foot distant lay one of the faceless men, on his back. The arms were splayed to either side and a slit across his throat told the rest of the story. Another lay in the opposite direction face down. In Cassandra's free hand she held her knife.

No other sound came. No one approached. No shout of alarm, though the faceless people made no noises at all. Cassandra approached the body while Shaw recovered. She pulled on the dead man's face. It had some give.

"It's not a face," she said. "It's some kind of covering."

One foot on the man's neck, she pulled, giving the mask some slack before pulling again.

Shaw got to his feet and approached, watching her progress. It gave, like a thin rubbery mask, but stronger than could be pulled away.

"Give me your knife," he rasped.

Shaw dropped beside the man, taking the knife, while Cassandra kept her foot in place. He slid the blade under one edge of the blank face. It wasn't a scalpel and lacked the precision, but the blade was sharp at least. He wondered if these had been normal townspeople, taken over by some spell. Could the mask be removed and allow them to reclaim their lives?

A stream of black-green liquid oozed out and across the dead man's chest. With a ripping noise, like a burlap sack giving way, the face separated from the man.

"No!" Cassandra shouted.

Beneath the mask was the depths of space. Stars. Comets. A sun in the distance. All of it in movement. One nearby planet.

And a vacuum.

Within moments the face had started to draw loose debris from nearby, sucking them into the endless void behind this faceless man's mask. Shaw staggered forward, pulled off-balance by the same vacuum. Cassandra grabbed his arm, pulling him back while trying to resist the pull herself.

Books from a nearby table were pulled into the void. A scrap of paper on the floor.

The pull increased with each passing moment. A table was pulled an inch closer.

"Put the mask back!" she said.

The mask?

Shaw pulled the thin covering up before his eyes and flattened it. Again he staggered forward, the fleshy mask held before him, and collapsed on top of the dead man, replacing the covering. Pulled away from the man, he and Cassandra gave several feet of distance, avoiding the other body as well.

"What the hell was that?" she asked.

Shaw shook his head. He didn't know and didn't want to. "It should be burned."

"No need."

Already the strange man started to decompose, shriveling and collapsing. No odor, no sound, but in moments all that was left were the two men's clothes.

"Let's get the hell out of here," Cassandra said.

He had never agreed with her more.

"Where though?" she asked.

"There's one place they won't look for us."

"Where?"

"Watkins's house."

"Are you out of your mind? We just escaped—"

"Exactly. It's the last place we would go."

"You're right there."

"We should find Matthew's letter, too."

"Why?"

"I noticed while you were gone that the words from your tattoos started to fade in my mind. Now the ones from the letter have faded."

"You *want* those words in your mind?"

"No." Shaw shook his head. "But that spell is important."

They stayed to the dark corners of people's front yards. Most of the ghasts and faceless had moved farther afield in their search, but there were still a few, moving in the direction of the university. Shaw and Cassandra traveled from one pool of blackness to the next, looking around for danger with each step.

"One more block," she whispered.

He nodded, though knowing Cassandra wouldn't see.

One last block, edging in the darkness, and they stood across from Watkins's house. All seemed calm, quiet, deserted. The front door sat open a crack. This was not the time to rush, except …

"It must be close to sunrise," Shaw said.

The sky had started to lighten, and had been for several minutes. It was still night, but not for much longer.

"Wait here." Cassandra rushed across the road.

Most of the darkness in Watkins's yard was gone as the day started to take hold. Soon the sun would rise above the houses and paint the entire town in light. They needed to be quick. She looked into each of the downstairs windows, giving Shaw an all-clear wave. He made his way to her as quickly as possible. Cassandra drew both knife and revolver and headed to the front door. Shaw followed her in, closing the door softly behind them. They made their way forward into the hallway, listening to their surroundings.

"Nothing," she said.

"Not yet."

They searched, looking into each room. Signs of struggle here and there. Broken knick-knacks, overturned furniture. Area rugs knocked aside.

"No sign of Amelia," Shaw noted.

In the professor's den they found Matthew's letter inside the desk once again. Cassandra held it toward Shaw, who stepped back.

"It might be better if I am not the one carrying it."

"Will that make any difference?"

Shaw had no answer for that.

CHAPTER 35

April 23, 1912
Professor Watkins's Home: 8:44 pm

Shaw!"

"Mmm...?"

"Wake up, you idiot."

Shaw's eyes shot open, and he struggled upright. Once again he was in his bed at Watkins's house. For the briefest moment his mind convinced him the previous night had been a dream. Then he saw Cassandra, leaned back and asleep in the room's chair, knife and gun on the table in easy reach.

"Fool! You are doing their work for them."

Shaw turned to his right to find Stephen once again, at the side of his bed, looking as manic as ever. His gaze landed on Shaw but didn't stay there.

"What do you mean?" Shaw whispered, not wishing to wake Cassandra.

"You are bringing the pieces together."

"The spell?"

"Everything."

What else was there? Shaw shook his head, not understanding.

Stephen grabbed the hair at both sides of his spectral head in his fists.

"When the six are gathered, the portal shall open." He moaned, pulling hairs free. "Run Shaw! Take the girl and flee."

"Doctor?"

Shaw spun toward Cassandra, who jerked awake and grabbed both weapons, leaping to her feet. In the short space between movements, Stephen had disappeared again.

"Doctor?" the same voice repeated, muted, as if speaking from behind a gag.

In the doorway a shape, cloaked in the darkness.

"Please," the voice said, both hands up in surrender toward Cassandra. It came out closer to "Fleas."

"Amelia?"

She turned back toward Shaw. "Yesh."

Cassandra lowered her revolver, though kept it in her hand, ready to use.

"You ust leae."

"That was the plan," Cassandra said, looking toward the night outside the window. "It was too difficult yesterday."

"They know. You're in Arkha."

Something more to the voice than the slurring of words. A dreamlike quality, as if the housekeeper were somewhat distracted.

"Know we're in Arkham?" Shaw asked. "Who are they, Amelia?"

"I … I …" Again she shook her head.

"You can't say?" Cassandra asked. "Or won't?"

"Can't." It came as a dreamy whisper, prolonged.

Cassandra brought the revolver back, not quite pointing it at Amelia but close enough.

"Cassandra?" Shaw started.

"Come into the room," the investigator demanded. "Out of the shadows."

Amelia did as ordered, stepping forward. She stopped just inside the door, bathed in moonlight. Both Shaw and Cassandra gasped. Amelia's right eye and the mouth on that side were gone, replaced by a smoothness of flesh. She was becoming a faceless person.

"Oh, Amelia," Shaw said.

Cassandra lowered the gun to her side. "They did this to you?"

Amelia nodded. Remaining eye unfocused and half lidded, as if drugged.

"Because you helped us?"

She shook her head. Her mouth was pulled shut by the flat skin, giving less mobility to her jaw, making it more difficult to speak. "For sfeaking with you."

"Speaking with me?" Shaw said. "How did they know?"

Amelia shrugged, eyes off to one side, searching. "They know."

"Well, they can't know everything or they'd already have us," Cassandra said, drawing her knife. "Come on, I'll cut that away."

Amelia stepped back. "Can't."

Shaw was glad to hear that, after what had happened with removing the last mask. Was it too late for Amelia? Cassandra stared at the housekeeper for a moment then slipped the knife back into its sheathe.

"You ust leae Arkha."

"Will you tell them where we've gone?"

Amelia struggled to bring her gaze back around to them, tears welled in them. "Yesh."

"Unless we kill you," Cassandra said.

"Yesh."

The housekeeper gave no indication that she was in danger, no sign that she would defend herself. As they watched, the facelessness crept further, covering her nose.

"I ah bein' absorbed."

"Sit in this chair, Amelia," Cassandra said in an uncharacteristically soft tone, indicating the one she had slept in.

Amelia did as bidden. Cassandra stepped to the bed and pulled the top sheet free. Twirling it into a tight rope, she wound it around Amelia, bringing it together in the back.

"Tighter," Amelia warned.

Cassandra pulled it tighter still and tied the sheet at the back.

Shaw grabbed his satchel and cane and made his way around the bed.

"Thank you, Amelia. Again."

Cassandra gave the bound woman a respectful nod before leaving the room, Shaw close behind. They scrambled to collect some food from the kitchen. Enough for a couple frugal meals. Once again they departed through the back door, into the darkness with the hopes of making it a few blocks.

"Where to?" Shaw asked.

"The trains."

"Is that wise?"

"Probably not. What other option?"

"Head deeper into Arkham? There are several abandoned houses that I saw where we could hide."

"And wait for the end of the world?"

"I …" He shook his head. Cassandra was right. They needed to be on the attack, and to do that they needed to get to Kingsport.

She watched the streets. "Sneaking aboard a boat headed up stream'll be harder than boarding a freight train."

"Ah, a freight train."

It hadn't occurred to him. His thinking was stuck on passenger trains. It would be risky, but he had no better ideas … unless they escaped through the woods. Remembering what those blackened trees looked like at the edge of town encouraged Shaw to keep his mouth shut on that subject.

Nearing Main Street they found several people. None that looked like their pursuers but no point taking chances. They waited in the shadows of a park, watching for the last people to pass.

"Why did you think that flute would open a portal?" Cassandra asked.

Shaw was glad for the night so his blush could not be seen. He'd made a wrong assumption on that flute. It was no elder god's object. It was just a flute, an item dropped off in that store because it was no longer wanted. In whispered tones he told Cassandra about his dreams, the flute player, and of blind Azathoth.

"You saw more of these gods?"

"In a dream."

"You think that affects their impact? These gods drive people mad in their sleep."

That was true, particularly artists. Shaw remembered Doctor Neufeld from his days in India. The influence came through in his paintings.

"You have some sort of immunity," she said. "I would say from exposure, but the first encounter should have driven you mad."

Also true. First it had been that ugly idol of Cthulhu. Then the book, the *Necronomicon*. He'd seen Dagon and Cthulhu, and now Azathoth as well, and all those others assembled around the sleeping god. Who knew what he'd laid eyes on in that dreamworld?

Ten minutes were lost waiting for those people to disperse. Cassandra gave it still another minute, shifting weight from one foot to the other before starting forward. He kept pace as best as possible but always appeared to be losing ground. When Cassandra reached a fresh spot of shadows, she would look left and right for anybody spying on them while waiting for him to catch up. At River Street they stopped once again and watched from the darkness.

Cassandra looked to him. "Ideas?"

"The bridge on our left seems to be least used."

Any bridge would be dangerous and leave them exposed for the time it took to cross. If they were cornered, the only escape was into the water, and Amelia had stressed to stay out of the river. Shaw remembered the shapes he'd seen below the water. Cassandra eyed each bridge, undoubtedly echoing his own thoughts. She rolled her eyes at the idea of being so exposed.

"At least ten minutes to cross," she murmured.

Shaw didn't bother to point out that with him in tow it would likely be longer.

"Either way we are noticeable."

"Either way?" Shaw asked. "What other way?"

In answer Cassandra pointed toward the shoreline and a small rowboat sitting there, flipped over to keep rain water out. No other boats were in sight. Not yet.

"Keep an eye out."

He knew what was expected and followed her to the water's edge, wondering if this counted toward Amelia's warning. The idea of being on the water unnerved Shaw, but he planted himself as sentry, looking left and right as the investigator flipped over the rowboat and looked about for the oars.

"Ready," she whispered.

Shaw turned to find a dirty boat and two splintering oars in place. After a gesture from Cassandra, he boarded the boat and sat while she pushed it into the water. A moment later she sat across from him, starting the labor of rowing across the Miskatonic.

"Why not keep going?" Shaw asked. "Drift down river until we reach Kingsport, if it's in that direction."

"It is, but—"

Something brushed against the underside, shuddering the little boat in a protracted contact. When Cassandra looked at him he saw the fear in her eyes, equal to his own. No, there would be no long journey up the Miskatonic. She rowed faster, nearing the opposite shore as Shaw watched ripples in the water, trying to convince himself they were the product of their own passage.

He didn't let out his pent-up breath until reaching the opposite bank. Without looking back they fled the edge and kept going until what they hoped was a safe distance.

"I'm sure the roads out of Arkham'll hold their own dangers to follow."

Shaw nodded, wondering what they might find on a freight train in the cursed place.

CHAPTER 36

April 23, 1912
Arkham Train Station: 10:01 pm

They station was a mostly flat yard with tracks leading in both directions. Scrub brush and weeds grew in the open area. Yellow dandelions between the tracks gave the drab scenery its only color. One lengthy freight train, quiet, not advertising where it was headed. Paint peeled from the outside of most cars, showing the worn wood and rusting metal beneath.

Cassandra huffed. "Wait here a minute."

She set off at a trot, heading toward the front of the train and coming back a few minutes later, annoyance on her face. "Only identifying mark is the train number which tells us nothing. No destination."

They walked together toward the train's other end, which disappeared into the darkness. Between cars they could see a second train on the other side. At one point the gaps lined up to show yet a third train. No way to tell which direction either faced without seeing an engine. Cassandra grunted her frustration and continued on.

"Shh," Shaw warned.

They came to a halt, and he pointed to one ear then made a circle in the air, hoping his message came across. Cassandra listened.

Sounds of movement.

Shaw raised his eyebrows in question, and she gestured for him to follow. They crept along, Cassandra bending to look under the train. A flickering light came at one point.

"Fire?" he whispered.

She crawled under the coupling where two train cars met and glanced around the edge. Shaw considered following, but she made a gesture to stay where he was. With effort he hunkered down to see what she was seeing. Definitely a fire. Getting back to his feet he went to the spot where Cassandra had crossed over.

"Hoboes," she explained. "About two cars forward."

"They might know where the trains are headed."

Cassandra had already considered that, of course. A glance at the trains then toward the station as she weighed their options. Even without it being Arkham, a woman suddenly among some potentially desperate men would be in danger. Without a word she pulled her revolver free, keeping it concealed behind her, then started toward the fire. Shaw scrambled to get further along the train and keep pace with her advance. He came abreast of the fire and crouched, watching, then crawled forward. He managed to drag his leg over one rail and stopped there.

Cassandra was approaching as he got into place to watch. There were four men around the fire, each wearing brown cotton caps and thick pants of various colors. They leaned forward as if in conversation, but Shaw could hear no words. A warning sounded in his head. Shaw drew in a breath to call out to Cassandra even as she spoke.

"Hello, gentlemen."

The four men turned as one.

None wore a face.

Cassandra's arm came up and she shot the first man right through his heart, assuming he had one. Shaw was glad she had avoided the face, remembering that cosmic blackness behind the mask. Revolver swinging to the next, she dropped that one as well. The remaining two had already rushed forward and—

"Behind you!" he yelled.

It distracted the last faceless hoboes and Cassandra shot a third, but another two had come up behind her. She was surrounded and grabbed, even as three others came from the darkness, more than she had bullets for. Two kept hold of her while the rest started toward Shaw's hiding spot.

"Run, Shaw!"

She struggled, stomping on one faceless man's foot and shouldering into the other. Two of Shaw's pursuers turned back and helped subdue Cassandra once again, though she continued to fight like a badger. Two were left to chase him.

No time for gentleness. Shaw scrambled over the rail, between two great metal wheels that could chop him in half, and rolled in the dirt. With one motion he continued to roll, got his cane under him and jumped to his feet—as much as he ever could jump. Without thinking he started a quick shuffle toward the station house, not considering this was probably the last place he should head. It was the only lit structure, and light usually meant safety.

Too late to change course now.

They'd been waiting for them after all, as they had set others for them at the library. Given the numbers of faceless, they expected Shaw and Cassandra to try to board a train more than retrieve the book.

It would take the hoboes time to get around or under that train. How the hell did they see without eyes anyway? Hopefully he could be out of sight before they got clear. Ah, but then what? One crisis at a time. For now he needed a place to hide.

He reached the station house and skirted the outside. Inside would mean danger for certain … unless there were normal people there. Normal, what did that even mean? He stopped with his back against the wall facing the river. All was quiet here, a cool night breeze pushed around him bringing the river smell. With great care he peeked around the corner, looking back the way he'd come. No pursuers. No movement at all other than what the wind blew.

Were they content with capturing Cassandra?

No. That didn't sound—

An arm wrapped around his throat, tugging him backward and cutting off his airway. His cane clattered to the wooden floorboards as he scratched at the arm with both hands. It was like back at the library, only this time his hands were free.

"Loosen up before you kill him."

The one holding him spun Shaw around, toward the owner of that voice. That man was in the black robes of one of the cult, hood up. Did that mean he could be recognized?

"Loosen up," the man repeated.

The grip loosened, and Shaw sucked in a deep ragged breath.

"So glad to find you, Doctor," the hooded man said. His voice came out oily, like a cheap con man. "Please excuse my companions, they aren't too bright."

The man holding him gave no response. It had to be one of the faceless people.

The robed man continued. "There is someone very interested in meeting you."

With that he turned and headed toward the station house's far end. His captor held him in a strong arm, but not so tight that it cut off air again. He was frog-marched forward, several paces behind the robed man, who had reached the far end and disappeared around the corner. A soft sound. A grunt. Then the footsteps ahead stopped. A moment later, Shaw was forced around the corner himself.

A fist shot from the dark, narrowly missing him and connecting with the captor behind him. Shaw glanced back to see the faceless man collapse to the ground, then spun back toward the dark and his rescuer. A shape stepped out of the shadows. This man was tall, with wide shoulders, dwarfing Shaw. He wore a dark suit of middle-class London fashion but with a turban wound tightly on top of his head, keeping his hair concealed.

"Good evening, Doctor."

"Singh?!"

"Just so," his adopted son said. Singh pulled his knife from the robed man on the ground and wiped it against the man's pants. "We should depart."

"My cane." He hated how weak and mewling it sounded.

Singh rushed to get the cane while Shaw glanced around. A spreading pool of blood surrounded the robed man. Singh returned before Shaw could start to wonder if this was all a dream.

"Your cane," Singh said, holding it toward his lifelong friend. "Time to go."

Shaw glanced back toward the trains and Cassandra.

"I am afraid there are too many, and they have your friend's gun now."

With a nod Shaw followed Singh away from the station and the lights. They followed the path for several steps before Singh pulled him behind some brush and thin trees. Shaw looked around, hearing nothing, but Singh raised one finger to his lips in a shushing gesture.

The sound of footsteps on the path coming toward them. Several of the faceless hoboes came, carrying Cassandra between them. It appeared the investigator had given up struggling. Unconscious or surrendered? Knowing her it would have to be the former. They approached the spot where Shaw and Singh had hidden, eight of the faceless men in all. Shaw tightened the grip on his cane, but Singh placed one hand on his shoulder and shook his head. From the other direction came two of the robed people, one carrying a shotgun. Behind them crouched four of the ghasts, grinning and looking left and right. They gave the occasional yip of excitement, ready for the hunt. If those were let loose, what could they do? Could Singh dispatch these with only a knife?

Best not to have to find out.

Shaw watched the two robed people, both of equal height and roughly matching his own. One of those must be Armitage.

"Where is the doctor?" the robed person holding the shotgun asked.

Not Armitage. A feminine voice.

The faceless men gathered before the robed ones. No reaction. No expression. Still, the message was clear, they had lost him.

"Mindless fools."

Cassandra was placed on the ground in front of the robed ones, as if to say, *See what we have.*

"Yes, you did well with this one, at least," she said.

The other robed person, this one a man, took Cassandra's revolver from a faceless hobo and slipped it into his robe. He said something too low to carry, and the woman agreed.

"We have until he arrives to find Shaw."

He? Who was this *he*?

She turned to the faceless men. "Get her to the church."

The church? Now that he knew, but why there? What about Kingsport?

He had no idea where the professor and David had been taken, but it was likely the same place they were taking Cassandra. If Watkins's other nephew was in Kingsport, then he would have to wait for now.

The church.

Two of the faceless bent and retrieved Cassandra, waiting for further orders.

"The rest of you, find him," the woman ordered.

Both faceless men and ghasts dispersed in different directions, while Shaw and Singh continued to crouch in the dark. These creatures knew he was close and would likely continue to hunt him on this side of the river, but were not aware of Singh's arrival. That gave a slight advantage of surprise.

Maybe.

The robed couple and those faceless carrying Cassandra continued on. Singh gave some space before creeping from the bushes and following, Shaw in tow. Luckily, those searching for him had gone off in every direction except for staying nearby. Shaw and Singh followed Cassandra's captors to a flat-bed cargo truck where they unceremoniously dumped her into the back. The two faceless joined her there as did the shotgun-carrying robed woman. The truck started easily and pulled away, heading deeper into Arkham. It turned the next corner and disappeared.

"What next?" Singh asked.

"I know where they are going."

While transportation would be best, neither of them had Cassandra's skill at starting a vehicle without the proper key. The church was fifteen minutes away by bus, which meant an excruciating hike for him.

"How did you find me, Singh?"

"You told me to come to Arkham."

"In your room aboard the ship? That was real?"

Singh nodded. "Why are *you* in Arkham?"

"I was drawn here … or pushed might be more accurate."

"By what?"

Shaw wondered on that himself. Had it truly been Cthulhu, as Stephen had implied? Some other entity? The book? Fate? He had no real answer.

The area switched from train yard to warehouses after crossing a street. They followed the route Shaw knew rather than trying to follow the truck.

"Have you discovered why you were drawn here?"

"No, I—"

Azathoth is the god that other gods fear.

CLICK!

"Azathoth."

"Azathoth?"

"Another elder god. This one will destroy all reality if it wakes."

"Another sleeping god. What threatens to wake this one?"

"I don't—" *CLICK!* "When the six are gathered, the portal shall open."

"What does that mean?"

"I have no idea."

"Hmm. Should I ask who, or what, the six are?"

"I—"

"Have no idea?"

Shaw looked toward his lifelong friend. The hint of a teasing smile quirked the corner of Singh's mouth. "Essentially."

"Why is this Cassandra important?"

"She has tattoos of the book on her."

Singh came to a stop. "Monstrous!"

A backfire came from nearby, and the two looked around for its source. Coming across the next bridge was the bus which Shaw had ridden to see Arkham. It was excellent timing. Too much activity and not enough rest, his leg had been throbbing for the past block. Shaw knew the signs. Soon it would be an ache, then a pain, and it might come to the point where it refused to go on. Shaw stepped into the street, raising his cane to hail the bus. It rolled to a stop beside him, the door opening. The same unfriendly driver waited inside—at least he thought it was the same man. He leaned into the shadows with cap pulled low. It reminded Shaw of the blind man in the restaurant, all features obscured. Other than him the bus was empty. Singh boarded behind Shaw, and both took their seats. The bus did not move.

"We are ready," Shaw tried.

The man moaned out some message, then grabbed the wooden knob at the top of the shifter, attempting to put the bus into gear. A grinding noise came as it jerked forward then stalled. Another groan as the driver pitched over to his right. The man would have landed head-first on the floor if not for Singh's quick reflexes, grabbing the driver by his jacket and pulling back. Seams popped, but the descent was stopped.

"Mmmmnnnn," the driver said.

Singh pulled the cap from the man's head, exposing his features. Like Amelia, parts of his features were gone, covered. His nose. The start of his mouth. Shaw pulled the eyepatch aside to reveal that eye too was gone.

Singh made a noise of disgust and drew his knife, but Shaw placed a hand on his shoulder, shook his head.

"We removed one," Shaw warned. "Behind that mask was madness."

The man backpedaled from them. The sudden movement hit him like a hammer, and he leaned against the nearest seat, head in hands.

"Are you ..." Shaw began, trailing off when he realized how

ridiculous any sentence ending would be. No, the man was not well.

The driver looked at them.

"Why was this done to you?" Shaw tried instead.

"You."

"Me?" Shaw shook his head. "Because you drove me around Arkham."

A nod.

Insanity.

Singh leaned forward. "Take us to the church."

"The church?" The driver's uncovered eye went wild as the man shook his head and scooted further from Shaw and Singh. His fingers felt at the smooth skin across his eye. "No. I can't."

Without warning the driver rushed forward and grabbed for Singh's knife with both hands. Teeth bared. A low growl started deep within his throat.

"Look out, Singh!"

Singh's free fist came around and slammed against the man's head, just below the eyepatch. The driver's other eye rolled up, and he was propelled sideways into one of the passenger seats, collapsing like a sack of laundry.

"I suppose we must take ourselves to this church," Singh said.

The knife disappeared inside of Singh's coat as he headed to the driver's seat. For a minute he inspected the controls of the bus before starting the engine. It lurched forward, came to a halt, stalled.

"I have seen these in England, though never driven one," Singh explained. "I understand the concept."

The second attempt had the bus in proper gear and rolling slowly. Another lurch, the grinding of gears, as Singh tried to change to second. A stall and restart. The bus advanced again. This time, when the engine's sound rose in pitch, Singh managed to change to second without stalling, though the engine sounded as if it was grinding mercilessly.

"I've watched others drive."

"You're doing fine, Singh."

With each passing moment Singh got better and managed to keep the bus moving. It wasn't a comfortable ride with the jerking about, but still much better than traveling by foot. The idea was to not slow down too much until reaching the church. Shaw gave directions as best he could, navigating by landmarks he'd only seen during the day.

"Where is the book, Doctor?"

"It went down with the ship."

"I was afraid that might be the case. The message was delivered nonetheless."

"You met the prince's son then?"

"No. Inspector Abberline was going to meet him."

"Abberline?" Shaw remembered the inspector from the awful days skulking around Whitechapel, and the aftermath.

"He agreed to bring the message to London."

"Unimportant now, I'm afraid. I'm sorry you wasted your time."

"It was good that I went. Abberline needed help."

"Fred Abberline needed help?"

Singh almost laughed. "It's true."

The Scotland Yard inspector was the least likely person to ever need help, or admit to it, at least. He'd been a valued friend in the days of trying to track down the *Necronomicon* and the malicious ugly idol. Shaw owed the man, as much as Prince Albert Victor and Singh, his life and more.

Singh launched into the story of how he met up with the retired inspector in Springbourne. Then Shaw told all about his adventure on the *Titanic* and everything that had happened since.

"Singh … Another copy exists. Here. It was hidden in the university library."

"Was?"

Shaw nodded.

"The nightmare is not yet over."

"No, and there is more evil in Arkham than this one book."

CHAPTER 37

April 24, 1912
Arkham, Massachusetts: 12:16 am

Singh cut the engine a block from the church and coasted to a halt.

"What next?" Singh asked.

Shaw hadn't thought that far ahead, but he supposed only one logical move remained.

"We watch the church. Find a way in. Then …"

"Rescue Cassandra?"

Shaw agreed, it sounded overly simple and naive to his own ears. Singh opened the bus door. They made their way back to the driver, who remained unconscious between two seats. The mask had continued to creep across his face, claiming the other eye.

"He's an innocent in all this," Shaw said. "Like the housekeeper back at Watkins's house."

"Innocent?"

He waved a hand. "As much as anyone drawn into this world without their consent."

Singh tapped his concealed knife. "I don't mind killing with reason, but …"

"I agree. Leave him."

Singh kept his eyes on the seats until Shaw had left the bus, then backed to the door, watching for movement from the driver. Nothing.

"I wish we could tie him," Singh said, stepping off the bus.

"I believe by the time he wakes we will be long gone."

"Will defeating these villains free people like him?"

Shaw thought about Amelia. "I certainly hope so."

Turning a corner, the church in question came into view. On top of that low hill, scowling down on surrounding Arkham. Light flickered inside the windows. Eyes on the building, they started forward, each one searching for some plan other than storming the church.

"Does this not feel as if we are heading toward the lion's den?" Singh asked.

"You believe we are expected?"

"I do."

It made sense. "What do you suggest?"

"Suggest?" Singh shook his head. "It occurs to me that you may be the one they truly want, not these others."

It would not be the first time his ability to read the words without going mad got the wrong people's attention. That insinuated that his being here was from this cult's influence. Had they urged him to Arkham? Him and Cassandra? Maybe, but that somehow didn't ring true. She would be of great interest to this cult, with her tattoos, they both would.

If he were to leave, would that throw a wrench in this cult's plans? Maybe. What would happen to the others though? Watkins and his nephews. There was no reason for them to be involved. Just part of the catalyst to get them involved?

"I have been guided here for a reason. Forced. Coerced. I have no reason to believe I will be left alone if I should walk away."

"True. We know from experience that is unlikely."

The two watched the church's silhouette against the night sky. Shaw could tell Singh to leave, that he didn't need to be part of this, but after so many years together he wouldn't insult his friend in that way.

With a forced grin, Shaw looked to his companion. "Into the lion's den then?"

"We have a habit of falling into these circumstances."

"I'm sorry, Singh."

The hulking lad turned, head cocked to one side in question. Though he thought of Singh as a lad, it had been many years since he was anything of the sort. All the more reason for the apology.

"Would it have been better to leave you in India?"

"In abject poverty? To live on the streets, begging?"

"Without knowing about this other horrific reality."

"Hmm, no. I wouldn't trade my life."

Shaw opened his mouth to reply, when he caught sight of his friend's face. Singh was serious.

"Do we have a plan yet, Doctor?"

A plan? Shaw had been living by the seat of his pants, allowing circumstances to happen, rather than choosing his own path. No more.

"I saw a back entrance when I passed the church earlier," he said, forming plans as thoughts came into his head. "We sneak up to that back door and once inside we search out the others and free them. Then we escape."

Simplistic, but that gave less things to go wrong.

"This will put an end to it?" Singh asked.

"Doubtful. They will still chase."

They skirted the outside edge of the church, staying to the shadows. No movement outside. No robed figures. No faceless. No ghasts or night-gaunts. A path led up the back side of the hill, dirt and uneven, connecting to the back door. Shaw's leg ached just looking at it.

Up the path, step after aching step, until the two stood in the shadow of the one tree existing on that hill. The church a short thirty paces away.

"Look at that." Shaw pointed toward the church while leaning against the tree.

Singh stared a moment. "A basement entrance?"

More of a storm cellar, with two doors almost in parallel with the ground. Both doors were closed, but hopefully not locked from the inside. What other option did they have, other than abandoning people who needed them?

Into the lion's den indeed.

A yip in the distance.

Shaw looked behind and Singh withdrew his knife, holding it ready in his grasp.

More sounds, to the left, to the right. Closer.

"Too many," Singh muttered. He glanced at the church and gestured toward it. "Go!"

The two hurried across the open area, looking back when they'd reached the closed doors. Sure enough, several of the grotesque kangaroo perversions with powerful legs came from the darkness.

"Ghasts," Shaw said.

Singh handed his knife to Shaw then turned and grabbed one door. He flipped it open to land against the dust and dirt. The wood gave a cracking noise but held shape.

"Inside. Quick."

Shaw used the steps as fast as possible, followed by Singh. The Indian lad turned and pulled the one door shut behind them.

"No lock," he said.

"We'll have to hope they aren't smart enough to open a door."

They were not. Outside the creatures assaulted the door, battering it. They did not have much time. The basement was dim, with light from beneath a door on the opposite end giving some illumination, but not much. It was up from their position, as if elevated. Stairs? Singh took his knife back and pressed forward, moving as fast as he dared. Shaw came up behind, one hand on his friend's back for guidance. The area was comprised of shelves, but the light was nowhere near strong enough to see what rested on them. Probably for the best.

More sounds of the doors being slammed into. If the ghasts made it inside before they reached that other door, they were finished. If someone came to find what the noise was, they would also be finished. Across the dark room, step by step, punctuated by the sound of the door behind them slowly giving way. At the base of the stairs the light was greater. Singh started up with Shaw still on his heels.

The sound of cracking wood came from behind.

"Singh!"

"I hear it."

"No, look."

Singh found black robes hanging from pegs. "A disguise?"

"It might get us where we need to be."

No time for an alternate idea, they dragged the robes over their heads then bolted through the door. Behind them, the other door gave way with a splintering crack, and the sounds of several monstrous bodies falling inside. The yips of those things filled the basement. Singh locked the door behind them.

A look to the left. To the right.

They stopped.

In each direction, several of the faceless people, unmoving but with all attention forward. Those to the right were positioned close to a door, a plaque overhead stating, "Church of the Ancients."

"Bluff our way through?" Shaw asked.

Singh stepped toward the group on their right. Immediately each of the faceless became aware, adopting a stance of being on guard. Their arms bent, hands balled into fists, legs set to move.

"Out of our way," Singh commanded.

The faceless ones stepped closer. A second row left no possibility of forcing their way through. Singh was no stranger to a struggle, but there were far too many for even him. They would need to find another way.

"Retreat?" Shaw whispered.

Singh stepped back. "Where?"

They turned to find the second group of faceless had moved forward, blocking the other end of the hallway. From the basement came more yips and snarls. Five minutes inside the church and they'd already been captured.

They'd been expected.

CHAPTER 38

April 24, 1912
Church of the Ancients: 1:22 am

They struggled, of course, but each were placed into leg irons, the chain joining each shackle short enough to limit their strides. In this way, Shaw and Singh were pushed through double doors into an open room. Across from them was another set of doors, the twins of those behind. They staggered forward into this area, the main body of the church. To the right were rows of pews where the faithful would sit. To the left, an area raised maybe a foot with a lectern to preach from.

This had once been a Christian church, or had been modeled after one at the least.

Etched into the hardwood at the center of this open area was a faintly glowing depiction, reminiscent of the glowing stars in Watkins's basement. An eye at the center, surrounded by a great double circle large enough to hold a horse. At equal distancing around the circles were five smaller ones, each holding a unique pictogram. Scroll. Knife. Skull. Two matching people, one black and the other white. The center eye held an inkwell at the center.

Between the two circles were words carved, in that oh-so familiar script.

"When the six are gathered, the portal shall open." Shaw grunted at the sight of it, stepped back, suddenly dizzy. The words were inside his head again. Insistent, demanding entrance to his mind. The tattoos. The letter. His drawing. They were all near.

"Shaw?"

He spun to find Cassandra and David on the front pew. They rose and made their way awkwardly toward them, their own leg irons clanging with each step.

"Well, this must be Singh," Cassandra said.

Singh gave a slight bow of his head in acknowledgment. "And you must be Cassandra."

"I'm David."

"Where's your uncle?" Shaw asked.

"I haven't seen him since that night. I woke to those faceless nightmares over me."

"They brought you straight here?"

"They held me at the house for a while. I got the impression they were looking for something. Turns out it was you and Cassandra."

"Armitage was trying to catch us all at once."

"Armitage? The librarian?"

"You didn't tell him?" Shaw asked Cassandra.

"Hey, I just got here myself."

"Armitage is creepy and prickly, but he never seemed evil."

Shaw told David about the books he'd seen in the library's locked room and the hidden *Necronomicon*.

"Is that where the page Matthew sent came from?

"It is."

The look on the boy's face went from disbelieving to grudging acceptance.

"Why does he want me? Or uncle for that matter?"

"I don't know."

"Why are you here, Shaw?" Cassandra asked.

"To … well … rescue you."

"This is part of your plan?"

"Um … no."

A click of the door brought everyone's attention around, greeted by the sight of two faceless men entering. Behind came two others, dragging a body between them, legs similarly shackled together.

Singh launched into action, starting an attack on the faceless men, but forgetting his ankle shackles. He made it one step before the short chain tripped him and sent him sprawling across the church's rough wood floor. By the time he'd regained his feet, the faceless men had retreated and closed the door again.

The recent addition lay face down, unmoving.

"Matthew?" David said, hopping toward his brother. "Matthew?!"

David rolled his brother over while the others made their way across the room.

"Oh, god!" David choked.

The others reached Matthew. Shaw expected to see another faceless man, like Amelia and the driver. Singh had a similar thought, knife in one hand.

Losing his features might have been better. Instead Matthew's face was a mass of scratches and bruises. One eye was swollen shut. His shirt had been shredded by something sharp and undoubtedly hid other scratches. Something strong and vicious had gotten to the boy and beat him mercilessly.

"Matthew!" David said, slapping his brother's cheeks. "Are you okay?"

"Enough already," Matthew said around swollen lips. "I'm alive."

"They let you keep that?" Shaw asked, turning back to Singh.

"It was hidden."

Shaw noticed he still had the satchel over one shoulder, but nothing of any danger was inside, though he did have his cane as well. Armitage was either confident, or the faceless men could only do so much. They didn't appear stupid, but perhaps they needed certain orders. He looked to Cassandra, who shook her head.

"They took all of my weapons."

Matthew brought one hand up to his face and hissed with pain.

"What happened?" David sounded horrified. "Who did this?"

"One of those kangaroo monsters."

"A ghast," Shaw said.

Matthew nodded. He got his feet under him with help from his brother. "My punishment, for trying to escape."

"Your letter said you couldn't escape," David replied.

"I had to try once I knew what those letters were for. I had to warn you."

"What?" Cassandra asked.

"They were to draw us all together. I was the bait."

David shook his head. "I don't understand."

"Neither do I," Matthew admitted, "but they need us for something."

Singh looked to Shaw, a moment later Cassandra did too.

"When the six are gathered," Shaw repeated, "the portal shall open."

"What does that mean?" Matthew asked.

"It's a prophecy," a voice said.

CHAPTER 39

April 24, 1912
Church of the Ancients: 1:41 am

Four figures in black robes with hoods up, near the opposite door twenty feet away. The woman, still holding her shotgun, waited beside two of the men. The final one, taller and wider than the rest, lurked behind.

"Now that we're all here," the man on the right said, "I will fill you in on the why."

"Neville isn't here," the hulking man in back said.

"Neville is late," the apparent leader replied.

Shaw cleared his throat. "Was this Neville looking for me in Arkham, near the trains?"

Leader kept his eyes forward while the other three exchanged glances. "He was."

"He won't be coming."

Shaw made sure to keep an unwavering gaze on them, a hint of a cocky smile to his lips. He hoped to unnerve them.

The huge man took a step back, a quick shake of his head. "From six down to four."

"I only count five with your dead friend on the train platform."

Leader gave a chuckle, not unnerved at all. "Oh you've met the sixth, Doctor Shaw. James Wilson was one of our little group."

"Wilson!"

"He was meant to bring the book to me, but instead was corrupted by it. Weak fool."

"You're Marsh!" Cassandra said.

"Marsh?" Shaw repeated.

Why was that name familiar? The man from Innsmouth whose people chased Cassandra out of town? Yes, that was it. The mastermind behind James Wilson and his bid to steal the *Necronomicon*.

Another chuckle from the man. "Yes. We came close to meeting there, but it wasn't time."

"I wish we had met." Cassandra's hands were balled into fists.

"As it turned out, we didn't need the copy James was bringing."

Armitage's decaying *Necronomicon* was suddenly in his free hand. Even as Marsh held it, the pages appeared ready to crumble.

"A gift from Armitage?" Shaw asked, glancing at the robed man who hadn't spoken yet. "What do—"

Marsh pulled a revolver—Cassandra's?—from a pocket and leveled it toward them.

"You will not make it to me before I fire, Singh," the man said, calmly, casually. "And I assure you that I will not aim the first shot at you."

Singh was crouched, ready to spring and take his chances on the attack. A glance at the others, then down at his ankles. "You know me."

"Only by reputation."

Singh went no closer but positioned himself at the center. A human barrier between the gun and everyone else. At a gesture from Marsh, each of the congregation doors opened. Faceless people mobbed about each door. There would be no quick escape.

Shaw stepped from behind Singh's protection to stand beside him. He narrowed his eyes. "One more lunatic leader of another cheap cult."

"Not quite," Marsh said. "For one thing, we are only four. Hardly enough to be labeled a cult."

The Indian princess Ananya had been dangerous with relatively few followers as well. With nothing but the book she had been able to gather the disenfranchised and abused women of Whitechapel as her loyal supporters.

"You did well maneuvering them here," Marsh said to the one who hadn't spoken yet.

Armitage? It had to be.

"Going to stay behind those hoods?" Cassandra demanded. "That where your power comes from?"

Marsh laughed. "No, I suppose our need for secrecy is past."

He handed the *Necronomicon* to one of the closest faceless men and pulled his hood back. A moment later the others followed suit, revealing their faces. Armitage was not among them as suspected, in his stead was another familiar face.

"Uncle?!" David exclaimed at the man who had yet to speak.

"My god man, why?" Shaw asked.

"Power. Immortality. Do I need a better reason?"

"But your nephews."

"Are part of the prophecy, as are the rest of you," Watkins explained, with the tone of a professor explaining something patently obvious. "We need you all to open the doorway."

Marsh held up one hand and Watkins came to a halt. "We will come to that."

Watkins had a slavishness in the way he deferred to the man. The way they all three focused on him.

Watkins was not the only familiar face. The big man turned out to be Silas Miller, the hulking professor from the other Doctor Bell's office. The woman was strangely familiar, though Shaw knew he'd never met her before. She was around fifty, if he had to guess, her brown hair pulled back into a ponytail.

Marsh himself had a timeless look to him. Someone who didn't seem particularly old or young. His hair was dark and combed to one side, with a touch of silver at the temples. He was average for everything. Height. Weight. Complexion.

"A prophecy?" David spat, glaring at his uncle. "Is that why your friends did this to Matthew?"

Watkins's gaze slid to his other nephew, betraying no emotion.

"Why?" David continued. "This … This isn't like you."

"Oh, this is exactly like me," Watkins replied. "The *real* me."

A cloud crossed David's face. He took a step forward, looking ready to rush his uncle. The woman turned her shotgun sideways, ready to use it as a bat. So, they needed them alive. That was worth knowing.

"Is this what our mother would have wanted?" he shouted.

"I'm actually fine with it."

Both twins shifted focus, staring at the woman. Scrutinizing her. It explained the familiarity of her face. Same nose. Similar mouth. More than a passing resemblance to Watkins. Neither could deny this was in fact their mother. She made no move, no gesture of motherly love, and eventually returned her attention to Marsh.

"Maria and I were part of the cult where you started your life," Watkins explained. He glanced to the leader, who gave a nod. "They were idiot hedonists, like you, Matthew. They played at greatness and power, played at raising Yog-Sothoth, but had no real vision. What they did have was a complete *Necronomicon*."

"Tell it all," Marsh commanded.

"He found us there," Maria said, indicating Marsh. "Shared the prophecy with us, as we already had the ability to fulfill one-third of it."

"When the six are gathered, the portal shall open," Shaw said. "What does it mean? Portal where?"

"It's misquoted," Miller said. "It should be: When the six are gathered, the portal to dreams shall open. Once the portal opens we can enter and stay there forever, awake in a dreaming world."

Marsh chuckled at that, turning a half step toward his co-conspirators.

"What six?" Cassandra asked, looking around as if she knew. "We're only five."

Watkins grinned at them and turned to those faceless which had come in behind them. "Bring him out."

As if awaiting their cue, two faceless stepped forward dragging the form of Doctor Armitage. The librarian was dumped, unceremoniously, a few feet from them. Singh looked toward Marsh, who still held the revolver pointed in their direction.

Would Marsh shoot them? Or did he need them all?

Armitage rolled to a sitting position and glared back at the robed figures. He was not subjected to the same leg irons as the rest of them.

"The six," Watkins exclaimed, as if a magician proclaiming some result.

Maria stepped forward. "The Living Book," she said, looking at Cassandra.

Cassandra glared, but even she had to see how well she fit that.

"The Ripper, walking between worlds." She pointed at Shaw. "The Orphan Murderer." Singh. "The Corrupted Scholar." Armitage. At this she paused and looked on David and Matthew. "And twins, born of twins, one a hawk and the other a dove."

The room became silent as the two boys digested this information.

"You …" Matthew stammered. "You're …"

"Uncle *and* father."

David looked ready to be sick. He shook his head, backing away.

"While we kept you two safe, we also orchestrated the tattooing of a girl to become the Living Book."

Cassandra gasped. "Your cult was my cult."

"Indeed. All we needed was the opportunity to escape with our boys, you, and the book."

"*You* set that fire," Cassandra said.

"No," Watkins answered, "but we took advantage of it. The police came to roust our group but something went wrong. I rushed to get the book, Maria the girl. We both came up empty-handed. Someone had already escaped with each. The fire was raging, so we blocked the doors on our way out to encourage confusion."

"You knew who I was when you sent for me," Cassandra said.

"Why the wild goose chase to Ipswich? Why not just take us when we arrived?"

"You arrived early, and we weren't ready yet. The others hadn't arrived in Arkham, and we still searched for the other components. The Ripper. The Orphan. The Corrupted Scholar. And the *Necronomicon*, or at least the necessary spell." Watkins shrugged. "Shaw was a complete surprise, and I didn't know what to do with him once he read the words."

Armitage started laughing from his spot on the floor, silencing Watkins. All eyes moved to the librarian, even Marsh, who seemed content to watch and listen.

"What is so funny?" Watkins demanded.

"You're missing one of your six. I am no corrupted scholar. I kept that book hidden from the wrong eyes. I've done nothing to be corrupted."

"You—" Watkins turned toward Marsh, confused.

"Armitage is correct," Marsh said. "He isn't the corrupted scholar."

"Then who—"

"You are." With that, Marsh shot the professor in the stomach.

Watkins collapsed, screaming.

CHAPTER 40

April 24, 1912
Church of the Ancients: 2:03 am

The poetic justice of Watkins being betrayed satisfied Shaw on some level, though it didn't diminish the difficulties they were in. Neither Maria nor Miller looked even marginally surprised by it. They'd known this was coming.

"Maria," Watkins screamed. "Help me."

Maria looked at her brother then moved to Marsh again, kissing him on the cheek.

"Maria?" Watkins's voice was smaller, weaker. "I … I'm your brother."

The remaining three cultists pointedly ignored their downed partner and focused on the other five. They knew Watkins wasn't going anywhere.

"You sent the night-gaunt after me," Cassandra said.

"It was meant as added encouragement, in case you didn't want to leave New York."

"For my tattoos. For the spell."

"Originally," Maria jumped in. "Though that point is moot with the *Necronomicon*. We still need you for the prophecy, of course."

"And you sent me those nightmares as well?" Shaw demanded. "And the ghost? The push to come to Arkham?"

"Not our doing," Marsh said. "Damn! Is there any wonder we wanted you, especially after reading the words and not going mad?"

Shaw glanced to Watkins again. "Better than you have called on these gods for power or favor. They will destroy you."

"Show him," Marsh said to Maria.

She wandered over to her brother, placed her shotgun beside him, and ripped his shirt open. On the man's skin was one of the familiar glowing, five-pointed stars. The protection spell.

"They each have one," Marsh said. "Except for me."

He pulled a metal amulet from inside his shirt. The same one Bell had shown him.

"It keeps us safe from the influence of those gods you speak of, and when the six are gathered, the portal to dreams shall open." Another chuckle, as if he had some inside joke he wasn't sharing. The sound was starting to irk Shaw.

"So you've said."

"Yes. What I haven't said is that there is a misinterpretation on the word 'dreams.'"

"What?" Maria turned toward Marsh.

"Not a misinterpretation, I suppose," Marsh said. "A lie. I told them the word meant dreams. It doesn't."

"What does the word mean?" Shaw asked.

"Doom."

Doom.

CLICK!

"Azathoth!" Shaw said.

"Very good, Doctor. I shall open the portal to sleeping Azathoth. Once I cross over I will wake him, and destroy all reality."

"And you with it?"

"I should hope so."

"Why?"

Before Marsh could answer, Maria had taken several steps toward him. She brought the shotgun level and blasted him with both barrels, shredding his robe and the shirt underneath. Marsh was thrown back several steps to a point where the momentum had worn off. There he stood, head angled toward the floor.

He chuckled, a predator's grin across his face.

All the hairs on Shaw's arms rose straight up.

CHAPTER 41

April 24, 1912
Church of the Ancients: 2:26 am

You dare to attack me?" Marsh asked the woman, his tone conversational.

He didn't have so much as a scratch on the flesh visible underneath his clothing.

How was that possible?

The amulet?

No, that protected against the gods, and whatever else Maria might be, she was not a god. Irrelevant! Details which could be discovered later … if there was a later.

Maria stepped back, dropping the shotgun. She spun, ready to flee.

"Oh, I don't think so." Marsh raised the revolver and shot the fleeing woman in the back.

"Maria!" Watkins wailed, perhaps forgetting that his sister had recently betrayed him.

David and Matthew both cried out as well, for the mother they never knew.

"Enough!" Marsh spat. "She was no longer necessary."

Several of the faceless men stepped away from the doors to take hold of Miller. The huge professor struggled, until it was obvious these drones were stronger than they looked.

Marsh retrieved the *Necronomicon* and stepped closer to Maria. "You will see this until the end. Be content with that."

"The end!" Shaw said. "Marsh, waking Azathoth will destroy everything."

"That is the point, Doctor."

"Suicide? If you want to kill yourself, just be done with it."

Marsh spun on him with speed that was a blur. His eyes flashed with the force of his rage. "I am no pathetic human who can take such measures. I am one of these elder gods you so fear. Expelled from that existence and cast down with you."

Maria glanced to Miller and mouthed the words *He's mad*. Miller just glared at Marsh, an expression that said everything he believed was a lie.

"I was banished a thousand years ago. Do you know how long that is when you cannot die?" Marsh shook his head. "Once I was equal to Cthulhu, Nyarlathotep, but now I have nothing. No abilities other than this immortality."

"You can take a shotgun blast," Cassandra suggested. "That isn't nothing."

Marsh's eyes shifted, looking away for a moment with an expression of utter sadness. "A part of this accursed immortality. I am not permitted to simply die, but must live as one of you. Perform menial tasks as you would. I had to learn to call night-gaunts and ghasts the way a human would." He shuddered with … rage? Revulsion.

Shaw glanced toward the nearest faceless one. Marsh matched his glance.

"Not my creation, though they do follow my every order. They have worshipped me since time out of mind."

"Willingly?"

Marsh shrugged, less than concerned with that little detail.

Images of Amelia and the bus driver drifted before Shaw's eyes. "And they absorb people? Make us like them?"

"At times, and at my orders. They don't reproduce, and this keeps their numbers up."

How many of these faceless people were once normal people? Residents of Arkham? People who incurred the displeasure of Marsh? A nightmarish violation.

To Marsh, another unimportant detail to wave aside as he returned to his own story. "I have lived as human far too long and cannot die. I can wake Azathoth and destroy everything, however. My little revenge against those who banished me."

"Little?" Singh spat. "You are truly mad."

Marsh chuckled. "All gods are."

"That's why you need me and the spell."

"Once I could have crossed the dimensions with a thought. Now I could only access them if asleep and dreaming, and I do neither."

Shaw grasped at straws. How did one change an immortal being's mind? "You will be destroyed before you get close enough to wake Azathoth."

Marsh pulled the amulet free once again. It was free of blemish from the shotgun. Was it as indestructible as its wearer? The skin where it had rested was blackened, decaying, but with the moving of the amulet the flesh started to regenerate.

"This spell only lasts a limited time, but long enough to protect me from the gods surrounding Azathoth."

"*If* you get there," Shaw said. "I refuse to cast your spell."

"You have no choice." Marsh's eyes flashed again, this time a poisonous green. "Ah'azanafl."

Shaw was jerked across the room, back toward the symbol etched into the floor. He didn't stop until both feet were planted firmly on top of the skull pictogram. Singh, Cassandra, the twins, and even Watkins were also dragged by some invisible force to land in their respective circles. Armitage stared from his spot on the ground, taking everything in.

In leisurely strides Marsh crossed the room to Shaw. The revolver was gone, and only the crumbling *Necronomicon* remained in his hands. He held it flat, supported by one hand while the other flipped from page to page. He showed no adverse affects for looking into the heinous tome, more like a man perusing the day's newspaper.

Singh struggled against the force holding him in place, as did Cassandra and Matthew. Nothing, not even an inch of freedom. Watkins's eyes were wide with fear and pain, face pale and eyes red-rimmed.

"It isn't here." Marsh flipped faster though the *Necronomicon*. "The page is missing!"

Armitage laughed. "Of course it is. That copy came from their cult. The page was torn in three. One part you have. The other was tattooed onto the woman."

Marsh spun on the librarian. "And the third?"

"Who knows?" Armitage smiled up at the man, a look of victory. "And there is nothing you can do without the missing part."

The missing part?

The part he'd sketched his first night in Arkham. The part that completed the spell. The part inside his jacket at this very moment.

No.

"Throdog Azathoth," Shaw said, hearing his words as if from a distance.

The other five repeated his words. "Throdog Azathoth."

"What?" Armitage screamed. "No!"

"Yes!" Marsh cackled. "Oh, yes!"

Across the room Silas Miller took advantage of the distraction and threw off two of his faceless captors, then fought past the rest. He rushed forward, snatched the empty shotgun from the floor beside Maria and rushed at Marsh.

Horrified, Shaw continued. "Mgepogog ot mgepogor. Ah'n'ghft legeth'drn r'luhhor. Ah'n'gha'drn ot shuggogg!"

The others repeated, weeping at the words they spoke.

"Double-cross me?" Miller swung the butt end of the shotgun and connected with the side of Marsh's head.

Surprised but not hurt, Marsh dropped the book.

"You're tired of living? I can help with that." Miller cocked his arm back for a second swing.

Armitage leapt to his feet and rushed to Shaw. "You will doom us all, you fool."

One short flute note filled the room. It was inside his mind as well, permeating his being. It seemed this time that everyone heard it to some degree, even Marsh and the featureless men.

"Mgahnnn nglui."

"Focus, Doctor. Remember the word for Dreamlands."

Dreamlands?

"Fhtagn shugnahh," Armitage hissed.

And what was he supposed to do with that information? What—

No. He saw.

Instead of a portal to Azathoth.

Marsh spun and grabbed the more muscular Professor Miller by the throat, squeezing. Miller's distraction had broken Marsh's concentration, and the spell holding them fizzled. The six were once again masters of their own minds and bodies. Watkins sank to the ground and crawled away from Marsh and the inscription.

They needed to get away.

"Nglui Fhtagn shugnahh," Shaw muttered.

A glowing portal opened behind them, bluish around the edge and white at the center. Shaw bent and scooped up the *Necronomicon*.

"No!" Marsh howled, pulling Cassandra's revolver free from his robe, pointing it toward Shaw.

Miller continued to struggle, grabbing Marsh's arm. "I might not be able to hurt you, but I can stop your plans."

With that the huge professor pulled the revolver in his direction. Instead of fighting it, Marsh let the arm be pulled, firing one bullet into Miller's arm, then a second one into his forehead. Miller crumbled to the ground with a wet splatter.

"Go, Doctor," Singh said. "Get that book out of here."

He and Cassandra both got between Shaw and the elder god. A

moment later Matthew joined them, then David. The four made a wall that would at least slow Marsh.

"No!" Shaw said.

There had to be a better way.

The god turned back, revolver leveled in their direction.

Armitage rushed at Shaw, tackling him. The two passed through the portal and into the Dreamlands beyond. The portal closed with a pop.

CHAPTER 42

April 24, 1912
The Dreamlands

The rocky ground underneath dug into the small of Shaw's back. He groaned. A weight pressed him down harder still. Armitage? The librarian was spread crosswise on him, unmoving. Had he died coming through the portal?

"Get off," Shaw demanded, voice struggling.

"Unhh!"

So the man was alive. Armitage tried to get a weak arm under his body and rise, but the muscles refused to obey. Shaw gave a hand and at least was able to roll the man off, though an elbow dug into the meat of his left leg in payment.

"That was unpleasant," Armitage said, arm across his face.

Was it? Now that Armitage no longer pinned him, Shaw felt no adverse effects from the transition itself. He forced himself to look around. They'd landed in the dirt and rocks which appeared to be part of some canyon's edge. Ahead the rocks rose to create a passage between shear rock walls.

Shaw rose to his feet with a dumbstruck expression. He raised first one leg, then the other—as much as the leg irons would allow

—looking at the cane which lay against the rocks and dirt. "I can walk."

"How wonderful for you."

"I mean, the pain is gone. The lameness."

Armitage opened his eyes. "That makes sense. We are in the Dreamlands."

Enjoying the newfound use of his legs, Shaw turned a slow circle, taking in their surroundings. To the left was a valley with green knee-high grass stretching for miles. On the right, a rotting dock which led to a river coursing past. A lounging serene cat on one post, eyeing them curiously. Behind them a city with houses and towers, ancient Egypt or something equally grand. Looking to the front again, the canyon was gone, replaced by a library. This last was the most enticing and had even encouraged Armitage to his feet, no doubt reminding the librarian of the one in Arkham.

Arkham!

Everything came back in a rush. "Singh! Cassandra!"

"They're on the other side," Armitage said. "We were the only ones through."

"I have to get back. Marsh. The gun."

"Calm down and think, you fool. They ensured you, the one who could read the spell, would escape with that book. Do you want to return and hand Marsh everything?"

"I—"

Another groan. Both turned toward the sound which had come from a rock, wide as a man but half as tall. The cat from the dock now rested on top, licking one paw. Another groan.

"Come out!" demanded Armitage.

From behind the rock rose the pale, bloody form of Watkins. The man swayed in the mild breeze. One hand was pressed against his head, as if he had the most monumental headache of all time.

Good.

"I thought I saw you crawl through ahead of us," Armitage said.

"Of course," Watkins managed. "Should I stay there and be sacrificed?"

"Sacrificed?" Shaw shouted.

Watkins shrugged, gaining some vigor. "No sacrifice without you I suppose."

Shaw stormed toward Watkins, fists balled and ready to strike. The other man stepped back, tripping over a rock and coming down on his back.

"Tell me exactly what you mean," Shaw said to the other man.

"The prophecy, the process for the reading. It drains the six of their life to open the portal."

"That ... That's not necessary."

"No?" Armitage asked.

"No ... At least, I don't think so. I opened the portal on my own."

Watkins rose again, wiping the dust from his clothes. "Whatever the case, Marsh thinks they need a sacrifice."

"And my son and Cassandra are back there with him," he said, fists clenched again. "Your ... *boys*, too."

"Yes, well ..." Watkins's lips worked in some attempt to offer an explanation. "Would it help if I apologized?"

Shaw seethed a moment longer before dropping his fists. There were more important considerations than challenging insincere apologies. Disgusted, he turned from Watkins and examined the area where they'd landed, then calculated where the portal must have been. Nothing remained of it. The dirt was not even disturbed.

"Damn it!"

"What now?" Armitage asked.

"The portal is gone," Shaw explained.

"And?"

"And they're still there with Marsh."

"Isn't that what I already said?"

Shaw ignored him. "I have to get back."

"Don't be a fool."

He'd changed the word of the spell, opened a portal to the Dreamlands instead of to Azathoth. The intention had been to give an escape for all of them, not only him and two people he couldn't care less about.

Change a word.

"Nglui … Nglui …"

"Nglui what?" Armitage said. "Do you know the word for the waking world?"

No. He didn't. All he knew were the words to get here to the Dreamlands, and those that would bring him to Azathoth. Both swam within his mind. Unwanted. When he'd returned to the waking world in the past, he had simply woken. How did one return while awake?

"Do you know it?"

Armitage shook his head.

"Would you tell me if you did?"

"I would tell you that I knew, but I wouldn't give you the word."

"Why?"

"You would rush through the portal without so much as a plan?"

"Yes!"

"And bring Marsh the spell and person needed to reach Azathoth?"

"I … I …"

"No answer? Good. You are showing sense."

Armitage was right, he needed a plan.

"You want some sense?" Shaw pulled the spell's third part from his pocket and crumpled it, throwing it as far as he could. "There!"

"Check your pocket."

Shaw did and pulled the same paper free again. This time he ripped it into pieces and allowed the breeze to take them, floating them away into the distance. Once again it was still inside his pocket.

"I can't get rid of it."

"No."

"If it makes you feel better," a soft, slow voice said, "that is an entrance, not an exit."

The three turned and found no one in any direction. The cat stretched and leapt from the rock.

"Humans," it purred, sounding exasperated.

"You can talk?" Watkins marveled.

"Obviously."

"Where is the exit?" Shaw said, recovering. "I need to get home."

"No." Armitage shook his head. "You need to stay away from there."

"Mrowr, only thing for certain is *that* cannot stay in the Dreamlands."

Both followed the cat's gaze to find Armitage's *Necronomicon* in the dust. The book was less decayed than when he'd first seen it. Was it … healing?

"Yes, it is."

Could the cat read his mind?

"Hmm, maybe," it purred. "If that book remains here long it will corrupt the Dreamlands and turn everything to nightmares. It must return to the waking world."

"Very well." Armitage stooped and retrieved the book. "I will take it back."

"You will need to travel to the exit, on the far side of the Dreamlands."

"How far is that?"

"A dream away."

"Can you be any more vague?" Armitage snapped.

"Mrow. I could," the cat chuckled. Not Marsh's disturbing chuckle, but one with actual warmth. "Now, do you want a guide or not?"

Armitage shut his mouth and gave a curt nod.

Watkins staggered forward and joined their group, not asking permission or seeking acceptance. He merely placed himself there. One of his hands continuously played with the bullet hole in his shirt, looking at his stomach beneath. It was a mess of gore, but no longer pumping any fresh blood.

"Incidentally, Shaw," the cat said, turning its green eyes on him, "throwing that spell away is not the way to defeat Marsh."

"Why can't I get rid of it?"

"I can't give you all the answers now, can I?"

"You haven't given any yet."

"Haven't I?" The cat spoke with a slow languid pattern, as if nothing would ever be a rush. "Here is something. It is easy to get distracted here and end up somewhere you do not want to be."

"What does that mean?" Armitage asked.

"It means what it means."

This was shaping up to be a frustrating journey, but they all somehow knew that the cat could be trusted to guide them, though none could say how they knew that. The logic of dreams.

"Why are you wearing those?" the cat asked.

Shaw looked at his leg irons. "I don't have the key."

A purr-laugh and the cat came closer, touching the leg irons with one paw. They fell from Shaw and landed in the dust.

"Shall we be off then?" the cat asked.

They journeyed on, following the cat from one section of Dreamlands to the next. The borders were defined with immediate changes to landscape and theme. They passed by and through places which would have been maddening or incredible if in the waking world.

A desert filled with pyramids, stretching back to the horizon. One land with multiple series of staircases, joined at right angles and going around in an impossible square forever.

The first place to provide clear danger came with an army of snakelike people who rushed for them, ready to make the kill. The cat stepped forward, between the two groups.

"If you are ready for Azathoth to wake, then by all means, kill these three."

The lead snake-person stared unblinking from cat to the humans and back, fangs bared. The cat waited, licking one paw until the leader hissed and turned back, giving the signal to his followers.

"Would the Dreamlands also be destroyed if Azathoth wakes?" Shaw asked.

"No dreamers, no Dreamlands."

Some cities were identified by their guide: Ulthar. Thran. Lost Carcosa. Others were more easily identified such as Victorian London and Bombay.

"You seem wise," Shaw said.

"Mrowr, all cats have wisdom."

"Would you answer a question?"

"If I can, and am so inclined."

"If Marsh needed the prophecy to reach Azathoth, how could I reach him by myself?"

"Hmm, you had help. Other gods that wanted you to see."

"Other gods, like Cthulhu?"

"None want reality destroyed," the cat added. "It would interfere with their plans."

"Plans?"

The cat gave no reply, and they soon came upon a city populated by cats. They were welcomed warmly because of their guide and had a banquet of dream food and drank dream wine, all of which was the best that their minds could imagine. The many cats watched them leave.

It occurred to Shaw that this journey had already taken several days, but it felt as if mere moments had passed at the same time. The paradox of dreams.

"Where is Watkins?" Armitage asked.

"He departed us at Lost Carcosa," the cat said.

"But … No. Carcosa came before lunch at the City of Cats," Armitage objected. "Watkins was with us then."

"Yes."

As if for emphasis to the maddening time perception, they came to a field of clocks, ticking and tocking and chiming. Running forward and back. Hourglasses with grains drifting upward. Some had no hands, others too many. One huge clock at the center ran in seven time directions, which Shaw understood as undeniable logic, but was certain he wouldn't once back in the waking world.

A city of living music, each note speaking in their pitch and duration.

One shadowed city made of strange connecting hallways. On each wall hung mirrors like the ones in Watkins's basement, speaking enticing words to them. *You will be rewarded.* Armitage broke into a sweat that lasted out of those corridors and well into the next area.

"Mirrors hold the soul," the cat said enigmatically.

"Why not simply destroy the six?" Shaw asked. "Why haunt my dreams and force me to Arkham?"

"Hmm," the cat purred. "Your dreams are haunted because you have seen gods. You are manipulated because those gods do not care about the whims of men."

That all sounded about right. "And the six?"

"If one pawn is destroyed then Marsh could engineer another," the cat explained. "How difficult to find another Orphan Murderer, Corrupted Scholar, or Living Spell? The twins born of twins would take more time, but still attainable."

"And the Ripper, walking between worlds?"

"Mrowr, that one would be more difficult. Be glad the gods chose to manipulate rather than obliterate you."

Armitage made a noise of disgust, as if questioning the gods' decisions.

An area of spiders made Shaw's skin crawl, Armitage's too by the expression. Their guide changed direction and headed around it, explaining that the spider people had their own agenda.

"When will this endless march be done?" Armitage grumbled.

"When you have asked the correct question."

Shaw and Armitage lapsed into silence for several of the next areas, which didn't affect the cat at all. In time Shaw realized what to ask, wondering why it had taken so long for him to see.

"If throwing the spell away won't defeat Marsh, what will?"

"Mrowr! An excellent question. How *do* you defeat him?"

"I … I'm asking you."

"You know how." The cat came to a stop and looked at a staircase spiraling up out of sight. "Here is your way out."

"But you haven't answered my question."

"I didn't agree I would answer. I just said you needed to ask."

They climbed for days without end. Up past the clouds and the sky until stars existed all around. It should have been exhausting. They should have needed to rest, to eat, but they did not. Still they climbed.

Armitage was not a conversationalist by any means and that left Shaw to his thoughts, churning around and around. One topic.

How could he defeat Marsh?

He had no idea, but had to find one. If not, it was only a matter of time. As the cat said, Marsh could engineer a new six for the prophecy, and somewhere there existed at least one intact copy of the *Necronomicon*, even if it was on the ocean's floor. In fact, Armitage's copy had healed back to its original state while in the Dreamlands. Had it also regrown the missing page?

Inevitable.

This mad *god* needed to be defeated.

"The cat thinks you know how to defeat Marsh," Armitage said, the first thing in days.

Shaw wondered what key piece of information he'd seen in the Dreamlands that hadn't clicked into place yet.

Something.

Could he go back without knowing? Hope it will all come together in his mind?

Another step in a series of thousands and Shaw came up flat against a closed door, even though the stairs had stretched into infinity a moment ago. He stepped back, scrutinizing the door.

He wasn't ready.

Perhaps if he just looked through.

Shaw gave the surly librarian a glance and reached for the door. It slid aside and ceased to exist, revealing a shimmering blue-white portal beyond. On the other side was a tableau he'd seen before from the opposite perspective. Marsh aimed Cassandra's revolver at Singh, Cassandra and the twins as they struggled to block the mad god. Marsh's finger applied pressure to trigger.

Beyond all of this was another portal in the process of closing.

No! This was the last place they should reappear. If they must return in Arkham, it should be outside of this church with a chance of hiding the *Necronomicon* away.

They needed more time.

"It isn't moving," Armitage observed. "There's no need to rush through."

There was sense in that. They could stay here until a way to defeat Marsh presented itself. One thing they had in the Dreamlands was time, and he was prepared to stay here for all eternity if need be. Armitage sat on the steps, *Necronomicon* in his lap, apparently having come to the same conclusion.

You know how, the cat whispered over and over inside his mind. *You know how.*

I know how.

Only … he didn't.

"Something is coming," Armitage said.

Shaw turned and watched where the man pointed. Down the steps, many thousands away from them, came a shape. It would take some time for it get—

"Waiting?" a voice asked.

The speck below was now next to them.

Their cat guide. Thankfully nothing more menacing.

"I don't know how to defeat Marsh," Shaw said. "I can't go back."

"Hmm, you have been shown how."

"Shown?" Shaw shouted. "Shown? What have I been shown?"

"The way."

"I don't—"

"The Dreamlands cannot keep you any longer."

Armitage stood. "No, you must—"

"It is time."

The world tilted so that stairs were suddenly to their right, and the open portal was beneath them.

"No!" Shaw said.

Gravity took them.

Then they fell.

CHAPTER 43

April 24, 1912
Church of the Ancients: 2:34 am

Shaw fell with a painful thud onto the church's wooden floor, only a few steps behind Marsh and the others. With a shout of outrage Armitage landed immediately behind Shaw, almost on top of him. Marsh spun toward the noise, revolver up.

The man's expression changed from anger to shock.

"Doctor, you do continue to surprise me."

Already Marsh's faceless minions had closed in on Singh and the others, immobilizing them through weight of numbers. More closed on Shaw and Armitage, forcing them back to their feet. Shaw sagged, unable to put weight on his leg, and stared at the cane which had come through with them. Marsh made a gesture, and one of the faceless retrieved and handed it to Shaw.

"Where is Watkins?"

"He was lost."

"Ah." Marsh reacted as if this were expected.

Yes! Shaw realized. The church no longer held a corrupted scholar.

Marsh raised one hand, and two of his faceless grabbed Silas Miller and dragged him toward the etched symbols in the floor, dropping him on to the Corrupted Scholar's circle.

"But … he's dead," Shaw said.

"Not ideal, but they're all destined to die," Marsh said. "They're easier to move around if alive. Now—"

"Stop. Please." Shaw held up one hand, playing for time.

Marsh raised an eyebrow while Shaw shook off the two faceless holding him and leaned onto his cane. In the moment he stared back at this banished god, his subconscious raced through their journey through the Dreamlands.

Lost Carcosa where Watkins still existed. The City of Cats and their surreal lunch. The city of living music. Reptile people. Spiders. The unending hallways with whispering mirrors. The—

CLICK!

"I'll cast your spell. I'll take you to Azathoth."

"No!" Armitage screamed. "Shaw, you can't!"

Marsh ignored the librarian and looked at the portal behind Shaw. It was as wide and tall as the doorway they'd passed through, still showing enough of the stairway in Dreamland for the destination to be obvious.

"That is not where I wish to go, Doctor."

Shaw shook his head. Falling back into this world had awoken his mind again. He was thinking now and understood many things he hadn't minutes ago. One was that, having completed his dream quest, he was now able to conjure the portal on his own.

"Nglui Azathoth."

The portal shifted, displaying a more terrifying scene. The vastness of space. Rocks floating in orbit around a hideous monster which, at this moment, continued to sleep.

The music of flutes drifted through the portal into the church.

"Why the change of heart, Doctor?" Marsh asked, suspicion clear in his voice.

"I'm tired, too." Shaw leaned heavily on his cane. "Tired of the endless battle. This struggle's conclusion is inevitable. One day you will gather the six again, either this six or another. You will find an intact *Necronomicon*. One day you will win."

This piece of logic he had seen while still in the Dreamlands. It was as sound here as it was there. As things were, this was inevitable.

Marsh glanced to the portal, then back at Shaw. The expression on his face made it plain that he wanted to believe. How long had Marsh been working toward fulfilling this prophecy? Years? Decades? Centuries? A wary expression reached the man-god's face as Shaw ran through what Singh had taught him about steeling his mind against others. The other man's eyes narrowed.

"I don't trust you," Marsh said.

Shaw nodded. Of course he didn't. Marsh would be a fool to trust him, and one thing he couldn't be accused of was being a fool ... But, Marsh couldn't *not* believe him either.

"You will accompany me."

Another nod from Shaw, looking down. Resigned. "Just ... let them have what time is left." He shifted his gaze to Singh and the others, not daring to look too long.

"No!" Singh shouted, mirroring Armitage's objection.

The others struggled in the grasp of the faceless men. Marsh gestured and more rushed forward. He wasn't taking any chances with them derailing his plans.

"It's okay," Shaw said.

They continued to struggle, but nothing he said could help them.

"Tell your followers to let them go once we pass through."

Marsh narrowed his eyes at Shaw, teeth bared. Then the anger of being ordered passed, and he told his followers to do exactly that. A god gracious in his victory. He turned to Shaw. "I will go first."

"Fine."

Marsh made no move, staring at Shaw until he felt like the man-god could see every thought inside his skull.

Defeated. Resigned. Tired.

It felt like eternity, but Shaw waited.

"No," Marsh finally said. "*You* go first."

Shaw looked at Marsh and shrugged. Another moment of hesitation, then Marsh gestured toward the portal, hand open, palm up.

After you.

Moving slow, weight on the cane, Shaw made his way to the portal. Without hesitation he stepped through. What he wanted was to look back to Singh, to Cassandra. To give them some final gesture. He did none of that. On the other side he endured the focus of all those gods, their glares burning into him. Anger and disappointment and sheer hate. Shaw ignored them and hunched forward. To look back into Marsh's face would be foolishness.

No.

The scuff of Marsh's foot against the church's stone floor. The swing of Cassandra's gun, brushing against his pants. Marsh told where he was in many unspoken ways. The change to his stride as he prepared to step through.

Marsh hesitated. His shoe not coming down on this side of the portal.

Shaw remained still, cane in hand. Patient.

Another scuff, this one of Marsh's shoe against the stone behind him.

One last thing that Shaw had realized on hitting the church floor. He recalled one particular area of the Dreamlands, and in that instant he knew how to defeat Marsh.

"Nglui mirror," he whispered and turned.

The portal's scene shifted, from the realm of Azathoth, which Marsh had been watching, to the calm reflective surface of a mirror. The timing was perfect, as it needed to be. Marsh tried to press through to the realm of Azathoth and instead passed into the empty mirror of Watkins's basement.

"No!" the man-god screamed. "No!"

"Nglui church."

The portal changed once again.

Before him stood Singh, Cassandra, and the twins. Just behind the unsmiling presence of Armitage, holding the tome for which he would remain the guardian. The faceless men hesitated a moment before turning toward the portal and giving a quick bow. They left the church en masse. Was that bow for him, or for their master?

Relief spread across each of his friend's faces.

"Come through, Doctor," Singh said. "Quick."

Shaw's expression changed, a quick shake of his head as he tried to appear content.

"Shaw?" Cassandra said.

"You cannot return."

Shaw glanced back to find the hooded elder god, tentacle-shaped flute in one hand. "I know."

"I warned you to not come back."

Shaw nodded. "It was the only way."

"What do you mean, you can't return?!" Singh demanded.

"I knew as much when I crossed over," Shaw replied. "I had a fifty-fifty chance that Marsh would go. No such luck."

Singh started forward.

"Stay right there. All of you. I knew this was a one-way trip, and I made it to keep you all safe."

"Why?" Cassandra asked.

"It was the only way to defeat Marsh … the only way I could see."

Singh shook his head.

The portal had started to shrink from left to right, as if a door were closing.

"Shaw!" Singh wailed.

"I have limited time and a few things to say. David and Matthew, there is a mirror in your basement with Marsh imprisoned. Keep it safe."

The portal had become thin enough that a person would need to turn sideways to get through.

"We will, Doctor," David said. "I promise."

Matthew looked from Singh to Cassandra and nudged his brother. "Maybe we should go make sure of that now."

The brothers retreated from the mirror, leaving the church at a trot. Shaw wasn't sure the faceless men wouldn't know where their god had been imprisoned, but he didn't think so, or maybe they would know but not care. After that bow, he got the impression they were fine with how things had turned out.

The portal had shrunk to being wide enough for one eye to see through at a time.

"Cassandra, thank you for one last adventure. I have no regrets."

The tattooed woman nodded but said nothing, unable to look at Shaw.

"Singh my lad. You have made this life worth living, and I hope you feel the same."

Singh wore an expression of torment and misery. "Just … so."

"Look after each other," Shaw said as the portal showed a sliver of the world left behind. "Goodbye, son."

"Goodbye, father."

CHAPTER 44

Shaw stared at the spot where the portal had been.

"Nglui church."

Nothing happened, as he suspected would be the case. Any ability he'd been granted had been taken away.

"You have your flute," the hooded god said.

"Flute?"

A glance at the other being's hand, then to his satchel as he realized what was said. He reached into the bag across his shoulder, pushing the sandwich aside and pulling the flute out. It was a match for the god's instrument. Was this why he'd found it, to deliver it here? Shaw held it toward the hooded being.

"That is yours."

Shaw looked at the flute again then back, not understanding.

"You are one of the players now."

"Oh." Another glance at the flute in his hand.

Silence. The flutes had stopped.

In the distance the great beast Azathoth twitched as Shaw

realized it was his turn. He raised the flute to his lips, blowing a note that sounded nothing like music.

"Why don't I go mad?

"Perhaps you shall."

"At least my wounds no longer hurt." He raised and lowered his bad leg in a way he hadn't in decades, gave a kick. "I can only have so many years left. Surely I will die before too long."

A low, rumbling chuckle, like an earthquake. Several other gods joined in.

"There is no time here, Archibald Shaw."

No time.

No death.

Eternity in this way.

CHAPTER 45

April 24, 1912
Arkham, Massachusetts: 3:16 am

Cassandra and Singh abandoned the church, heading toward Watkins's home for want of a better destination. David would give them a place to sleep while they worked through the pain and numbness. Both walking in silence for several blocks, lost inside their own thoughts. Cassandra knew no words existed to relieve the grief Singh felt. Only time could do that.

What of her own pain? She'd known the doctor for all of a week, but he had wormed his way into her trust. Unheard of, and unexpected. Now that she had opened herself up, Cassandra found she would miss that, much as she hated to admit it.

Ahead a half block staggered Armitage, that damned book clutched against his chest, the way a mother might carry their child. That would go back into hiding, masked by the other horrible books in that library. Too much danger there.

She glanced at Singh, making a decision she may regret later. "You know, there's a lot of evil right here in Arkham."

Singh nodded.

"As it turns out, I got used to having a partner. Interested?"

Singh turned toward her, misery plain on his face, but still he found his voice.

"Just so."

It was enough. Two loners could learn to work together in time, the memory of a good man spurring them onward.

OTHER WORDFIRE PRESS TITLES BY JOHN HAAS

Our list of other WordFire Press authors and titles is always growing. To find out more and shop our selection of titles, visit us at:

wordfirepress.com

ABOUT THE AUTHOR

John Haas is a Canadian author, born and raised in Montreal before moving to Calgary where he lived for twelve wonderful years. Now he lives in the nation's capital of Ottawa, but misses those Rocky Mountains in the distance.

John has been writing for most of his life but only became serious about being published in the last decade or so. In that time he has had more than twenty short stories published in various excellent publications, including *Writers of the Future Volume 35*. This novel marks his sixth published book, and he has no plans on slowing down.

His goal is to become a full-time writer (rich and famous would be nice too, but one step at a time).

He lives with his girlfriend, Michelle, and two wonderful sons who all continue to give him lots of motivation, support, and time to write.

www.ingramcontent.com/pod-product-compliance
Lightning Source LLC
Chambersburg PA
CBHW020419110726
47899CB00006B/2056